Reviews of T

'*True Colours* reads like a love note to
and by a cast of illustrious characters v
to Dickens with a detour via Flann O'Brien. Wry, playful, rich, surreal,
this is an absolute romp of a read with genuine affection at its heart for
the people and places and histories of the city.'
Bernie McGill

'An endearing cast of eccentrics and a strong sense of people and place.'
Martina Devlin

'An indulgent pleasure… a contemporary fairy tale; even a morality tale, a
clever and subtle satire on the way we live in Derry; a comedy with laugh
aloud moments and rich in cleverly, witty phrases that had me smiling…I
love it that characters on their quest for love are in the older age bracket,
unashamedly flawed …and far from conventional romantic protagonists.
It may well say more about post Good Friday Agreement Derry through
the eyes of its marginalised than many a socio-economic-economic
analysis. Leaves us glowing with the possibility of a happy ending.'
Felicity McCall.

'*True Colours* is Derry on a plate. Prose that absorbs you with lyricism,
character and a wry mastery of everything Maiden City. Like Ms Marrón
and Mr White, you will read this with the wind at your back and a
ballad in your heart.'
Sue Divin

'A cast of amazingly colourful characters, as though you stood on the walls
or the top of Shipquay Street and looked at the city in the round and
through a kaleidoscope. This is a story that puts Derry in the position it
believes it deserves-at the centre of the universe!
Like the very best comedy, it is only just at a little remove from reality…
there were times I cried with laughter, not least at the foray to Strabane…
the shenanigans in the "Poetarium"…and at the brilliantly-caught spoken
words and names of the inhabitants… A joy.'
Maureen Boyle

Also by James Simpson
Smokes and Birds

Reviews of *Smokes and Birds*

'Unexpected runaway brilliance.'
Ian Sansom

'An atmospheric, beautifully crafted collection that showcases James Simpson's acute powers of observation, keen ear for dialogue, lyrical mastery of language, dry wit and breadth of imagination. This is a collection to savour, time and again; it will linger long in the mind. A compelling new voice in Irish short story writing.'
Felicity McCall

'These are stories in which entire lives, complete worlds, are held in a reader's mind as they read.'
Martina Devlin

'Was ever there written a more damning indictment of the social aspirations of an Ulsterman than that he "had abandoned the glottal stop, was buying his shirts in Arthur Street"? In these atmospheric stories James Simpson parades before us a colourful and lively cast of characters who populate pre- and post-partition Ulster, from the glamorous drawing rooms and expansive gardens of the merchant classes, to the cramped terraces and filthy yards of working-class Belfast.
'These are stories that deal with important conversations, around identity and allegiance, around solidarity and probity, taking place as they do at critical historical junctures in Irish history: on the eve of world war, on the night before the signing of the Ulster Covenant.

'There is a savouring of language here in this senses-filled writing, a precision and attention to detail, and a resonance in the imagery that capture the atmosphere and the concerns of the women and men of this northerly province in the first half of the twentieth century.'
Bernie McGill

True Colours

James Simpson

Artwork by Bridget Murray

First published in 2024 by
Colmcille Press
Ráth Mór Centre, Derry, BT48 0LZ
info@colmcillepress.com

Text © James Simpson, 2024
Cover illustration © Bridget Murray, 2024

ISBN: 978-1-914009-42-6

Project management: Dingle Publishing Services

The moral rights of the authors and contributors have been asserted in accordance with the Copyright, Designs and Patents Act, 1998.

Colmcille Press gratefully acknowledges the support of Creggan Enterprises Limited and the John Bryson Foundation.

James Simpson gratefully acknowledges the support of
Arts Council NI and Derry & Strabane District Council.

A CIP copy for this book is available from the National Library of Ireland and the British Library. All rights reserved. No part of this publication may be reproduced or transmitted in any form or by any means, electronic or mechanical, including photocopy, recording, or any information storage or retrieval system, without permission in writing from the publisher. The book is sold subject to the condition that it shall not, by way of trade or otherwise, be lent, re-sold or otherwise circulated without the publisher's prior consent in any form of binding or cover other than that in which it is published and without a similar condition including this condition being imposed on the subsequent purchaser.

This is a work of fiction. Unless otherwise indicated, all the names, characters, businesses, places, events and incidents in this book are either the product of the author's imagination or used in a fictitious manner. Any resemblance to actual persons, living or dead, or actual events is purely coincidental.

For Jen with love and gratitude

'Inhale possibility, exhale creativity.'
Laura Jaworski

Excerpta ex Libro

Miss Black's ball gown was of the most translucent apricot, which caused her hair to glow, fusing, so it seemed, with her immortal soul.

Like Derry itself, of late, Mr White had grown all out of proportion, his thoughts branching off like crazy limbs and leaves tangling his brain.

Miss Marrón had descended, she maintained, from a nucleus of strong women who married sailors spilled ashore from galleons, onto the northern coast of Ireland, then a savage corner of Christendom.

Mrs Green set off with purpose, down her somewhat hazardous path. Careful not to trip. A white and yellow profusion of feverfew shoved through the slabs, many of which were cracked.

'All it takes, sometimes, is one disaster to bugger up your life,' said the Blue Two.

One of the lingerie ladies, fair play to her, came out to ask if John Orange was OK. 'He's a bad colour,' Miss Black said, 'but it's pure annoyance.'

How Judge Scarlett's spirits lifted as Miss Black came into view. He glimpsed her standing there in his wide hallway, adjusting a loose strand of hair.

Rev Gray, for his part, owing, no doubt, to extensive training at clerical college, appeared to have little interest in practicalities.

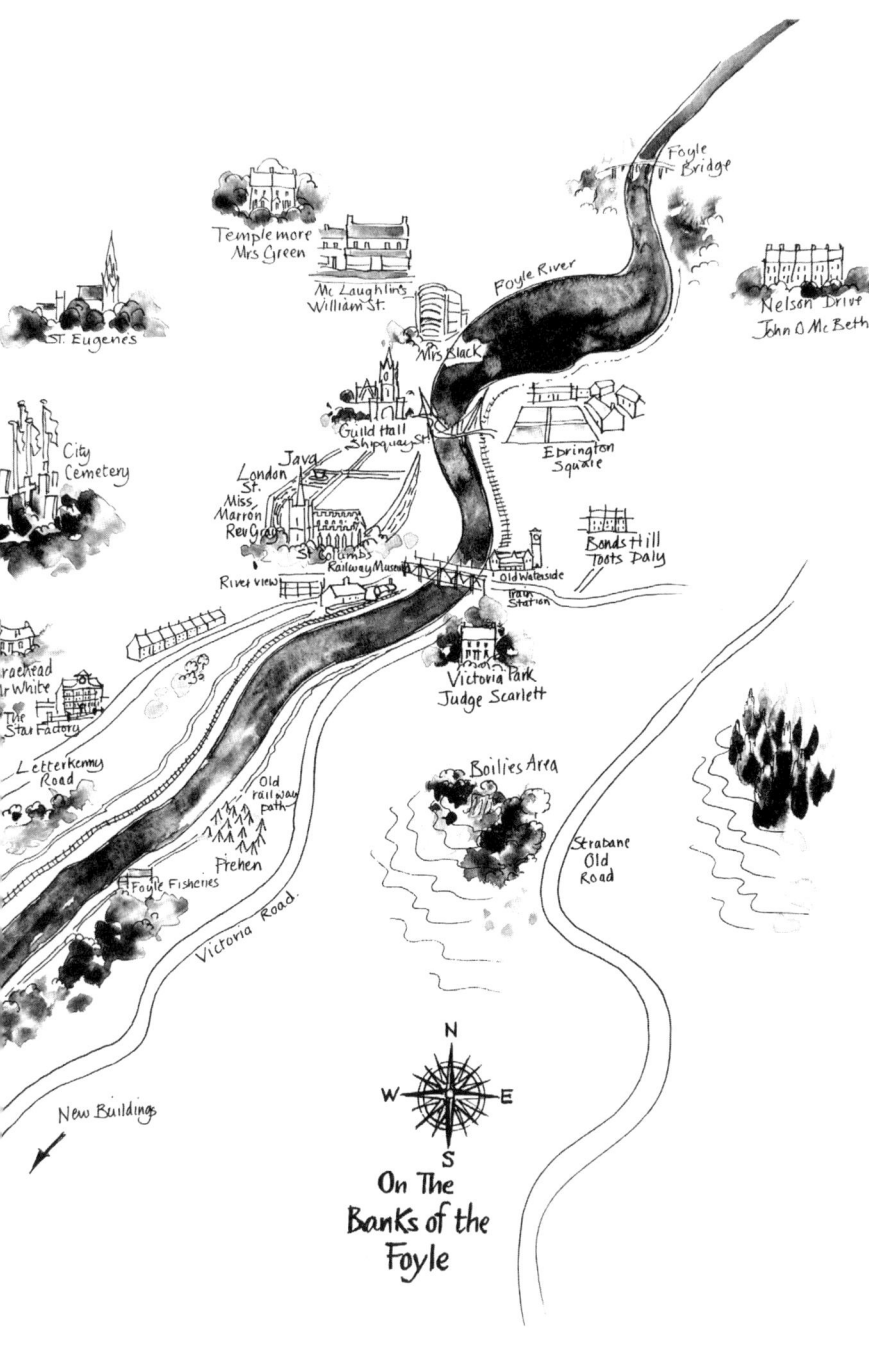

Contents

Part One
1

Part Two
49

Part Three
137

Part One

Heart Music

It has been the most amazing election result for Miss Indigo Black in the noblest of cities. Soon it will be dusk. On the airy balcony of her fifth-floor, Art Deco apartment, she surveys the world, as a newly elected Councillor. In the sky above, a bank of cloud is etched in red and gold. Below, the River Foyle travels easily to the sea. Flow. Ebb. Flow. Sail boats clink at their moorings. Swallows swoop. She is ideally positioned in tonight's twilight zone for buoyant thoughts to fill her mind. Not everyone is so blessed. Civic possibilities already abound, but for the moment, she is at rest. Allowing the day to sink slowly. What a terrific turn of events. Thank God for fluidity, and liberty to be.

In some future world, she will come back to the earth as a cat, to dwell again in the cradle of her dreams. Her eyes will be Egyptian. She will teeter like a ballerina on pure, white paws, and in that by and by, she will possess the pinkest tongue ever to lick double cream. Her coat is to be thick and sumptuous. Her tail flicking in nuanced concentration. She will pad the city's walls like a shade, marvelling again at the throb of history, pondering the superior knowledge of the stones.

All that, undoubtedly, is the future, but in the meantime, she must secure the artistic interests of the splendid people she knows and has yet to meet. Listen to their heart music, and with them, bask in the glory of the Oakgrove. Tonight, she celebrated her victory, re-dedicating herself to the aesthetic, knowing that the beauty one creates in all its forms is marvellously banked. Naturally, Miss Black will turn down other incarnations; a golden Irish hare perhaps, an elusive, soulful selkie off Ballyliffin. But that can wait. Tonight, she will reflect. What a triumph, to take the seat against the odds, and by a margin of miles, to pass her surplus to other non-aligned independents. Hooray for free spirits. Bad luck to the big battalions. A cat has nine lives. Right now, however, she has but one in which to make a difference. In which to promote her dream.

Beginnings

Indigo has been open with the media. 'I was an only child,' she told them, 'born and reared in Georgian Clarendon Street, on the Cityside, to an alderman and his wife Florence. And, yes, frankly, I was born into privilege. I know that.' She had been a protégé, from the start. Well, her record spoke for itself. Music. Transposing at six. The Eleven Plus at nine. One hundred per cent in verbal reasoning. No, not one slip. At fourteen, she had read Chaucer, come first in a national drawing competition, and skied in Zermatt.

At the very beginning she had been treasured as a toddler. A warmly dressed infant in home-knitted woollens, who never got her feet wet. The story went that she had wept one frozen January morning, upon spying a tiny, hatless baby in North Edward Street. Does she recall this small event? Not at all, but her empathy, it seemed, had extended to mangey stray dogs, and wilting dray horses hauling too many barrels. 'Poor horsies,' she had evidently said. It seemed she had grasped the misery of that perished infant imprisoned in its pram. The drudgery of the mongrels, the harsh restriction of noble beasts wedged tight between the shafts.

But what of her childhood? Her growing up? Perhaps she had been frivolous, but, honestly, style had dominated. She had the look, you see. That *Picture Post* eye for haute couture. Classical, French, whatever. Every whim had been indulged by mother, so that from the beginning of her journey as a human, to where she is tonight, she has worn, with more than a touch of class, the florid trappings, not of convention, but of her imagination. She has dressed, always, with precision and flamboyance according to her sense of the wondrous. 'Turning heads' had remained high on her agenda.

No one will tie me down. This was an assertive, risqué work she wrote at the age of fifteen. The *Derry Journal* had partially published it, omitting the more lurid parts. Those were different times. But, indeed, it had caused a right old stir. Who was she? Where did she get her ideas? Some praised her. Others mocked. Young women were getting above themselves, and where would it all end? But fair play to her headmistress. The spectral Miss Tyrrell, a gaunt, surprising figure had claimed Indigo as an incipient pearl on a par, say, with Amelia Earhart who had conquered the Atlantic. That had been something like endorsement.

When a valedictory June brought the end of her school career, Miss Black and her friends prepared to take flight like swans. They became adults in a splash of indulgence, enjoying at last a legal glass of bubbly, strutting the waxed dance floor of the Golf Club with a new, brash confidence, exposing with daring, acres of bare flesh. Especially Miss Black, whose body was the envy of every female. The desire of every male. What a night of frolics. How they had revelled on the very rim of life, as it tilted with uncertainty. And God, what a lurching it would be.

Her ball gown was of the most translucent apricot, which caused her hair to glow, fusing, so it seemed, with her immortal soul. Truly, something monumental and molecular had taken place as they danced till after four. To a nine-piece band.

That same October of nineteen sixty-eight, Indigo went up to the neo-Gothic Queen's University, in old Linenopolis, where she installed herself like a common mortal at a standard desk for ordinary students, as though she were not divine.

'But is she real?' the students asked in Belfast.

How she had flitted like a moth, under Lanyon's cloisters, continuing, without fear of opprobrium, to wear that self-same low-cut dress. What a sensation.

But back then it was a hard time in Ulster. An historic meltdown, A rude, bloody awakening. In those years the very fabric of compliance ripped apart, as upheaval upended expectations. Violence erupted stark and raw. Having bided its time. Seismic readings were recorded.

Certainties shattered. She had turned out for sit downs. Sit ins. Seen heads cracked wide open. Skulls splashed with blood. A returning plague, a resurrected Famine ghost, had knocked like Willie Winkie. With his infectious rat-a-tat. As the students responded with new-found energy, Miss Black became incensed. No one then doubted her indignation. She dug in and joined the other young warriors who were headline news, and notably, gave a furious interview to the *Belfast Telegraph*.

'Government Minister says he's "prepared to... kill," she told the world. 'To kill. Do you hear me? His very words. How bloody well dare he?'

'Dynamite in taffeta.' Her persona grew, as protests swept the streets.

'Glamour in the gutters,' some papers said.

This, at a time when bin lids beat harshly on flagstones. When drums pounded and men bled to death.

Turbulence, new order and realignment were all the chat in the smoky chambers of academia, in the fug of the junior and senior common rooms. But often as not, the conversation returned to – 'that woman from over the Sperrins.' It was not so much what she said, as who she appeared to be.

'But have you seen her? Have you been in her company?'

Had she pursued a formal career in politics back then – oh, dizzy heights. By now, she might have ruled the world. Meantime, she signed petitions, attended rallies, obstructed highways. She squatted with the rest in sleet, played guitar, sang protest songs. Once, she'd been held by the RUC on a public order charge.

'Two nights in the slammer, on a bench. Peaked caps aplenty. Bread and water darlings.'

And then, swiftly, a sudden shift of direction. Was this perfidy? It had been inexplicable to the world. To the *Belfast News Letter*, and the *Irish News* – to whom she had been Joan of Arc. There had been many in the movement who blamed her. Who called her 'self-serving.

A fake. An opportunistic bitch.' Who said her heart had never been in it.

But she had not explained. Nor would she. Life had become intolerable. Pearse Donnelly, leader, orator and strategist had thought he owned her. To be a pioneer was one thing. To become a chattel was entirely another. She had been almost broken. The movement could not contain them both. Sanity took pride of place. 'Let him go to hell,' she'd said at last. Once decided, she could not be turned. Freedom was needed in every sense. Too many women were enchained. She would be no one's spare rib. Some circles could not be squared.

Even as she disengaged, the waves of hatred swelled. Reaction had been unleashed. Sinister, local, earth-shattering uprisings flared magnesium in dead end streets. Terraces burned. Gun-toting men roamed on motorcycles. Hunting down victims. Stupefied, beyond belief, Miss Black wept for Sam Devenney, who died in Derry, murdered by the police. For Victor Arbuckle, the first policeman to be shot in Belfast. She wrote a scorcher to the *Irish Independent*, about bigotry, pogroms and brutality. Murder was wrong, so very wrong. Her heart for the deliverance of all had remained strong, but she needed another path.

As the conflict boiled unchecked, she proclaimed in the midst of chaos, that true, inner freedom could be fully achieved only in a world of creativity. That after collapse would come reconstruction. A new heaven and earth. Hearts and minds uniting in the love of art. Healing through unity. Unity built on diversity. There would be tolerance for self-expression. Difference would be celebrated. Compassion and connection would trump everything. They had called her a conflict denier. An escape artist. A fantasist. A deluded idealist. Whatever. She knew the truth. Ducks' backs and all that jazz, though she had been hurt. But they would see. In the midst of turmoil, she had kept her dream alive and built on it. Had it been revelation or retreat? Let others judge. Courage or avoidance? With growing conviction, she had stayed on course, as theatre became her hallmark, and education her passion.

But how awfully high-flown that all sounds. In truth, Indigo's nineteen seventies, eight-by-ten foot undergraduate room in Ogilvie Hall, in the soulless, multi-storey Elms, had become a cavern of chic. A bower of fragrance. It had been a heady time.

Miss Black smiles as a soft breeze strokes her skin.

Queen's. Ah, so long ago.

Monday, Wednesday and Friday, at two minutes before ten, she had swished up the steep steps of staircase R, specks of quartz glinting underfoot, her entrance awaited by drooling young hopefuls. Fat chance for them.

Always, she had beamed at the redoubtable Professor Brock. Unsettling him with her gaze and Chanel. It was said she forced him, without so much as a word, to deal with Grattan, and Tone, whilst mastering his own desires. Parnell, the Fenians, Collins and de Valera. The whole gang. What self-control he must have had. What fun.

'How nice to see you, Miss Black. Good, good, we'll make a start.'

The tiered auditorium heaved in those unsettled days with miniskirted girls. Some in voluminous and multi-coloured maxi coats, for the January chill was intense. The less serious boys wore foolish grins. These were the late-night losers at poker schools in flats. The grants blown to hell brigade. Proud of their excesses. Chancers up to their chests in noble poverty. They were not for Miss Black. All around her, the scratch of Conway pens. The conscientious opening and snapping shut of ring binders. Clerks filing Brock's every word.

Irish History was serious stuff. There was no banter with the great man. Following lectures, he reached for his briar, rummaged for a match, gathered his papers, in that crumpled, flustered manner he had, and left without a word. Questions un-posed continued, presumably, to hang in the ether of that ancient, hallowed sanctum. Perhaps they are hanging still.

She had perched keenly in her stall, refusing to take notes. Occasionally, she opened a silvered handbag to retrieve a tissue. Sometimes she closed her eyes. In the main, she had simply allowed the past to infuse her mind, in a kind of marination. On Saturdays she skated alone among the throng of students at Balmoral. One Tuesday morning, in the Great Hall, she had asked Heaney to sign her copy of *Death of a Naturalist*. May I borrow your pen?' he had asked softly, patting the pockets of his shabby duffel coat.

'For Indigo,' he'd written. 'From Seamus.'

His poems are on her shelf.

She and Brock had been carved from the same block of marble. The sculptor had merely released them at different times. Their connection, according to those who knew them, could be detected in the merest tremble of an eyelid. Occasionally she too had said, like he did himself, 'Indeed, indeed,' and 'absolutely so.' They had worked in reciprocation. As if they were sharing some long-haul flight. He, unfolding history like a Japanese fan, she, in her resplendence, achieving total retention. They were improbable soulmates. But Brock had been beautiful in his way.

Their simpatico was even more evident in the Eyrie, his attic study. She was always arrayed in her finery. Brock let her smoke.

'Yes, yes, Indigo,' he'd often said, jiggling his size twelve feet. Read that last paragraph again. 'You have it completely. Do you see? The savagery of war. Civil war, especially. Damned apt. Exceptional cogency my dear, you've nailed the matter, entirely.'

Then Bloody Sunday and slaughter. My God. Corpses on the streets of Derry. How relative everything was. How many realities? How irrelevant academia had seemed in a world of snow. Yet she had stayed on.

After four stellar years, as the North descended into hell's deepest pit, Indigo graced the Whitla, to take her finals. A vast uncompromising auditorium, in which, day after day, she distilled the past, without so much as a cardigan in reserve.

With a flamboyant flourish she had clinched her First Class Honours. Not many were awarded then. She had read Miss Austen's *Persuasion* three times. Brock's favourite writer. On his advice, she had rested her brain, and hadn't cared who knew.

At the end of the final paper, Miss Black remembers emerging into glorious sunshine.

There was Brock, an old Daedalus lounging in cords. Olive green, she believes they were.

'Well, Indigo, I told you I'd set a corker.'

A corker. No one says that now. How words can become disused.

She had felt herself flush like a glass of Dubonnet. It was still so vivid. She had lighted a long Dunhill. No question of collusion.

Brock must have been seventy.

'You have it all to play for, Indigo,' he'd told her that tropical day.

His words came back tonight.

After the cream and strawberries, the Grenadier Guards had actually played The Queen. Imagine. The imperial national anthem. It was still done then. How times have changed. But even then, strong views had been expressed. Letters published in *Gown*. The mighty tribune, Pearse had sought reprieve. Said he had been stupid. Overbearing. Shortsighted. That he was miserable without her. How foolish that would have been. How little he'd known her. How crazy he'd been to ever think... but Brock had taught her wisdom.

They had been an unlikely duo that summer, often seeking coffee and privacy, in the Europa, Belfast's bomb-loosened hotel. How many times had it been rocked? Yes, someone had kept a tally. 'Two strands in history, my dear. The constitutional and the revolutionary.' Blown up twenty times, to date. Could that be right? How bizarre when she thinks of it now.

Brock had no one, apart from her. My God, what distilled loneliness. His books were his friends. When he died of a burst appendix, he breathed his last in Camden Street. Indigo had hurried home from

Aberystwyth, on a leaden November day, to attend a lifeless service in St John's, near Orangefield. What a dismal, cadaverous affair. She had stood at his grave in her long mourning coat. There was muck everywhere. And the rain came down in sheets. He and she had lived in the past. It had been their country. They had often addressed the issues of the world, but not of the world to come. Did she expect an afterlife? Perhaps, but as a cat. She believed in truth and beauty.

Art and the Needy

Oh, but she had fought such an energetic campaign for her seat on the Council. She had railed against disadvantage but been frank about her journey. There had been plenty of questions. Some of them unexpected. Had she not, as a student, in fact, simply abandoned her principles, when things got hot? What had been her motivation? But she had stood firmly on her record. On the success of St Gobnait's and her girls. On her expansive view of art, in the very widest sense. She had remained relaxed. It had been an honour to serve in education. In the city of her birth. To have been part of its resurgence. To have seen potential take to the air on wings of song. But how, asked some cynic, had a young, academic woman, 'reared with plenty of money,' ever become committed to girls brought up in want? Was it not, this creep suggested, a case of 'rent a cause'? Or to put it another way, what under God had been her angle in coming back to Derry away back then? Nudge, nudge and wink.

Miss Black's epiphany had occurred in her third year at Queen's, during a lecture given by the daughter of a black immigrant from West Africa, who lived in Creggan. Cindy Ash. Cindy was poor, but rich in brains and resolve, and fearless in the teeth of prejudice. A mighty union activist in the shirt factories. She had taken on bosses. Spoken up. Refused to be put down. Brought a slide show to Mandela Hall. Her celluloid transparencies, as they were known, showed women sweating over industrial sewing machines and out-of-work men walking greyhounds. Cindy was a great photographer. She had captured children eating bread and dripping in the streets around the Gasyard. Youths standing idle on Derry's corners on both sides of the river. Old grandfathers smoking fags outside the huts in Springtown Camp. Under each slide she had inserted a caption.

Resilience. Girls singing at work.

Leisure. Men in the bookies.

Rest. None for women.

'There was just me and a handful of other black women,' said Cindy Ash. 'Most of us weren't far from our last pair of pants, but we danced, anyway, in the Corinthian. No one had any money. I want hope today,' she said, 'for all the young women of tomorrow, whether they're black or white, Protestant or Catholic.'

It was then that Miss Black, doyenne of the History Department, and always resplendent, had committed her extraordinary talents to gifted, unnoticed girls. 'Extraordinary,' she had told the sceptics. 'Because no girl is ever ordinary.'

After her midweek lecture, and a light lunch of Ski yogurt, she had exchanged her ball gown for something more practical. A pair of tight jeans and a burgundy, skinny rib top. A pair of blue sneakers she'd bought in Clarkes, for the walk past Deramore Drive.

Drumlin View had been two houses knocked together. Brick looking at brick. A girls' home. A temporary address. She was a volunteer in the kitchen, though she couldn't cook. She cut up crinkly chips. A bit of light ironing. An attempt at producing griddle soda bread, with disastrous results. But that was how one learned.

Two of the Drumlin girls had been from her own city, and she'd felt connection. They were both 'expecting,' as Matron put it. Indigo was neither coy nor pregnant, thanks be to God. These two had been 'both ignorant and unfortunate,' or 'foolish enough to get caught,' depending on how one viewed it. Gemma and Roberta. Each of them sixteen. Both far away from home, and awaiting their babies.

The sense of guilt had never quite left Indigo. Guilt, for all she had been given. For inequality. For good looks and her brain. For the ease with which life had unfolded so far. Guilt for the lack of effort she had been required to make.

As a teenager at home, she had been broadly uninformed. Even as unrest lurked in her city's streets, and children slept three to a bed, she had begun the quest for glamour. And this had not left her. It was who she was. Still is. But also, the race for grades. The annual school drama production. Though what of the wider world? What of girls in her own place, who literally had no life? Who had not a cat's chance in hell of a future? Girls with artistic souls, but no means of realisation? That had come later.

She really hadn't known what to expect when she started in Drumlin View.

Gemma and Roberta had changed all that. God, when she thinks of them now. They each already had plastic babies of a kind. Fat dolls, bizarre and vaguely pregnant in a way. Grotesque, donated, ugly effigies. Not anatomical of course. The sort that people threw out in bits. Missing an arm or a leg. Dolls who had cried themselves to sleep, but who, somewhere along the way, had lost their voice. Perhaps the result of cruelty. Dolls dressed crudely, in crocheted frocks, with patchy ginger hair. With perforated scalps. Clusters of pinprick holes where their locks had come out in clumps. Dolls without softness. Unyielding, un-breathing, man-made reminders of retribution, cold, with unseeing, glass eyes.

No school for the girls. An occasional magazine. An unwelcome, strained visit from a clergyman. Awkward silences. Brooding mothers. On occasion, whispering little sisters. Detached fathers when they came. Silences. No books, save the Bible. Some childcare pamphlets. How to hold baby. Plenty of dishwashing. Squeezy bubbles to cleanse dirty hands. Oh, my glory. Tears abounding. Missing home. One girl from Horace Street. The other from Mourne Drive. And Derry was on the moon.

'I'm studying English.'

Blank looks.

'Novels, you know, and poetry.'

'Is Indigo a colour?'

'A blend of blue and purple.'

Short walks by the canal. 'Look, a kingfisher,' she told the girls. 'Orange, cyan and blue.'

At last, 'I like your top.'

A laugh. An exotic flash of youth. But where would the dash be later, for Gemma and Roberta?

'They want to know who did it,' the girls had told her. 'Are they mad in the head? Could you get us some lollies, Indigo? Could you say a wee prayer for us?'

Three Lyons Maids. They'd licked one each.

Three grew closer as two grew larger. Expected dates around the first of April.

'April Fools' Day,' Matron said.

The girls had never read a book right through. Their scribbles were big, round boulders. But their words were telling. They should have been going on to the factory, to support their mothers, but now, they didn't know. They wanted to keep their babies, but how?

'There's no chance Indigo.'

Babies, the real, warm flesh of their flesh. Their red-blood-pumping babies. To be given away. Yes, 'Given.' They weren't stupid girls, but they were dull with despair. Girls expecting pillage. In naked daylight. Outwardly Indigo remained herself. Inwardly she was emptied.

The girls had been allowed to cuddle their babies for up to half-an-hour. Thirty whole minutes in which to smell their skin. To spill bitter tears. To scald their babies' brows with grief before separation. Roberta and Gemma, breast-bloated and weary.

Indelible writing on her heart. A great deal of space between her world and theirs. Even as she continued to absorb the past at Queen's, part of her, at least, became realigned. And this had stuck. Memories of these two waifs from her own native town, whom she would never have met had she remained at home, have stayed with her. 'If ever I teach young women,' she had vowed back then, 'I will look past the apparent, beyond the outward façade. I will look inside.'

Drumlin View must be long gone but tonight, as she considers her success, she remembers everything about it. The reek of boiled cabbage, the sweet, acrid, lavender floor polish. The insipd, watery lamb stew. The narrow dormitory shared by six young 'fallen' women.

To hell with her critics.

In what way had art nurtured the souls of Gemma and Roberta? What had they known of Monet or Degas? Well, Degas. But then again. Two wonderful girls untouched by beauty. Sensitive souls. All but abandoned. Stripped of their prizes so hardly won. What were they doing in the Ireland of yesterday? Where are their babies today?

In Drumlin View they had dabbled in paint on paper she sourced in Smithfield. In Kavanagh's low-roofed cavern. The man who bought and sold everything. They had dipped their brushes as one, while Nina sang to them on a scratchy gramophone, whose stylus kept jumping. *My baby just cares for me.* They had all cried at that. It had been for her, at least, a precious, swaddling embedding time. And she had read them Keats.

A Brisk Move Up

After Wales, she had returned, as a teacher, to St Gobnait's. To a fractured, early seventies Derry of disintegration. Yet, somehow, in the midst of mayhem, life had gone on. Children were born and the old were buried. She remained zealous for her charges. If ever there was a champion of girls, it was Miss Black. How many times had she found herself stirring porridge with one hand and with the other, madly jotting? Neglect to grab a worm, and off it wriggles.

This election result was so rewarding. So affirming. Her intuition had been right. The people were ready to embrace something grander. The future was unwrapping. On her low, ceramic patio table stands the glass of celebratory Muscatel she had promised herself. The sun caresses the river. Love floats on its surface. Rays dance and fade. But heat radiates from the stones. Stones that would surely speak if only they could. It is not Nirvana, but how truly glorious it is, and somehow right.

Bats are abroad. Inside now, she partially draws a curtain. Lights a beeswax candle. Slips on a sloppy jumper. Turns on her lava lamp – how very sixties.

But how, people also asked, had she climbed the educational ladder so quickly? I mean, was there not something fishy about her fast ascent? This was the subtext. An inference that to have become headmistress, she must have pulled strings. Hence her detailed interviews with both the *Sentinel* and the *Journal*.

It was all merit. There had been no strings, but yes, it was true, St Gobnait's had appointed her to teach history at the age of twenty-two. And most certainly, she had become the youngest Head Teacher in the North when she was twenty-eight. Had she been driven by naked ambition?

Ambition, yes. But naked? Hardly. Though she had taken her chances.

The seventies had been a time of war. Of rockets, hostages, massacre, kidnappings, innocent young women smothered in tar, feathered like cowards by men. Men blown to bits. Combatants in and out of uniform, yet, somehow, and bizarrely, life had trundled on. The flame had continued to burn. Girls came and went. Success was celebrated. Always. Her girls had blossomed in the rubble, stray poppies waving in the debris. There had been death and destruction, but the birds sang. Tomorrow still followed today. School was the one stable pillar in the lives of many girls. And yes, there had been miracles. Theirs had been a community of hope, bright testimony to the positive. She had become part of the fabric. Sometimes, though, one could trace a leap forward to a particular event.

The Army had occupied St Gobnait's rose gardens without a by your leave. That particular spring, the daffs had bloomed gloriously, but the times were ghoulish. It was unthinkable to have a military installation, camouflage, guns, the whole paraphernalia and khaki squaddies as a presence in the grounds. The girls were at risk in more ways than one. The audacity of it.

'Miss Black, I want you to come with me to Fort George,' Miss Ryan said.

They had found themselves billeted in a cramped, airless room, with the smell of dusty mice. A finger-marked bank of grimy internal phones. Grey maps covering the walls. And on the maps, paper stick-on stars of varying colours, reds, blues and whites. Little sharp flags, conjured from cocktail sticks, denoting fortifications or pressure points. Rosemount Watch Tower. Piggery Ridge. Strand Road Police Station. The maps also sprouted dozens of green, white and orange-headed pins. The locations of republican suspects? Safe houses where they slept?

They were meeting Major Jinks, commanding officer of 'N' Division, at nine o'clock precisely.

'I am Head of St Gobnait's, Major,' Miss Ryan said, 'and this is Miss Black.'

Her lava lamp oozed.

What an astounding retrieval system lurked within one's brain.

'Delighted to meet you, Miss Black.'

The Major had given her the once over. Face, chest and legs. He pulled out a seat, like a waiter in the Hilton.

'Would Miss Black care to view the menu?' A sneer as he winked at Miss Ryan.

'Cigarette ladies?' How awfully Noel Coward. Naturally she refused.

'Now, look here,' the Major began, 'PIRA are upping the ante. I take it we are familiar with PIRA? Provisional IRA. Intelligence indicates an imminent attack. When, and on what scale, we do not know. But we will. Believe you me.' He grabbed some wooden pointer thing and thrust it at the wall.

'We have reason to believe that PIRA plan to make use of public buildings, and their green areas. A kind of herbaceous border strategy, if you like.' He waited.

This was supposed to be amusing.

'You get the picture. Hence, the need for pre-emptive presence. Deterrent. Do you see. Logic.'

He stabbed again.

'Foyle College. Thornhill. Templemore Secondary and last, but not least, I am sure, St Gobnait's. Digging in. That's what we call it. Do you follow me? Who was St Gobnait?'

'Bees,' Miss Ryan said. 'The patron saint of bees.'

'And when did he live?'

'St Gobnait was a woman,' Indigo had said. 'She could command the bees to sting an enemy. On the eyeballs, I believe.'

The Major had lit up. He blew second-hand smoke now, over Indigo and Miss Ryan. Then he scrunched his butt. A knock at the door.

A soldier, balancing tea on a tray, and three Nice biscuits.

'Iron rations,' said the Major, 'if you've no objections to sharing a cuppa with the enemy. Just joking. How we beat the Germans. Tanks, a few Yanks and PG Tips.'

He attempted a grin.

'Our chaps were offered ground glass sandwiches on the Falls. Generous Irish hospitality. No offence. World famous. Charming, but hard to chew. Sugar? Here in Londonderry, it's so much more civilised. Thank you, Lance Corporal. Don't bang the door.'

Miss Ryan must have been Principal since the mid-sixties. Rumour had it, she was thinking of a wig.

But was her eye on the principal's job already? Absolutely not.

'I dare say you think we'll change our minds,' Jinks had said. 'Do you care for milk?' He'd milked his own already. 'Forgive my manners. Too much male company. The way things are.'

She had taken in his grey eyes. His unyielding, metal, army issue desk. How soulless and rigid it was. There had once been a tiny window in the room. A high, square portal now sealed and painted out. Did the military not need to breathe? Fluorescent light glared acid. Jinks was a tall man with a youthful body.

You'll see,' he'd said, playing with a desk toy. Five polished ball bearings bounced off one another. Each nudging the next one on strings. 'We won't back off.'

A gauntlet. But what to say? Miss Ryan glanced at Indigo. There had been no pre-planning. No tactics talk. No reason given for the absence of Mrs Boucher, the Deputy Headmistress. But when the glance came, it was a signal, and Indigo was ready. In that instant, destiny had called. It was hardly premeditation.

'Are you married, Major?' she believes she asked him. 'And have you children?'

'Two girls.' He said it quietly. 'Emma and Charlotte.'

'Their ages?'

'What is this,' he said. 'Interrogation? They are fourteen and twelve. Both mad-keen, as it happens, on ponies.'

'I don't think your girls attend our school.' Indigo turned towards Miss Ryan. Where had these words come from?

The Major gave a twisted sort of smile. 'Tour of duty,' he said. 'All that pack drill. We're all human beings, you know.'

'We have five hundred human girls like yours,' she had told him. 'Same beating hearts. Same tears and dreams. Four Emmas in Year ten. One Charlotte in Year twelve. They have no livestock to speak of, and they live in tight little streets. Their daddies have no jobs. Are you with me?'

'That's hardly our fault,' said the Major. 'The Army is a worthwhile profession. As noble as teaching. We risk our lives, you see. It's from those *wee* streets you mention, I'm afraid, the no-hope flats and overcrowded slums that PIRA draws their members. The scum who kill our men.'

His hands were trembling.

Some silences live forever.

'Then it's touché,' she remembers saying. 'I'm sure you know the expression.'

'I do,' he said, 'but it's hardly appropriate.'

'Let me tell you something that is appropriate,' she said. 'You are making a very big mistake.'

She had shoved back her mug. Rejected his pale, cool offering. Slopped weak, cold tea all over his papers. But she did not apologise.

'We will not expose our girls. Whether to you or the Provisionals.'

'We are the *British* Army,' he said, shuffling a pile of imaginary papers. Cracking his English knuckles. 'And with the greatest of respect, it's not up to you two ladies, is it? Shall I tell you something more?'

He leaned forward, white teeth in her face.

'We intend to root out every God-cursed Republican volunteer, every Londonderry broom cupboard full of weapons, every priest-ridden closet of bulging ordnance. They will wish they had not been born. We intend to rid this city of vermin, and you and your teacher friends will help us. We do not shoot innocent men.'

'Or women or children?' she'd said. Miss Ryan followed her out. This had been her moment. Though it had not been intentional.

Next morning, Miss Black led all the girls, the entire school body onto their lawn, in full view of the traffic, with a billowing banner on poles. *St Gobnait students will not be targets,* in red, bleeding capitals, embellished by the Art Department. She phoned John Hume, though she'd never met him. Called to see both bishops. Gave an interview to *The Times* of London. Spoke on RTÉ. The girls had lined up like Amazons, in the cold, spring sunshine, in their racing green battle dresses. And oh, the spine-chilling harmony when they raised their anthem in Latin.

She would recall this now, keep it to the forefront of her mind, as she embarked on her brand-new mission. It had never been a case of taking sides. There was only what was right.

Jinks' orders had been rescinded.

Humble pie.

'All a bit of a crossed wire,' he told the BBC.

Before his transfer.

When Miss Ryan retired, Indigo's colleagues were persuasive.

'We want a principal with balls,' they'd said quite seriously. 'Age doesn't matter. Someone strong. Like you.'

Quite a number of parents sent well wishes in advance of her interview. She beat off two women from Galway, and a Frenchman with Esperanto. Such a bagful of notes and cards to treasure in her large Black Magic box. The rest is history. How time had galloped.

Would she do it all again if she could? In a heartbeat, despite Mr Cathal Martin.

The Cathal Martin Affair

The letter, when it came, was a shock. A nightmare, though the upshot should not have been a surprise to someone of her vintage. Yet it was an awful punch to the head. More than forty years of teaching up in smoke. But people advanced their own.

Cathal Martin had been a great catch, or so she'd been led to believe. Winner of the Earnshaw, PhD in Photonics. Keen on drama. A patron, like herself, of the Lyric. Adored by her girls, and, as it turned out, by one in particular. Nephew of Jim Carlin, the well-connected turf accountant, wheeler-dealer chair of Gobnait's Board of Governors. Though bookies, of course, had their place. She enjoyed a flutter herself.

Naturally, from the outset, Jim had declared an interest. He wouldn't sit on the appointment panel for the physics vacancy. 'Oh God, no. Wouldn't be seen dead on it.'

No brown envelopes. Propriety. Squeaky-clean Jim played it by the book. The book of track records.

'Good luck,' he told them as they assembled in the boardroom.

'Science is vital. And I know a bit about it. Without physics, sure, you're only guessing, do you know what I'm saying? A good physicist can tell you how a bee sees in colour. Did you know that? The way a horse works out his jumps. Everything is based on science. May the best man win. And by the way, that's not a sexist comment.'

Yes, Jim.

'You take magnetism... no, I'll give this panel a miss. It wouldn't be right with the young fella being my what do you call it. Phone me when you get white smoke.'

No pressure.

'Best candidate on the day.'

Seven on the panel. Set questions. Scoring sheets. All that malarkey. An advisor from the Department. Ultan Wright. Jim knew him through rugby. Had been yarning to him in the corridor before the panel assembled.

'Sound man, Ultan. Great chat entirely. Six Nations. Fancies Ireland big time.'

Two tickets no problem.

'Off the record, I gave him a nudge for Fairyhouse.'

No vote, but key.

'Ten applicants, you tell me. We need top-notchers. St Gobnait's is high end. Marvellous. Great resources. New labs.'

Mary Barton, one of the parent representatives. '... and after all the brainwork, my goodness, and what credentials, what else would you bring to the College, Mr Martin?'

'Drama.'

'Oh, would you really?'

'I'm into school shows.'

'And if you were needed, after school, I mean, to coach a particular child that was, say, neurodiverse, would that be a problem for you, Mr Martin?' Bronagh O'Driscoll. Her child was on the spectrum.

He checked her name badge. 'One hundred per cent, Bronagh, I'd be with you all the way.'

Ultan Wright. 'You've been in academia. Is there any possibility you could feel, how can I put it, a little restricted in this post?'

Cathal didn't think so. He wanted back to the city.

'I'm a pretty grounded fella,' he said. 'And there's more to life than research. I'm dually qualified to coach soccer and Gaelic.'

'Are you now.' Smiles and nods.

He had done more than well. But just the same. At these panels, one recognised the unsaid, the quiet intake of breath, the extension of a vowel, even the inflection of a voice. Indigo knew Jim's form. Machiavelli wouldn't be in it.

'We'll let you know this evening.' This was Henry, the deputy chair. Handshakes.

'Good luck.' Melanie Cooper, always tanned. Seen often with Chairman Jim.

Ten candidates. Long day.

'You couldn't go past him, Miss Black. What do you say?'

There was something about Cathal Martin which refused to be bottled. The other contender was a lovely woman who had worked for NASA, but they wouldn't entertain her.

'She'd be away above the children's heads.' But she should have been considered.

Can one imagine an undertow? Jim Carlin, like a lot of men, had seemed so solid at the beginning of his tenure. But he loved power. And time is a great unraveller. Had they all been nobbled? She knew about influence. Drinks late at night, and whatever. And, no, she wasn't being paranoid. Why had she not confronted them? Had it been an off day? For once she had taken the easy path, but she had certainly missed a trick.

What does Miss Black think?

Oh, very well.

'The appointment's yours,' she'd told him on the phone. 'Congratulations.'

'Okay,' he said, 'that's grand.'

Grand. My God. A teaching post at Gobnait's.

In the event, he'd appeared to settle in. She had not always been right. Just being Jim Carlin's nephew did not make him a criminal. And he did have chiselled looks. If looks were all, she could have become ensnared herself, had she been twenty-five.

The show. Synge. The Playboy. Terrific stuff. West of Ireland and plaid shawls. Callous stories and dirty deeds. In a flurry of exuberance, she had mucked in, to help paint Pegeen's kitchen. Appearing in green overalls. Slapping foundation on flats. That sort of thing. Going to the Whatnot to borrow props. Two snooty china dogs. Very supercilious. A pair of black granny shoes for the Widow Quinn. A cooling rack and crane. She even found a turf spade with a lip on it.

'Oh splendid. A loy for Christy.'

And yet, the unease.

She watched Cathal at work, Earnshaw winner, thespian producer in action. He was good. Maybe it was all in her head. A prejudiced bias spawned by distrust.

She had not frequented the staff room. Gossip came from the cleaners after school. Soft information, but vital.

'Hello, Miss Black. I'll dust your room.'

'You're looking tired, Miss Black. I'll water your wee plant. Boil your wee kettle. A Jaffa Cake, Miss Black?

'My daughter Geraldine has the toothache, Miss Black. Wild painful.' Isobel, who missed nothing. Red heat rash on her neck. 'Mr Martin's a hard goer, isn't he? God's sake, he never leaves the place.'

But a hesitation. Now what was this? A lingering too long at the door. Years of experience.

Sharpen up, she'd told herself.

Lucy Craig was a natural Pegeen Flaherty. Magical. She had the voice. The figure. The poise.

'Six yards of stuff for to make a yellow gown.'

God, Indigo was back playing the part. But she watched from the wings in silence. Listening to Lucy's modulation. If anything, she underplayed the part. Didn't overdo the brogue. She looked twenty-one. Hair clasped for the dress rehearsal. No overacting.

'You're perfect,' Cathal told her. 'You're dream girl.'

That was it. In that moment she had it. She knew the tone. The impact of his words. What lurked behind them.

'You're *perfect*.'

She'd been so blind.

Then a knock. Geraldine's mother.

'I'm sorry, Miss Black. I thought I should say.'

It all fitted. The body language. The illicit electricity.

'Are you sure? It's a serious accusation.'

'I saw what I saw.'

Geraldine's mother had seen what she saw until she was needed. Until the PSNI called on her to speak up. And Lucy denied it. Any of it. All of it.

'Malicious,' she said.

There had been no case. No evidence. No answers. No child protection. No need. But there had been repercussions.

Dear Indigo. The Board of Governors cannot begin to thank you for all you have given to our wonderful College over the years... etc, etc.

It referred to the onerous responsibility of running a school in modern times. Jim would spend more time with her. Join her for lunch. Act as a sounding board. A turf accountant. It was reprisal, sexist and ageist. But she still had her pride. There had been no option but to walk.

Even on this night of victory, as she looked ahead, she supposed there was more to be processed. In time she would leave it all behind.

The Guildhall clock struck twelve.

Midnight. Night music on Classic. She would sit a little longer.

Goodbyes

Indigo stared from her window at the Peace Bridge. How long had they wanted rid of her? The unexpected travelled downstream. She lit a cigarette. She had yearned for more years. But in the end rejection had married treachery. To be as good as shown the door. It had been the worst of times. She should have had more resilience. But what use was cognition when one's feelings had been mangled?

She had governed with such energy, sometimes, in retrospect, to the dismay of the Board, shedding staff who refused to put girls first, struggling, if she were honest, not to bloody well lay hands on them. In the O'Brien case she had appeared before an Industrial Court in Belfast's Linen Hall Street, accused of harassment. Three days of grilling by two men and a woman from Bangor plastered over the *Irish News*. It was nonsense, of course, but the Board had been upset. It ought to have been a warning. One can miss one's footing so easily.

Quite simply, she had been satisfied if her students left the College with song in their hearts, and that distinctive St Gobnait quickness of step. Especially those who had been unfortunate. When a girl became pregnant, she had honoured her as a mum-to-be. Miss Black was never a stranger to the maternity ward, often shopping in the Craft Village for soft, knitted lambs and comforting cot blankets. Each new little bundle was a gift.

The girls had produced their own plays, sung duets, strummed harps. Their paintings hung in every cranny of the school. A kind of Bayeux tapestry had grown and grown of their unspooling work. They had produced short films that played on loops and written first novels. Gobnait's had won prizes for child-centredness, though she'd never referred to her charges as 'children.' They had read Heaney with passion. Valued Woolf and Piaf. They had trashed regrets together. When Liam Neeson visited, the girls had melted, and so had she. But in the end, none of this mattered.

Retirement had struck like a gong.

Bong bloody bong.

'Miss Black, retiring? Can't be.'

'Not old enough.'

'Have you seen her skin? How smooth it is. The slimness of her ankles. Her hair, no split ends.'

It was vanity to think of this. But how bruising it had been.

'It's a pure sin, Indigo.'

'… and personally, I would fight it.'

Of course you would.

So unreal. Her farewell party at The Beech Hill, in its gorgeous surroundings. The peacocks and pheasants. What an eternal place, and yet how dismal she had felt during the venison and asparagus tips, the soufflé and truffles. Afterwards she had walked limply around the pond. A dying sun had kissed the lilies and the arch of climbing roses.

Her goodbye speech faded like a lament. It was a night of mourning, an evocation of the Irish wake. Shaken hands. Head down.

'Sorry for your trouble.'

The hugging and kissing. The offers of a lift.

'Let me.'

'No, me.'

There would be chats to come in Nero and Costa, jolly meals in Browns in Town and a thousand other fine eating houses during half term holidays –

'We'll keep in touch.'

The scrolling, tapping, summoning of husbands.

'Taxi?'

'That's yours.'

'Take care, Concepta.'

'God, Malachy, is it really all over?' she'd said at last.

What a faithful caretaker.

For all her time at the wheel, what had she honestly known about departures? Now *she* was the blubbering one. Her empathy for others had been like something from Enid Blyton. Tears for exiting teachers had been for her own departure. Could one even come close to inhabiting the heart of another?

'A drama queen,' some must have said. And that naturally was true.

But what was new? Her energy, all along, had been boundless. At that low point, she had wondered if she would ever again take pleasure in her walks at Inch.

Then things had moved on. 'Moths,' she said. 'Gossamer wings.' She closes the windows. Lights twinkle in the Foyle. Damn it, she's had a fine night and there's little sign of rain.

A Good Doctor Is a Find

Thank God, all had not been lost. The stars, whatever they are, had opened a way, thanks to her friend and General Practitioner Barnaby Toland, whose practice is merely yards away. A good doctor is money in the bank. Tonight, Indigo Black will think of him, before she succumbs to sleep alone in her apartment, in her amazing waterfront building. For he has helped her turn the corner.

'You certainly have the blues, Indigo,' he'd said. 'I know to look at you, but we'll run the tests. Blood is the big thing. How long are you on the happy pills?'

Did his computer not store all that? But he had wanted to talk.

'How many years were you teaching anyway? Forty. My God. Withdrawal. It's not unusual.'

'Thank you, Tom Jones. Neither is it, I suppose, unusual to cry?'

'Indeed not.'

He was looking more serious now. Back stretches in his swivel chair. An old injury. He had driven fast cars. Almost goodnight. Crashed near Slieve League.

'Men often cry,' he said, 'between you and me and the wall.'

She had broken some hearts herself.

'You might be surprised,' he said.

Such a long time she'd known him – once, amazingly, he had threatened himself with a knife.

'I might as well end it,' he had said drunkenly, on the Ha'penny Bridge.

This after a visit to the National Gallery. Lavery and luminescence. Toland had stared at the darkness of the Liffey for a long time but wishes could not be enforced at the end of a dagger. Blackmail would never have secured her. And he had survived.

'It's been just too acute,' she told him, in his untidy office.

'Get into something,' he'd said at last. 'Go back to the Operatic. Tread the boards again. Audition. Be a principal, no pun intended.'

Toland would never be a plain old almost-ran. She regarded him, she supposed, in much the same way as she did her late father's roll-top desk, battered, thran and smelling of dependable tobacco.

He had ordered bloods. Full profile.

'Full marks. All clear. Nothing nasty. No shortness of breath? Palpitations? How are you on Shipquay Street? Can you climb to the Diamond without stopping? I wish I could myself. Lower Bennett Street? I'll check your lungs. Blood pressure? One hundred and fifteen over seventy-five. God save us, you could be twenty-eight. Not a thing wrong with you. It's in your head. We'll do an ECG.

'I'll not be giving you any more of the you-know-whats. Long live the euphemism.'

He leaned forward to peer at his screen.

Too damned small a font.

'Find meaning in life, like me,' he'd grunted, toying with his stethoscope – what a primeval smell of rubber – 'pull up your top now would you.'

Cold, shiny steel on skin. Tap, tap. 'Everyone needs purpose, that's what I find.'

She had sweated profusely, despite a new antiperspirant. He took her pulse. Twice. 'Sometimes it elevates with anxiety.'

But no, it was normal.

Now, incredibly, he offered her, 'a ciggie.' How very quaint.

'For later, of course.'

A hidden pack of Bull Brand in his drawer.

'Some doctors still smoke, you know.'

But then, he'd found the words. Real words. And strong. There was still that old dissolute, Donleavy look about him, when he told her straight.

'Stand for election. That will teach them. You haven't thought of that. Be a public representative. An advocate of the people. I'm telling you. You'd play a blinder.'

'But I've never considered....'

'Well, it's time you did. This city needs a clever, independent, and – beautiful woman in the Chamber.'

He would never give up.

'Go and show them,' he said. 'Take it to them in The Guildhall, or wherever they meet nowadays. Force them across fresh frontiers. We need positivity, especially with all this Brexit bollocks. Grab them by the short hairs, Indigo. Bring hope.'

'What would I *be* though?' she had asked him. 'I could never join a political party. I'd be neither green or orange.'

'Precisely. To hell with alignment, Miss B. Take your purity to the people, without filtration, unpasteurised if you like, God damn their labels. Present the voters with yourself.'

She should probably have switched to Dr Laverty, a younger man, devoid of baggage or charisma. But there was also the ethic of human connection. Some sticky electrodes had remained on her person, the gluey ones he missed. She would remove them later. At this point she heard him sigh.

'But would it give me room?' she'd asked.

'Good God,' he said again, now forced to check his watch. 'You will be your own person, like you've always been. Become a scriptwriter and produce your own manifesto. *You'll* be the Wonder of the Western World. I went to see it, you know. Of course, I didn't know then about the… that's right. The other. But these things happen. You will bring so much life. Same as you've always done for me, and all us fellows who still worship you. Think of your students. The artists, and dancers, the actors, who got there, thanks to you. Who was it lit their fuses, Indigo, if it wasn't you? This sense of loss will pass. You are still in good shape. Make the most of the now. Expose yourself to the people and they will reach out to you.'

'Write my own production, is it? No pill to cure my ill.'

'Pretty much. I often prescribe for the sake of peace, you know, and I know I shouldn't. But I won't today. I'll soak up the patient's wrath. No more bloody chemicals for you, my girl. I'm calling time. How's that from an old admirer?'

He had held her hand for a fraction longer than one's doctor ought. Though hers was not yet an *old* hand. His, though, was soft like putty.

'That's fluid,' she told him.

'You stick to aesthetics,' he told her. 'I'll heal the sick.'

Strange how one accepted firmness from so weak a man. Was it weakness that made her love him?

She thinks she will make some toast.

Fresh Start

Miss Black had left the surgery that day with resolve, to run her own show. To win loyalists and republicans to the cause of beauty. What a challenge. But the spirit of humanity was well beyond Catholics and Protestants. She would fight for the ecstatic. It would be her recovery. In time, she would make the city a cultural adventure park, a place of revelation for ordinary people, whatever their flops or failures. She would create vision, fulfilment and possibility. And teach again, of love.

All this she had included in her promotional material, with the help of past pupils and the business community. There was such goodwill. She had taken with ease to the airwaves, enhancing the experience of listeners with auditory colour. Her voice, she was told, had the mellifluous timbre of a late-night jazz presenter, with that 'attractive allure of quality.' Which made her 'relatable.' Her style, as always, was unashamed seduction.

In Little Acorns Bookstore, two customers said, 'Good on you Miss Black.'

She bought new clothes.

'Bring on the elections,' she had repeated with increasing confidence, 'I love the bunting's flutter.'

Her appearance on promotional posters had been ectoplasmic. Such a transformation. One had to admit, she had looked spectacular in yellow, and as for her hair…

Leaflets, fliers, press coverage are the tools of your average wannabe. But Indigo had tapped into something more substantial. Something at the core of her persona. Of her essence. When she spoke, listeners glimpsed, with pleasure, comprehension. She made sense to them in violet and ultra-white. Greyness was banished. Miss Black created clouds to lie on, sea horses to ride, nautical charts to lend direction. Her words were received with joy by coal men and stevedores, butchers, bakers and artisan candlestick makers in Pump Street. Asda delivery men and BT engineers rang in to speak with her. Beauty, she assured them, was for all, and an ever-flowing fountain. 'We are all children of wonder.'

Where and when had she received her vision?

'I was washed up,' she confessed openly. 'But a dear, straight-talking friend pulled me through. My back was to the wall. So be encouraged out there.'

Toland had come up trumps.

Her appeal, indeed, was wide. She had targeted the middle ground. The left. The right. The floating voters and voters who had never floated or voted. Those who believed in something. And in nothing. She had courted support from across what is still referred to, appallingly, as 'the sectarian divide.' Reached church goers, the heathen, nudists, herbalists, and lapsed royalists who wanted more wonder. She had extended the net to include Sinn Féin, the Church of Irelands, Methodists and unknown numbers of closet Presbyterians, some of them said to be Free. She welcomed everyone who wanted to self-actualise. Won applause from closet disciples of Charles Rennie Mackintosh, and Markey Robinson. She revelled in the cheers of emergent art lovers, who yearned for Cezanne, Leonardo and, more locally, Dillon, and dear Colin D. What absolute skill and heart he has! And Dali, for crucified madness. It was fine to be eclectic.

'More art, please, in schools,' she had preached. 'That is my slogan. More painting in Pine Street and Florence Street, more books in Creggan and classes in Nelson Drive.'

There would be dulcimer sessions in Irish Street, and poetry for all. Her vision included cars speeding with seekers towards Bellaghy, writers of prose on bursaries, on chartered buses, bowling towards the Bawn. More grants awarded to aspiring practitioners of whatever genre, to facilitate retreats. Municipal help would be lavished to an ever-increasing extent on lonely sculptors and gay dancers. Miss Black would launch a superhuman revival in creativity. 'Stand by,' had been her injunction, 'at last, together, we will find release.' She had also healed herself.

'I mean, honestly, is that not a bit hyperbolic?' asked the Long Presenter on his show, one dismal afternoon.

Indigo was instantly alight. 'We will have pilgrimages. Why not? Our Derry wans are marvellous. Look at the Millennium. The Playhouse, Waterside Theatre, The Wee Theatre at Skeoge, beyond the horses, don't talk to me, just think of Pat and Pauline, Felicity, and Olly G. Are these not our local wizards? Try to keep up, young man.'

The Long Presenter had smiled in his engaging way, when he said she was a marvel, like La Trinidad Valencera and the Broighter Gold.

'Good grief,' she said, 'now, steady on.'

'You know what listeners,' he had said, 'this is a complete waste of time. 'It's pointless talking about art to this one. She *is* blooming art.'

Now the Guildhall clock chimed one.

What progress there had been.

Gate Crasher

Tonight, in bed, Indigo Black should not need to open her new Claire Keegan. She will douse her lights and sleep. But sleep is a challenge when one is poised.

By way of thanks, she had taken Toland and Barbara to dinner at the delightful Bishop's Gate Hotel, once a club for the wilting ascendancy. The sort of place where a certain sort of man might have sought solace. Where he could have whiled away his nights at cards and whisky, listening with half an ear, for the sonorous bells of St Columb's

Cathedral. At special times, for the beat of drums. This, despite brewing upheaval, incipient street violence and revolution. In those days, the Queen had still hung languid on a hook.

As usual, she reflected, Toland had got quite squiffy, but for once, had kept his hands to himself. He *was* after all Miss Black's mentor and physician. And Barbara reined him in. This, his second union, had appeared not to waver. In any case, Indigo adored them both, but she was also lured by the dogs in wigs who stared from the textured walls. These learned canines would mete out themed justice in calibrated barks. What an amusing thought. Her spirits had been understandably high. 'Light, woofy sentences for first offenders. Snarls and savagery for the more serious felon.'

How wonderful it had been to celebrate one's new start with the Tolands in the grand kennelled style, in one's own town. She often calls it a town, for, here, everyone knows everyone. Their mother, their cousins, their sisters and their aunts. Indigo has inwardly made a vow to stay grounded as well as resolute, whilst reaching for the planets. And, above all, to be true to herself.

If sleep should come tonight, so be it. If it refuses, let it go hang. She has plenty to think about.

The mussels in Bishop's Gate Hotel had been outstanding. The Sperrin lamb, superlative. But should she have had the crumble?

'I think so,' said their waiter without hesitation.

Clearly a fine judge of rhubarb and of women.

'You know you want to.'

It was true. She had wanted to.

'If you say so,' she told him.

She had not needed to be cajoled.

'And where would you be from?'

On reflection, this had been a little intrusive. Certainly, she had no interest in his religion. Whether he had a faith, or not, was crassly irrelevant. But when one achieved a certain vintage, it seemed one took more chances.

'Northland Avenue.' He said it readily enough. 'Not far from Radio Foyle.'

'Don't tell me.' She had studied his cheekbones. 'You have to be a Doherty.'

'The town's full of Dohertys.'

'But I taught your sisters.' It was good, she had placed him. 'Sinead and Bridget. Cello and trombone. It feels like yesterday. Christmas carols in Pennyburn. Of course. Methinks they went to pagan England. Tell them I said, "Hello."'

'I will, Miss Black,' the boy had been so polite. 'They live in Stockport now,' he said, 'and work in Bramall Hall.'

'Bramall's a Tudor pile,' she told the Tolands. 'They've done so very well, and all in pursuit of art. Two of our finest young women.'

'You see, I told you,' said Toland.

After the meal, she had drunk Sambuca. Eight seconds of intense cold blue. Life is full of anomalies. Quench the flame and down the hatch. Giddiness had been mandatory on such a night, as beauty was being reborn.

The Guildhall clock chimed two.

'Romped home, though. You really did.'

Toland had been scanning the dining room. 'Some noses well out of joint.'

He had said this sotto voce.

'Love conquers all, and so will beauty.'

'I know,' said Toland.

Throughout the evening, many of the diners had segued to her table. Hesitating for an uncertain moment before taking their leave. Like fans approaching an idol. What a vain thought. This had been pleasant, though, if superficial in its way. Mostly they were men, some of them tight as ticks. 'Yes' and 'good luck,' they said, in the familiar Derry manner. A number were large assertive males, with little, thin, anxious wives. There were also, among these men, the designated drivers. The short straw brigade, forced to stay sober. Who wished they'd stayed at home.

'Go for it, love,' a woman told her, 'we need more artists like you, and what d'you call the gorgeous singer? Ursula. Wullie loves her, don't you Wullie. And that other beautiful Anne one, from Moneymore. There's not a pick on either of them.'

'Great voices,' Wullie said.

'Personally, I'm dying about jazz,' the woman said. 'I wanna sing like them. I used to do an odd turn, you know, in the Social Club at Gransha. Before I had the weans. Wait till I tell you, this city is just bustin with talent, pet. God bless you anyway and your new party. G'on you shake us all up with beauty, and you'll have my vote and my Wullie's. Won't she Wullie?'

Wullie jangled his keys.

'I'll do my best,' Indigo told the woman. 'Just watch this spot.'

'What spot?'

'Come on, Assumpta.' Wullie had marched her out.

Indigo turned now in her bed. Plumped her pillow. It was just as the woman had left, on Wullie's arm, that she noticed Shugh Henderson and his jackals. Ties loosened, at the bar. Jaws slack. Beads of sweat. On a hard night's elbow bending. Consolation pints of the black stuff. Little rejoicing in his camp, for she had wiped their eye. Mother of God. How long had he been there?

So far, Henderson had shown no sign of recognising her, with his cobra eyes, but she watched him take in the colour of her dress. He must have been sixty-five, but with his belly, he looked a lot more. He steadied himself, one hand on the bar, amber liquid in the other, to plough an unsteady furrow right into the dining room. He was a blundering, florid, ill-fitting man on walkabout, perspiring heavily, bumping between tables like a big, blunt bullock. A man on meander, badmouthing as he went. Using his bulk. A bully in need of a pee.

'Titipu,' he said, obliquely, as he reached her table. 'How are you at all at all?' 'Gilbert and Sullivan.'

Poor Toland groaned. Henderson's trigger finger pointed at Indigo.

'Great to see *you*, after all this time.'

No reference to her win.

'*Mikado*, in 'eighty-five.' She'd been in the chorus. Had he really seen the show?

'I hear you're back?' he said, 'it can't be easy at your – ah well,' he hesitated, gathering himself, 'we used to rehearse in this very place,' he told the Tolands, 'up there you know.'

We. He waved in the direction of the grand stairs.

Had he been in the Society?

'But wait a minute. Weren't you one of the little maids, or am I or wrong? My God. Would you credit that? A little maid.'

He studied her closely. 'Doesn't time, I say, just fly.'

Henderson inspected her fingers one by one. No ring.

'You wanted to be Yum Yum,' he said, 'but the voice was too weak. The McCrossan woman was top drawer. I'm too busy to sing these days.'

He had rocked on his heels.

'This must be the second Mrs T,' he said, looking for the first time at Barbara. 'How are you doing love?'

Indigo had refused to speak. No one had spoken.

'Long time, long time,' he said. 'I believe I'll be seeing a lot more of you, Miss eh, Black. Truth and beauty. Isn't that your catch phrase? No word about the rates or the shitty bin collections.'

The staff were gentle but insistent.

'Thank you,' Indigo had told them, and meant it.

She had let him make an ass of himself. Often, she reflected, as she waited now for sleep, there is no *need* to say a thing.

Henderson had threaded his way in the general direction of the gents and turned his back on her, ambling off, much as a dancing bear might have done in medieval Europe. Sober enough to know he might fall. Too drunk to rise if he did.

'He's a lout, but watch him,' Toland said. 'Him and his hoodlums.'

'He's a hack,' she'd said. 'Nothing lovely in his soul.'

'Hack or no hack.'

'Barnaby's right.' Nods from Barbara. 'I know a bad person when I meet one.'

She had patted Indigo's hand.

'But I also recognise a strong woman. Who else could have seen off a boor like that, without a single word?'

At first, Barbara had refused Toland. But Toland had insisted.

For a moment now, under her duvet, a shiver threatened Indigo. Toland had a nose for things. Had he been right when he'd spoken of villains? She felt instinctively that what they had witnessed was not so much a case of bad losing as an opening salvo. But if Henderson wanted a fight, he had come to the right woman. With this last affirmation, she surrendered to sleep as the Guildhall clock struck three.

American Dream

Next morning, refreshed, her town stretches its limbs. Over muesli and heather honey, she begins to plan her Happening. Many might shrug at the idea. 'A what?' Those who had missed the sixties. This uncertainty will pass. Before long, they will grasp its potential. Its unifying, kick-starting cultural power. She added more hazelnuts.

Naturally, any Happening she could conceive would not obliterate sadness, or remove the scars of pain – how trivial to even contemplate such a thing – but it *would* release a momentous, explosive surge of power, to build momentum and enhance the artistic legend of Colmcille. It would strengthen the cores of her fellow citizens. No wonder she had barely slept. The thought filled her with purpose.

As for Henderson, he could not even begin to know the essential Miss Black.

Wearing only her robe, for clothes are restrictive on such a portentous morning, she floats through her polished kitchen, lifting a plate here, a saucer there, rattling a silver spoon, steadying the crimson roses she received from Quiggs, courtesy of an anonymous admirer. She trills a little, inhaling the perfection of the moment. Adjusts the Aboriginal bark painting brought back from Uluru. This is a time to think, but the call of the African Grey upstairs is compelling.

'Stroke City isn't shitty.'

On this new day of promise, and despite being under-slept, Indigo is happy in her skin. How blessed to have summer as one's friend. She nurses a companionable hot chocolate. Is she a little hung over? Well, yes, perhaps. On occasion her use of alcohol has been awe-inspiring and led to impulsive moves. Once, she flew supersonically with an RAF pilot, who dropped his aircraft like a stone over Horn Head, strictly illegal, in Irish airspace, looping the loop with almost cataclysmic results. And all because he had liked the way she sliced his lemons.

'Oh God, so thin,' he'd said, 'So very wafer thin.'

She had dibbled them into his glass with such seismic little plops.

Her brain is already at work, but she can take her time.

Aeroplanes. Instantly, she is transported to another place, where strong coffee was drunk, on a different morning after. Years ago, she had travelled west and encountered the incredible Billy Grail. And now, between mouthfuls of oats and pecans, and beyond the shadow of hesitation, she knows that she must have him – for The Happening. That he will *be* The Happening.

Through her inviting window flutters a painted lady with messages of affirmation. Here it is, alighting on her finger. How can such a living creature be so thoroughly fragile. Yet so persistent. How far has it travelled for this connection? The insect's arrival is one of those occasional blessings which visits the truly chosen. Indigo welcomes it, as one might the return of a priceless, stolen painting.

'Oh, there you are,' she says.

She had met Billy Grail in Philadelphia, following the receipt of unexpected funding from the Robert Emmet Society and the Presbyterian General Assembly. An unusual, unifying, and poetic moment of acceptance had followed on the steps of Magee College. Much reported by the media. She would take her girls to Boston.

'Radicalism is art,' she had maintained, 'we shall revisit the scene of the Tea Party. Then off to Pennsylvania.'

She peels a ripe banana for the potassium, and brings to mind that first, preliminary flight to Massachusetts. She had travelled at her own expense, to prepare the way for her girls, to iron out wrinkles, though who can say what cogs were already spinning. One memorable afternoon, she found herself on opposite sides of the Liberty Bell, from – a man, who, like her, was presumably intrigued. His face was obscured by the bell, so he couldn't catch her eye. Each time he moved, she also shifted in a game of cat and mouse. Somehow each found the other, and the circuit went live. What foolishness, but what a different experience from the beginning of any previous relationship, and there had been quite a few. Until they called it quits, she had no idea who he was. But then he emerged. And so also did she. Indigo Black, Principal of *the* quality city school, behaving like a teen, in a physical charade with Billy Grail. *The* Billy Grail. As a student of history, she regarded the bell with gravitas, but this had proved a challenge, as Billy, purporting to be just a simple musician, questioned its utility.

'Well now,' they'd said together, abandoning their cast bronze cover and smiling broadly. 'What a delightful movie to be in.'

'I give up, Ma'am,' he'd said, 'I really do. What is the point of a bell with a crack in it. With no ding dong. I mean a bell that cannot ring? Is there a name for that?'

Americans were not devoid of humour.

'I just can't imagine,' she had said, all those years ago. Her words still echoing with hypnotic amusement. Oh, how they came back.

It might have amounted to nothing more than a passing flirtation. Except that the flames flared hot, because Billy's soul was set deep in the bluest of eyes, reminding her of the young Presley. Before the peanut butter and the jello that destroyed him. Poor, vulnerable, betrayed Elvis. Billy, beautiful as Elvis, could have been his brother.

'I'm only a singer,' he had said. 'I'm really not real.'

But her heart had stopped. Here *was* the real Billy Grail, this young, slim, supple, but also, after a fashion, hungry looking boy, who was reaching out to her. A young man who needed the care of a woman.

'I sing a little myself,' she had told him stupidly – oh Lord, how utterly embarrassing.

At that stage she had still retained a voice.

'I did not know him from Adam, only by reputation,' she would venture afterwards, a tad ashamed of using such clichéd words. Later, during her stay in the stuccoed Ulysses S Grant, with its themed shingled roof, she had reminded herself of the late general's credentials.

Yankee soldiers were billeted 'right here,' according to the bellhop. Tipping was endemic, but she had gladly parted with ten dollars in gratitude for that image, conjuring, as she brushed her teeth, some rocky Union officer, sleeping in this very feather bed. Doubtless it was fanciful to imagine his animal scent, but God, one could dream and tingle, even in one's middle years.

Billy took her to dinner next evening in The Jakob Ammann, a plain but select Amish place, with exposed wooden beams, and all the rest of it, where the waitresses wore Dutch, Vermeer, linen caps and crisp, white pinafores. There had been a healthy pink glow about their cheeks. By contrast, the delft was intensely blue. Indigo, who had visited Holland, recalled for Billy the Clog Museum of Zandaam, the great paddling windmills and Edam cheese. She told him of the Rijksmuseum, of Bruegel's skaters and cannabis brownies. How her heart had clouded for Anne Frank, trapped like a rat above the jam factory. She and Billy ate ground beef with apple chutney and elephant eye corn. They drank farm cider from a barrel and finished with Snickerdoodle cookies. Such embedded memories.

Framed by her morning window now, a Derry man's pert face appeared quite suddenly, popping up like a cheeky brush from a chimney.

'Morning, Miss Black,' he mouthed, waving his chamois wildly. 'Can I do your wee windows?'

Perhaps she had taught his mother?

'You won't believe this, Billy. I actually wore a fringe on top, when I saw *Oklahoma*, for the very first time in the Hall.'

'You didn't. In the hall?"

'I did. In St Columb's Hall.'

Billy had been wonderful. The unworldly Amish had loved him. He was a mega star, even to them.

Perhaps she had not fully understood Billy's genre until then, but that night, in the restaurant he had sung 'Motherless Child,' a cappella. And she had managed a harmony. So many mingled tears. Had that been superlative, or what? 'Bloody visceral,' she'd called it. Billy was the motherless child. She, the mother who took him in. At that moment she had been a woman leaking love. With the urge to be with him forever, though that would have been impossible.

'If that was us, I loved our date,' she told him next day on a rented cell phone.

'Damn the age difference,' he said up front. 'I'd like us to meet again.'

He was wall to wall with gigs, but her ticket for his second show in Symphony Hall arrived at the Ulysses S Grant by courier, along with magnolia blooms.

Never had she imagined any American, apart from The King, wringing her soul the way Billy Grail did.

'What are years,' he said, 'when passion burns? It's the soul that matters. Bodies are a means to an end.'

On stage he had been a sinewed, muscular man. Yet off stage, he needed her. Oh, but what rippling tone. What a diaphragm! A rival to Feargal, his range was two and a half, with ease. How life-changing, to be lifted higher. A challenge, truly, not to feel orgasmic. He was a Leo, like herself – something she discovered over dinner. In all honesty, who could have blamed her for dreaming?

In the event, she had settled for a promise.

Billy was on tour, from Sacramento.

'In other circumstances,' he said – she had never forgotten his words – 'you and I would have been a big team, Indigo. I mean one hell of a big team.'

She had glimpsed his core. Believed his words. And he had felt it too. Of that she had been certain.

'I *want* to visit Ireland.' Lounging in his blossom-strewn dressing room. 'I really do.'

'Then come,' she'd said. 'Visit my jewel of a city. See where I walk and live and have my being. Imbibe my air. Dublin is fine, Belfast is lively, but come to Derry, for Derry is a jewel. Visit a big, warm village full of characters. Our walls were built by Docwra, in the sixteen-hundreds, but our hearts have always been wide open. We'll do you proud. I'll fete you at my school.'

The rest of that second night had been spent in sensuous mirage. She had talked, and Billy, though drained by his performances, had listened in the rapt manner of a student hearing a legend for the very first time.

And so, they had become rather more than friends. That same starlight she dreamed of now had been shining in his eyes.

'Damned right, I'll come to Derry?' he'd told her. She can read his pouting lips.

More coffee, she thinks.

Some promises, no doubt, are worthless. Especially when uttered by men. But there had been something steady about Billy, which spoke of solidity.

'If I'm wrong,' she later told her confidante, Judge Scarlett, 'I'll become a harlot.'

But time is a mystery. It had splashed away. She had seen triumphs and trials. Girls who excelled. Girls who went to Oxbridge. She thought of teachers who had let her down. One who had stolen from their little charity shop. My God in heaven. Second-hand novels and HB pencils. But she had dealt with it all. Shared the euphoria of families on prize day, accepted invitations to graduations. Attended funerals of grandmothers, mothers, brothers. Given evidence in Courts One and Two. Been threatened by both sides. Biting bullets had become a necessary part of her job.

She had once reported explosives found in a store, which exposed them all to horror. The English papers had covered it. Julia Greenaway, from *The Guardian* had flown in from Manchester. Perceptive woman.

Long column. Words like 'disadvantage,' and so forth. And that was all true. But the hearts of the girls had been subverted and misled. A bad time, but she had praised those girls, explaining to the world, a life of duress. She had extolled their many good points. How, inspired by St Gobnait, they had helped to set up beehives and deliver hot lunches to the old.

There had been the usual excoriation from predictable critics. 'To hell,' continued to be her response. Those same girls, she was sure, would be at The Happening. They would meet Billy Grail and kiss his neck.

It will be a glorious new beginning. Billy will flash like a scimitar. Turn the earth red hot. In her womb, she has conceived something outrageous, and already incubating. The appearance of Billy Grail will be climactic. With this erotic thought, she enters her tasteful bathroom.

To a stranger, such ceramic opulence might come as a surprise. But Miss Black, when one thinks about it, wears rimless spectacles, and is a member of Mensa. She has briefly been a Soroptimist. Can scan *The Times* in an hour. Complete brain teasers in half the time permitted. She is not perfect, because hers is a complex persona of colour. Certainly, she knows the words of Socrates, but when one weighs them up, can one really know oneself? Neither has she ever aspired to complete coherence. And this, though sketchily grasped by many, is her charm. Intellect and – how would one describe it, sensuality – have entwined like vines in this city of surprises. Throughout her odyssey so far, and please God it is far from over, she will treasure ambiguity. 'Who wants to be boring, darlings?' she had often challenged her girls.

She runs her shower. The gentle notes of nocturnes waft from speakers in elevated locations. As the jets play, it comes to her that one is never entirely alone in the company of Chopin, or Mozart. Having tested the temperature with her elbow, she yields with pleasure to this freshest of immersions, in water so hot, it might easily flay the skin of a less imaginative woman.

At last, and with purpose, she rinses off the scented conditioner, remembering its silkiness and above all, her determination not to slip. She reaches for a cinnamon towel. This moment of fluffy swaddling is the climax. Sighing, she allows her juices to be absorbed. She is on her way again. Caressing herself with love, she remains convinced beyond measure that this project, this Happening – is exactly what she needs.

What her city and its people need. Those whom she knows already, and those she has yet to meet.

Part Two

Hello, Mr White

Someone, as yet unknown to Miss Black, is undoubtedly Mr White, who had always been pale as an Easter lily. As a boy, growing up on the straggling periphery of the city he had set new records for pallidness. Other lads of his age were ruddy from climbing trees and chasing rabbits. But Mr White's complexion remained that of a sickly child. 'Blanched' was the word which sprang to mind, like an unripe plantain, a peeled parsnip, or the anaemic flour his mother had used.

She would shake it, he recalled, from a pewter dusting pot, an overgrown salter, which, as she said about herself, had a broader bottom than a top. Instead of her pinched grey head, there was a rounded dome, like you got on steam trains, before his time, or on a Muslim mosque, pleasantly symmetrical but with a dozen pin holes punched through its roof. As he lay on his horsehair couch, covered for warmth by a crocheted blanket, despite the roar of the range, Mr White's mother had sung along in a clear voice with Mary Black on the radio; 'Sonny, don't go away...' This as she'd steamrollered her buttery pastry back and forth, with the Old City Dairy milk bottle, he'd found for her, manoeuvring it smartly on a doughy, wooden parade ground, with precise little turns.

'Ironing it out,' as she often said. 'If life were only so simple.'

But look at him now without her.

'That's a good one, Mr White,' she'd used to tell him, when he was seven, complimenting him freely, though he was her son. There had been a surprising light feel to the shaker when he'd held it, no matter how full it was. The thin beaten metal was the sort of tin, he imagined, gypsies had hammered once, in the open air, with ringing blows, in woodland camps. He supposed they'd hawked pots around the houses. You got the same cheap fabrications, he discovered, from a pile of old National Geographics, in the artisan craft shacks of Iznik, which was in Turkey. Cramped home-cabins where lean men banged alone till late, fashioning lamps and decorative bird cages, while they smoked and fasted. He'd like to have gone to Turkey.

Once, there were weevils in the shaker when she'd gone to refill it. 'Look, Mr White,' she said, 'at those bad little buggers.' She'd swung open the door of the old Doric stove, and pitched them in. Together they'd watched, and listened to them sizzle, like tiny sausages, writhing for a second, before they were no more.

'Life's short,' she said, and 'they're full of protein, Mr White.' She'd told him this, he was to realise, in a strange prophetic way. Then whoosh, and they were gone. 'Nourishment down the drain.' Or up the chimney. Up and down, for once, meaning the same thing. Now she was up the chimney and people bred cockroaches to eat. In less than twenty years, he'd heard, the whole world would be munching the legs of insects. That business with the weevils was the one and only time he recalled the shaker being washed. There had been no fuss at the time. All she did was switch to McDougalls flour because it sounded Scottish, like the settlers of Ulster. 'I can't abide a weevil, Mr White, no bleeding harm to them.'

He'd always been Mr White, from the hour of his birth, as far as he knew, until she left him on his own and went to *you know where*. He'd never asked her about it before she went. Never said, because he'd never thought she would go off to heaven without him. Death was an inaccessible place for the young.

He still thinks of her every day, imagining himself as a small wean, and her bringing him home in a taxi from the maternity hospital to Carrickfergus, where they started off, he thinks, the pair of them. If he listens carefully, he can hear her telling all six pounds of him – he'd made enquiries – that this was where King Billy landed from his ship.

'Oh, such a castle they have, in Carrickfergus,' she'd said, 'now take the nipple, Mr White.'

She must have told him this a million times, for the words come to him naturally, and how else could he know them?

'You nearly pulled them off me, you devil,' she used to say, so he knew she'd admired his pluck. 'Eh, those were the great days too.'

She wasn't from Carrick. She was from England. How she'd got from Binton, wherever that was, or why, he didn't know. After the *something awful that happened*, they'd arrived in Derry to begin again.

Not everything had worked out well. Yes, there had been the high spots, like the day he won a prize at school for being well turned out, in his royal blue sweatshirt. In his perfect grey pants and knitted socks. Children weren't wearing them by then. Time had passed. Fair play to his mother, but the boys said he looked like a pansy. Wan anonymity, he discovered, forged a smoother path. At times his life had been full of maggots, like a bad dream and there'd been nothing he could do. The big Gnomes had been after him all along and now it was the Ogre, himself, who owned the tip he lived in, and was the grossest weevil of all.

Sleep had deserted Mr White, as an orphan, at eight. Mr White, the single handed. Of late, and out of dire necessity, he had become convinced that music could save him from despair. Caught in a coma of insomnia, the ukulele would be his salvation. The light, Hawaiian, plinking sound of it would resonate inside his bones – in the hollow, empty spaces where the marrow should have been. In a peculiar way, it would excite him to become a human echo chamber.

'What is wrong with me, though?' he must have asked his mother when she was still alive. When he couldn't go to school.

'Weakness, no doubt,' she'd said, not paying attention to psychology. 'Sensitivity and lethargy. They're all connected.'

There'd been no reason to doubt her. Well, a good son doesn't.

'Are there no pick-me-ups?' he thinks he may have asked. Was there no tonic like other boys took, to make him grow sturdy? He'd probably been lacking in iron.

'You know when I tried to dye my summer coat maroon,' his mother said, 'and it wouldn't take, well, it's the same with you. Flesh won't stick to your ribs Mr White. It's in the nature of the beast. Eh, Dr Galbraith's at his wits' end, he is. He sits in this kitchen when you're at school and tells me you won't do.'

Why would he say that? Why would his mother? Had there ever been a Dr Galbraith? Why had he been with his mother? And sitting in the kitchen, on days when he *was* at school?

'He comes to check my veins,' she'd said, reading his mind.

Galbraith had sounded like the milkman with his little buff book that he signed each week using a bitten pencil. Or the electric meter man.

Like Derry itself, of late, Mr White's mind had grown all out of proportion, with his thoughts branching off like limbs, leaves tangling his brain. What lay ahead? No one could tell. So many frightening possibilities, but there again, like the town, he supposed he would survive. The Maiden City. The Oakgrove. Derry, in the end, had raced ahead and shown the way to peace. Perhaps he would be saved by Bruno Mars. 'Marry You,' is a good tune. He is still unattached, but you never know.

He joined a uke group on Trench Road – a fair, good walk. Sean, the freckled young fella that leads the singing in the group, sounds just like the record. At first, Mr White borrowed a uke, which had been a discovery. Like relativity. Left hand creating tension. Right hand working on his own strum, keeping time with a musician's foot, rejoicing in those combinations of notes which we must have hummed since Adam first serenaded Eve – before the apple poisoned them. He has always imagined the Garden of Eden to be fringed with date palms, an oasis sprouting allotments, like a tropical Brooke Park, in its special corner of Paradise. But with the serpent, chewing gum, though serpents have no teeth.

'Fork off,' he'd have told it.

He didn't blame Eve, but Adam was a mug. He should have thought for himself. Oh, but the wonderful, bare naivete, the fulfilling, satisfying wholeness of the universe before it went belly up.

He recalls two spots of solder attaching the handle to the shaker, which was mouse-grey dull with dust. When he thinks back now, it reminds him of the cunning little camping kettles someone bought for boiling on a Primus. Squat, ugly, gluggy, flat-bottomed, and like the flour shaker, unnaturally light. It was never on the Primus. The Primus was kept in his kit bag, because he never became that boy scout happy wanderer on active leisure service, marching like a ranger. It stayed unlit. Instead, he had lived in staggered mists and low cloud, beginning by languishing at home for years while his mother baked. Or so he told himself. It was all so hard to grasp. Time and again he'd tried. But he could not deal with time. Somehow, he had become an ailing spaniel needing comfort, wanting desperately to be called Lucky, or, sweet God, Sunny Jack White.

Sometimes though, Mr White is in the *present*, when he has to insert pound pieces into his outdated, 'pay more as you go' box in the cupboard above his door to his narrowing hallway. The Ogre inflates the rate. Mr W keeps a shallow pile of coins on the mantelpiece, to feed the bear, next to the jar of pebbles he brings home from his walks at Greencastle. The coins are dull and dead. The stones, little planets or eggs laid by some tiny dinosaur, a gentle one, with a narrow back passage. They must have lain in mud for millennia, hardening with the centuries, until one day, by accident, if such are things possible, a determined wave pounded the beach, unveiling the clutch for him. They still wait in vain, no doubt, to hatch. Ah now, potential. What kind of world was it at all, in which a mother wandered off, and left them to time and fate? Yet still he dares to hope.

And there is the mermaid's purse, the skull of an animal, probably a seal, and of course, the Tio Pepe bottle, worn smooth in the belly of the ocean, bung still in its mouth. Inside, there is a folded piece of paper, God knows how old, but Mr White, despite his curiosity, has not disturbed it. Nor will he yet. He had simply lifted the bottle, with the eggs, having made a mental note of their formation, and plopped them with reverence in his galvanised collecting bucket – gaudy with green weed and wrack. He uses it in the Ogre's garden, to bring on a plant or two. Following some brutal and unfortunate locations, in various shanty shacks, he had dragged all his treasures to Stone Cottage, at Braehead, where, in a land of hanging gardens, he clings precipitously to existence, despite the Ogre's threats, overlooking Prehen on the east bank, and upriver, though he does not know it yet, from Miss Indigo Black.

These trophies, for want of a better name, now rest upon his makeshift nature table, a focal point in an otherwise angular room, should some passing naturalist ever want to see it. This isn't likely, but nor, he supposes, is it impossible. Mr White has arranged the stones like menhirs, now that he comes to think of it, with reverence, faithfully positioning each in a simulated birthing circle, on the vacant lot to the left of his peregrine feather and adjacent to his concave rib of driftwood – an evocation of some primal creature, washed clean, and scoured of meat, and, certainly, in that sense, quite like himself. He is proud to keep faith with prehistory and with the aesthetic, though, truly, no one has set eyes on his treasures for years, or seen them, apart from said Ogre.

'This place is an octopus' garden,' the Ogre says, but not in a good way, as he grabs the rent. He likes to stand clicking his extra-thick tongue, while he counts the money twice.

'Will you sort the spoutings?' asks Mr White, in a reasonable manner.

'The spoutings is it now?' the Ogre says. 'I've never met a tenant like you for complaining. Never had such a useless scrounger in my rented houses. In all the years of taking in hobos. It's the same every bloody time. You're always looking for some damned thing to be fixed.'

Mr White mentions the spoutings only because, when it teems, water pours off the mossy asbestos roof onto the external wall of the cottage and seeps through its deepening cracks. In the winter these cracks widen in the frost. This has been the way of it for years. There is now a forest of grass thriving above the soffit. A majestic buddleia has taken root in the mortar, waving blooms on willowy stems. Tendrils invade the property with persistence all year round.

'You're a nuisance,' says the Ogre, scowling at Mr White, and his puny little gems. 'Bringing in minging scrap. Remember fella, no vagrants, no pets, no nancy boys. No guests at all. House rules. Or you'll sleep under Craigavon Bridge. And that will larn you.'

This is no good-natured exaggeration. Mr White would gladly move, but where would he go? He's done the rounds of John Street. Been given a caring coffee in Damien House. But group living isn't easy. The strangest people coagulate in impermanence. Once, in a hostel he stayed in, a man kept a gun.

'Do you see what I've got,' the man had said to Mr White, who wouldn't have crushed a fly. A homeless woman whom he'd known as Maeve had been murdered near Inch, in a caravan at Burt.

He needs to be rehomed, but he suffers from inertia. And he owes the Ogre money. Admittedly, though, like Miss Black, he draws solace from the view, from the morning sun which shines afresh on the west bank. Briefly his spirit soars as he regards the ancient woodland rising as it does, beyond two redundant railway beds. Prehen is the place of crows. He values the rising horizon across the Foyle.

After a time of meditation, he'd found the ideal place for the Tio Pepe bottle – next to his sweet wren's nest. Sometimes he nurses it like a foetus, wondering when it will be right to fish the message out, to read it for what it says. But he is a procrastinator, our Mr White, and it may be in a foreign language. All that could be years away. Perhaps it will be never. Still, it is a comfort to consider a mystery that he may share, in the end, with someone special.

The paleness of Mr White's youth was noted by health visitors and the gruff school doctors who'd checked his testes long ago. His testes had dropped, but his colour had not changed. It remained present by its absence. He has heard the word 'pernicious.' They tested his blood. Sharp scratch. Sharp scratch. Something was amiss. He has anaemia. 'Eat liver. Here, swallow these ferrous pills.' Capsules of red and green. Full of little nodules, if you could see them. He'd swallowed them for Ireland but had remained translucent. Though he was not a ghost, for he knew corporeal pain. Long needle. Iron in hip. Flick finger tap to clear the bubble. Sunk deep. Other children had wondered and asked if he were real, in those dislocated days.

The Troubles are over. But his are not.

For a long time, Mr White believed that the bottle, like a rabbit's foot, would bring him luck. This prompted him to polish it and think about it steadily, on tight, sharp nights on the Braehead cliff, when his chickens are dry and snug – he makes sure of them, at least. But when the storms hit hard, he curses the Ogre, as witless run-off sloshes spoutless, and the deluge surges wild.

So far, there had been no sea change, but after an hour on the ukulele, his mind clears, his head de-mists. His very own instrument when he got it was a handsome ebony, etched with sandalwood. He'd bought it on a generous plan, in Bishop Street, from a lovely man who gave him a discount, and threw in a nifty Snark tuner. With a battery in it. Happy days. He wants to play like a pro. Even take the lead, for he has a passable voice and a deep love of Johnny Nash. Someday, with the help of Almighty God, he will see clearly, and the bad times really will disappear.

Mr White Meets Miss Marrón

Agatha Brown is of a swarthy complexion. She descended, she maintains, from a nucleus of strong women who struggled ashore from wooden galleons, spilling onto the northern coast of Ireland, then a savage corner of Christendom, circa 1588. Her theory, rooted in passion, lacks evidence, but undeterred, she shares her story with anyone who listens.

Indeed, she also imagines herself in the swirling red petticoats of a flamenco dancer, believing that she and the women Paul Henry painted as they picked potatoes are also in some way connected. If her beliefs are rich in colour, her conclusions are steeped in the crimson blood of fantasy. Moreover, Miss Brown is persuaded that the young Spaniards declaiming loudly in the cafés of Derry, such as Claude's, are undoubtedly her kin. Although her grasp of the Spanish tongue is scant, she has, nonetheless learned to call, 'Hola,' in the most authentic accent. This is especially so following writing workshops at Holywell Trust or the grant-aided mouth music sessions she enjoys with a blond musician from Sheriff's Mountain.

Someday she will, without a doubt, learn more actual Spanish words, but then, in a sense, hers is a lexicon of sounds. Sounds of the soul, the agony of the immigrant, the emigrant, prelingual and intuitive. It is clear to her that she is attached to her heritage by some invisible but enduring umbilicus. With relish, she inhales Camel Blue pavement smoke, allowing Iberian chatter to infuse her brain, without the need for ostensible comprehension. It is, in truth, her heart which responds when she sits in the shadows, allowing the raw honesty of Janette Hutton's voice to haunt her powerfully, to embrace her, as a woman. On good days, she returns to the counter of the Sandwich Company and waits for a refill, standing expectantly with her tall mug by the Coke machine, waiting to catch the eye of whoever is on duty. And let us be clear, they abhor the idea of charging her extra, and exercise discretion.

Often, and imagine this, she claps her hands smartly to the staccato of guitars playing in Seville or whatever cities she will someday visit on the pilgrimage she'll make, in order to fully find herself. What communion it will be, to worship her ancestors on La Noche De Los Muertos. By heavens, she will squat among the graves, like a native, lighting commemorative candles and for the very first time, feel totally at home in the vastness of the peninsula which spawned her antecedents in the days of El Cid, and Isabella the Catholic.

Consequently, and for good reason, she had changed her name to, 'Marrón,' and instantly felt better. Nothing can shake her on its permanence. 'Marrón' is so much better than plain old 'Brown'. She, Senorita Marrón, is a flouncing beauty from a family close to royalty, yet, tragically, stripped bare for generations, of – well, everything, but memory.

Lingering alone on the shingle, in those distant imperial times she had awaited, embryonically, the kindness of some peasant family who fed her porridge, spooning it into her belly, to sustain life. She had undoubtedly learned to speak in Irish in those old days, and to hoke in the earth the way people did, as a wife, then as a mother, whose daughters had more daughters. Sadly, through time, though, she lost the Celtic language, in the teeth of domination. Yet, she had never abandoned her destiny, enjoying more than a glass or two of Campo Viejo in Sandinos, when funds allow, which sadly is not often.

Her name, Agatha, was her father's idea. Honestly, he'd been like a soft aunt. Refusing to fist fight in bars, or use a sword, preferring to crouch in cowardly fashion around an electric bar-heater, and read the Derry news. A man who was keen on mysteries, with the whiff of fantasy on his breath, but in every other way, quite unlike herself. He had consumed every Agatha Christie volume held by the City Library. Strangely, and without precedent, according to the staff, who refused to pursue the matter, he had removed one vital page from each, to increase the challenge for the next borrower.

'I'm going to make a book of them,' he'd said, 'which will be worth a fortune.'

Some fortune. There was no Spanish blood inside his veins. Not one single drop of plasma. God help us all. Spanishness had been transmitted by the female side, travelling in ova, and not in the seep of sperm. Her mother had been reared in Nailors Row, now tragically no more, in a doll's house, outside the Walls. Her mother's mother's mother, she believed, had been as tough as boot leather, and she'd had to be. Her man was a docker. Some dockers were fine, brawny men, but legend had it that *he'd* been a wife thumper. Friday night, according to the story, had been beating night.

But the Spanish in her great-grandmother had triumphed in the end. One famous night, he had perished with a blade in his heart. The rope in Derry's jail, however, had swung empty. For no one squealed. Whoever killed him was a hero in the eyes of Miss Marrón. It lifts her to think of them. She pictures her great-grandfather roaring like a bull, his pants filling, the lifeblood draining from him. It is pure theatre. And it was his destiny. His only moment of pride. The reason he'd been born. Her own prince, she remains convinced, will be a musician and a lover of the sea, and he will find her ready. She had got rid of Agatha in favour of Laura, which she pronounces in the Spanish manner, with much rolling of the r. Her future is, therefore, demonstrably bright.

At present, however, and curiously, for one so stylish, she rents a shabby flat in London Street. Some of these days, when the time is right, she will attend to it with paint, but on the upside, her rear lattice window overlooks the Garden of Reflection, and often, when more established writers gather there in the sunshine, she is reassured that she too, most certainly, will read her work to such an audience, outside the studied safety of a class. One day, though perhaps not yet.

On balmy days she walks alone from The Diamond, sometimes straying off Shipquay Street, into the Craft Village, with its pristine thatched tea shop, where she whispers a silent prayer for the soul of Paddy Bogside, RIP. What a time she had in the Village, one blazing afternoon, in the euphoria of the Jazz Festival. She had worn her fullest, most flamboyant skirt to reflect her buoyant mood, and a young man, not just any young man, had picked her from the crowd. They had boogied joyously for Spain and Ireland. The young man wore expensive tweed, and, like the Duke of York, may not have sweated. A Donegal cap, quite jaunty, was balanced on his head. He sported a well-cut jacket. His hair was especially well-trimmed, as was his tidy beard, and his shoes – she always noted a young man's shoes – were two-tone, like a golfer's, from long ago. Tan and white. No smudges. The young man, let us say, had been pure performance. Scarcely real, in the sense of flesh, rather he was an ethereal, spiritual young man, so dainty and nimble on his feet.

He did not speak but how gloriously they had danced, the good-humoured crowd clearing a space, while the Limavady Swing Band played marvellously, mutes held in trumpet mouths. They had enjoyed a transitory but perfect union, moving in coital calypso.

Then too, there was something amazing about the young man's lips, the manner in which he held his head. After the dance, which had, in the way of all magical things, lasted forever, but also for a moment only in the life of Laura Marrón, the young man, Lorenzo, as she now thinks of him, bowed to her splendidly, but tragically, to the cheers of the *turistas*. Then he lifted his cane-handled umbrella – guarded by some well-wisher – and melted away. Indeed, on reflection, he may have entered Soda and Starch, with a certain young woman who wore red, green and white Basque ribbons. If that were so, then Laura's heart would break. But her core was strong. Instead, she chose to treasure the memory, and add it to the installations in her mind, which she viewed at night before sleep came, though often, alas, it passed her by.

Today, the town is also packed with visitors. She walks the roads, swinging an old Moroccan leather handbag, high stepping through Shipquay Gate. The gracious Guildhall has assumed an ochre gleam. Exercising her civic right, she goes in to use the bathroom. The signage is, inclusively, in Irish, and Ulster Scots, as well as English, the language of the invader. 'Buenos días,' she calls to the usher in the hall, a McGrory from Malin Gardens, whose mother works in the Omniplex. God love him, he spends his days with the stone statues of British monarchs, Queen Vic, who'd got her hand blown off, and some of the lesser Georges.

The toilets are great in the Guildhall. When you use them, you felt quite elevated. Like you have more right to be there than British royals. Especially as you are, after all, *Spanish* nobility yourself. The towel dispensers are full of soft paper and the taps shine, like the city really cares. And so it does. There is hot water in the pipes, and salve in the liquid soap dispensers swinging on well-oiled pivots. The locking bars in the cubicles all work grand. They slide and don't jam. There is no felt tip graffiti on the walls. No disgusting scrawls. No mobile numbers prompting you to ring for sex and chips. There are no screws missing. Nobody bothers you. It is a good feeling to relax in there and do your business in safety, at the Council's expense. You could sit for as long as you liked on your own private throne, just you in a centrally heated chamber, with your thoughts, in the citadel of your temporary adoption. Like Badgers Bar, with the Derry Girls on its gable, it is sheer heaven.

When she dries her hands, she stands in Guildhall Square where Clinton had talked to everybody that day he came and said, 'Hi,' like he was your mucker. Where Cameron had apologised on the big screen. She meanders below the walls, under the London Companies' cannon, and reads the plaques. She imagines them blasting away. Smoke billowing, recoil and the reek of gunpowder. The fountains are playing today. Sudden waterspouts rise randomly, like life, falling back in uncertainty.

A dozen unemployed pigeons try their luck, pecking, and dodging the spray. A bare footed wee boy of four or five zigzags between the water jets, ignoring his granny, a stout, lumpy, bedraggled oul wan in ankle socks, who shouted and blows smoke. The wee boy leaves damp, dark footprints as he dodges the crowds, but the granny yanks his arm.

'Come on, you,' she shouts, 'and stop your carry on.'

The footprints fade in the heat. Then they are gone. Life is evaporation. She heads down the Strand.

It is the time of the clippers. Yachts that sail round the world.

Miss Marrón queues at The Coffee Tree. It will be worth the wait. She shows surprising patience, despite her hot blood. Lost in ozone, she is inhaling Colombian roast when an ashen-faced man in front of her says something not unpleasant, and before she knows, not that she often does this sort of thing, she says, 'Qué?' like one of the lads from Madrid. And he, God bless his wit, smiles back. He is hungry looking, but his teeth are not so bad. And she hadn't been winding him up. Her greeting was spontaneous.

'How're ye doing, are ye fond of the sun yourself?'

Something like that, which is a friendly way to speak to anybody, from anywhere, and he says, 'I thought that you were Spanish.'

This pleases Miss Marrón.

He is a Mr White, from up the Braehead Road.

Braehead? Her geography of Ireland is iffy. This is not, all things considered, her native land. 'Where is the Braehead?' she says, engagingly, 'is it near the gander's neck?'

No, it isn't.

She tries again. 'On up Park Avenue. Is it beside the shirt factory?' He seems a civil being.

'Naw,' he says. 'Naw, it isn't. He is busted flat, he says candidly, but here he is splashing out on a cinnamon swirl to go. Then he turns and tells her he's fond of Spain and would she like a bit?

It isn't a bad oul joke. Miss Marrón smiles. She walks with him, sipping coffee down the quay to look at the boats, and his face has brightened.

The Foyle is festive. Festooned. And a thousand flags are flying. 'All the Fs,' says Mr White.

'Nice one,' she says.'

'This is a bit of alright,' he says. Then he's quiet. Surprised, maybe, at what he's come out with. They both smile a lot. And it is good. It feels like forever. Everybody is out walking. Buying burgers. Pulling pork. Squirting strong barbecue sauce like cowboys. Lashing on Ranch. Weans with balloons. Ones stopping to collogue. The water shimmers with positivity. It could be Barcelona, or anywhere. People trip along the ledge, like in the song. Hundreds cross the Peace Bridge, taking selfies. The big white concrete stanchions are just like the masts of ships. They're gleaming, just gleaming.

'Do you think they scour them things with Daz?' asks Mr White.

The seagulls perch high, the ballsy cheek of them. Trees wave, across on the Waterside, light streaming. Mr White and Miss Márron watch a slinking train, all sleek and aluminium, and hooting with life, as it heads towards Coleraine. 'There she goes,' the crowds roar, cheers bouncing on ripples. The day-trippers won't hear them inside their hermetic carriages, but what the hell? They'll get the picture. This city is alive. The Foyle is a powerful river, even on bad days.

Something, too, feels right about Mr White, though she doesn't tell him yet that she is a famous, undiscovered writer or where she hangs her hat. He, on the other hand, though shyly, makes no secret of his love for nature and assorted bric-a-brac. Old toasters, coasters and posters. Traffic cones, heavy, black phones, 78 RPM needles, which he calls 'wee steel thorns.' He keeps them, he says, in tiny metallic boxes, with tiny pictures of dogs on them. And in pipe tobacco tins. Walnut Plug and that. He also loves anything made of Bakelite. 'Underrated material,' he says. Old postcards. Four hundred at the last count.

'To be honest, though,' he tells her, 'my life is limited. Even with my extensive nature collection, and a special bottle, I often feel alone.'

'I know what you're saying,' she says. And that is true.

Mr White, it transpires, somewhere possibly about the Pyke and Pommes pop-up, is a lover of poetry, and of Mr Heaney in particular. God rest him, the poor man went before his time.

'My surname is Marrón,' she says in the end. 'Laura Marrón.' Mr White, whose Spanish is also rudimentary, says that is perfect, and that their colours are complementary. 'You know, the brown and white. The Yin and Yang.'

'I adore poetry in a man,' she says, as they gaze at the waves, 'and a nice sense of humour. Do you like my name?' She gives the r in Laura her customary burl. 'My people have lived in Ireland for more than four hundred and fifty years, but still, behind the caul of my soul, in some secret harem I hear the clack of castanets.' Her eyelids flutter, and Mr White seems moved.

'I know what you're saying,' he echoes, endeavouring, she is sure, to take this in.

'Would you like to meet up again?' he asks. 'Maybe, you know, we could – take a bus trip to Culdaff, no hurry, like?' He says this rather quickly. Perhaps he has not said it often, or at all before, owing to reticence, poverty or indeed, like herself, good breeding. Already she feels a rush of blood.

'In Java on Friday afternoon,' she suggests, more modestly, taking charge, as she was born to do. 'They will look after us well.' She will be honoured if he can join her at half past three to share a traybake.

'Thank you,' says Mr White, 'I may come dressed as a beachcomber, but I'm partial to a brownie.'

'Bueno,' she tells him broad mindedly. He can dress as he likes. She will not be distressed. 'So, it's a deal? Adios amigo,' she says. 'I for one am looking forward to it.'

Rev Gray and the Lean Young Man

Rev Gray, who *is* known to Miss Black, is no longer a clergyman. To be fair, he was never one entirely, in his head. It hadn't been his idea to become a minister of religion. Not for a minute.

'But' – as he had often remarked, wistfully to his wife, 'your life is not your own.' His path appeared to have been chosen by forces other than himself. Call it his parents, the Lord, the fates, or the stars above, but then, as Joxer had famously uttered, 'What is the stars?' And he'd said it more than once.

Gray, despite the dullness of his name, had, in happier times, liked to think of himself as a jolly chap, in a Calvinistic kind of way. The sort of decent boy at school who was *meant* to crack a joke at the back of the class or to let off a sinful stink bomb in a chemistry laboratory and still excel in the summer tests. His winning smile was legendary for innocence and amusement. In all probability though, he had unsettled teachers by the depth of his questions. He might even have been responsible, though who could say now, for single-handedly getting rid of the conscientious pastor who taught RE, a man beginning to suspect, much to the consternation of his flock, that the theory of evolution might, after all, hold some merit.

For all his boyish mischief, though, he was undoubtedly of a helpful nature, often carrying parcels for infirm neighbours, walking with them slowly, refusing to accept the proffered coin with a toss of his tousled head. Always on the look-out to do good, he helped, with patience, the slower members of his class with 'problems' as they were then known. *How many hours would it take four big men to shift ten tons of Kerrs Pinks from a pit, if two of them worked twice as fast as the other two, and one of the shovels broke half-way.* That sort of thing. Some children cried at the thought of such conundrums, but his Reverence had chuckled, though he wasn't a Rev then, never turning down the chance to turn a puzzle into an opportunity for *x*s and *y*s, and to secure an answer. Clearly, he had a gift for mathematics and sensitivity to others. This latter quality – perhaps his undoing – it appeared over time, had less to do with God, and more to do with his bursting love of his fellow man – or woman. Hatred, point scoring and all that tripe was not his style at all.

His loss of faith – and it was a big loss – if it may be located, went back a long way, to an engaging radio presenter and guru, who scoffed at false prophets on his show, between debates about ferrets and lost poodles. Somehow, the two of them had got on well, drinking a convivial glass together, in a house near Grafton Street. Discussing Confucius, the blight of sectarianism, and various puzzles which were causing Gray sleepless nights. It was around that time he grasped the impossibility, as he saw it, of remaining in holy orders. For years, it seemed, he had wrestled with these burdens until, one Christmas Eve, in the capacious environs of a first-floor drawing room, in Crawford Square, he renounced his faith terminally, with some dark regret, and considered the possibility of further revelations. But such was his confusion, at the time, that a plan for the future entirely eluded him.

'Find yourself a wee job in the wireless,' the broadcaster had told him. 'Go to the Beeb. I'll give you a reference. Write little homilies for the punters. I'll get you a spot.' But the broadcaster had jetted to America, to be a cowboy for a while, and so he hadn't got round to it. In the hiatus, Rev Gray gave up his church, and shortly afterwards Amanda, his wife of twenty-seven years, an inoffensive lady who often wore a beret. They'd had no children. At a touching valedictory service his Reverence said he would not 'go gentle into that good night…' This was lost on his congregation, who had heard a rake of rumours. 'God help him,' they said, allowing six weeks before he should quit the manse.

'You see,' they said, 'we knew there was something wrong with him all along. Something about the way he held himself.'

They also left him two bags of purple beets and a voucher, as blood money, for a cheap weekend in Sligo, off season, to mark his years with them. The elders wished him well as he plunged into agnosticism, and God only knew what else, all of which appeared to be growing in popularity within the walls of the city.

Most Protestant clergy retire to Donegal. To Portsalon, or The Downings. But Gray was a true Derry man, who, in the end, refused to abandon the fanlights of Pump Street or the elegance of Great James Street. Accordingly, he rented a bachelor pad, not far from Miss Marrón, with whom he was now on nodding terms. The pad is adjacent to the practice of an excellent acupuncturist, close to a nurturing café, and when he stops to think, when his mind unclutters a little, he can hear cathedral bells and listen to jazz. He continues to enjoy antiquity, and hopes for some peace of mind.

Gray has taken to burning joss sticks and writing fiction early in the mornings, when he cannot sleep, to divert himself from the clackety-clack of machine gun magpies and the din of irreverent crows. At night, before retiring – having abandoned prayer – he strolls down Waterloo Street for a novel pint in Peadar's, where he listens, with growing interest, to rebel songs, enjoying new freedom of expression. Earlier in the day, for old time's sake, he often frequents The Holy Shop, where he has developed, of all things, an interest in icons. He is known now as the Wandering Prod. A lonely, familiar sight on the ramparts harmlessly watching life in the Bog, from the vantage point of the Double Bastion. The quality of his own existence, without the pressure of preparing sermons, would, one would imagine, have increased a hundred-fold. But behind that winning smile, who can tell what spectres lurk? Old habits are hard to break. He is still inclined to visit hospitals, to comfort other loners, and to share with them seedless grapes, in the absence of Communion.

One day, to his surprise, he was invited to review the papers. But in a startling departure, he soon began to compose his own headlines, adding colour where there had been none. Injecting dull, boring items with life. This did not go unnoticed by the listeners, many of whom asked, 'Is that the same man who was in… such and such a parish?' They named the church, and said he was 'some laugh.'

Homeless problem explodes like Semtex.

Bum note. No one wanted to think of Semtex.

Doctors' appointments; a game of chance. Stormont dances on graves. This was more like it. A perceptive amount of bite.

Mixed through it all, he had hoped, was an emergent germ of levity designed to enliven and amuse. Perhaps he was rediscovering himself.

'You'll catch your death of cold,' magistrate tells man convicted of mooning in Marlborough Street – in January. 'Away home and put on your pants.' This one was without foundation, but it parodied a member of the bench.

What was going on in the mind of Rev Gray in these harrowed times? Did he display a certain loosening of bolts?

Randy walrus makes advances to female sailors in Labrador.

A project, wait for it, funded by Southern Baptists – in The States of course – in association with some cult crowd here, will study evil sounds. Sounds. I mean, come off it.

Gray had leaned to the unacceptable.

One morning he said he'd found an item in 'An Fhírinne' (The Truth). 'Wait till you hear what they're saying now,' he told the listeners, *British Queen spotted in Westland Street without drawers.* More stuff about pants. They were too slow to beep it. A dog-eared politician said the Queen's underwear was sacred. That republicans should have their backsides well kicked for daring to violate the monarch. That in the 600 plus years of Britain's investment in Ireland (sic), the dissidents had *never* (sic) possessed enough cash to buy a decent pair. 'Transparent fact.'

The Fianna, in keeping with the politics of escalation, felt demeaned. They wanted compensation for the hurt he'd caused them, on top of everything else. No one asked the question, why? And isn't this sometimes the way? What was going on with him? Face value was face averted. Let's be amused and let a man go down. It is not the Derry way, but there are always those who'll knock a man in a muddle. Even in this most holy of cities. Rev Gray's pronouncements were the whole chat in corner shops and mobiles, from Curryneirin to Carnhill, from Lincoln Courts to Bradley's Pass. Polite people also discussed them in Hinton Park, in their greenhouses, in the herbaceous borders of Troy Park, not forgetting the barbecue belt at Clearwater. Slogans appeared in Sperrin Park about the Pope in Y-fronts. There were a lot of Parks. It was getting out of hand. An unhealthy quid pro quo. Years of solid work put in by long-suffering negotiators were going down the pan. The High Sheriff, a handsome young woman with high hopes and whitened teeth, gave a statement on Q102. She didn't go round the houses. Rev Gray, supposedly once a man of God, had done untold damage to community relations. Yet the people had loved him for it. The fat controller whipped him off the air. End of. Life had gone on for his erstwhile Reverence, but it had not gone on well. There is something 'other' about a sudden single man. A professional man dwelling mostly in his head, and publicly on his own, in cafés, bars and civic spaces like the Eternal Flame Garden.

'Scandinavian?' asked his ex-Reverence of a Lean Young Man upstairs in Waterloo Street, as he drank a herbal tea.

The establishment was vegan, an oasis for thinkers, isolated or otherwise. The proprietor was writing a book, with her partner Michelle. They were both supportive to Rev Gray. The Lean Young Man had the long, flaming red beard of a Norseman, and strong bronzed arms, possibly from rowing in fjords. To an emergent soul like his Reverence, this Freyr of the Vanir tribe amply fulfilled his dreams, although he wore no horns. But then, horns weren't everyone's thing. And perhaps they were a myth. The Lean Young Man was reading Hewitt, that disappointed Ulster titan of poetry, museums and peace, though also troubled in his way.

'Where are you from, please? asked the young man, looking up at Rev Gray, the way people did, casually. As though by staring into the middle distance, some literary riddle might suddenly become clear. The young man, it appeared, had decided to notice Gray, who jumped a little with nervous surprise.

'I'm just a local,' he said.

'I have been to Norway,' said the Lean Young Man in a neutral accent, 'may I join you? This is an enchanted land. Sweden also. They had times of conflict in the times of Charles 12th but are a cerebral people now. Though peace can crack like ice. They make a lot of furniture and no longer fight. I'll say no more. Do you like noir? I am not so keen on Russians, but I like the Nords a lot.'

'The Nords?'

'Yes,' the young man said. 'I call them that.'

He was certainly not from the Fountain or Carnhill.

'I admire clean lines,' the young man said, developing his theme, 'also Greenland. But I am not entirely a pacifist. I met a Finn, one time, with sapphire eyes. They glinted like pebbles and had a frosty look.'

Gray nodded. He had once almost managed a Danish girlfriend for a week. But then… 'Go on,' he said.

'He was a most intelligent person, of perhaps fifty,' said the Lean Young Man, 'who still swam naked in winter, and was whipped with birches. His ancestor, you see had fought the Bolshevists, travelling many furlongs each day, with a frozen rifle on his back, weighed down by skins, on skis. Most brave and admirable. The whole platoon, I believe, resembled polar bears. But still, there is, I think, generally, a certain flatness in the rationality of the peoples steeped in snow.'

For once Gray failed to link a man's accent to his turf, or mouthful of lichen.

'I've come to your city, you see, to find emotion,' said the young man earnestly, but, as yet, without a smile.

'Is that a fact?' asked Gray.

'Oh, yes,' the young man said, continuing to use impeccable English. 'I wouldn't say it otherwise. I need a transfusion of affect, so to speak. New life force, if you follow me. Like personality dialysis. I believe one can think too much, don't you? Are you too an intellectual?'

Gray grinned.

'Oh well…' he said.

'I take you for a modest person,' said the Lean Young Man, 'but tell me, where can I learn visceral songs of angst? Maybe you can recommend such a place?'

'That's what I need myself,' said Gray. He had not lifted his Eko guitar or played with anyone for years. 'Are you staying in Derry long?'

'*Derrylong*. Where is this city?' The young man was unsure of its meaning. But Gray pushed ahead. Had he been in town for some time? Did he intend to stay much longer? These questions appeared to race on thin tyres, and at speed through the mind of the Lean Young Man, taking bends, no doubt, at lowish angles, pedals scraping the concrete and sending up sparks.

'We'll see,' said the Lean Young Man, at last, with more composure. 'I am most comfortable lodging with a lady in Dacre Terrace, where I enjoy all your local delicacies, and from where I may look upon the dawn and those peculiar Peace fellows on the strange glass traffic island, the gentlemen with cones balanced on their heads. I plan to stay as long as necessary. I wish also to become unleashed, you understand, and free.'

'More coffee, guys?' asked the proprietor, always the perfect host.

'I am ashamed to tell you, that although I am twenty-six, I have never, to date, done a really wild thing,' said the Lean Young Man.

'You've come to the right place, then,' said his Reverence, who, at that moment, felt his own wildness might, at last, show signs of fledging.

He had recently met a poet called Voodoo, an interesting chap. Given him his number but, alas, received no calls.

'I'll take you to Tinneys some night for the full-on folk,' Gray told the Lean Young Man, with only a little premeditation.

'Don't worry. It will also be a first for me.'

'Spotty dog,' said the young man. 'I have heard this saying, though I am ignorant of its origin. I like it though. But, first, let me buy you a bowl of the excellent soup. No nasty sodium glutamate. It bulges with herbs and is truly life changing.'

He mouthed these words as if they had struck a chord.

'To celebrate our union,' the young man said.

Rev Gray is about to expound on some nuanced thought, but as he strives for articulation a visceral banging of bodhrans kicks off directly opposite. A manic, churning rhythm of hearth music explodes. This is both Gray's and the Lean Young Man's introduction to the Belgian Waffles, an emergent group from Bloomfield, who sound most unrestrained.

'You see,' said the Lean Young Man, smacking the tabletop in time, 'this is what I am after in your amazing metropolis.'

At that moment a fierce pounding also begins above their heads on the flat bitumen roof of the café, which lies ruminatively against the famous, never-breached Walls. The lure of the space has proved too much for the leaping lords of Fahan Street, who like to breakdance, stripped to the waist.

'Are you perhaps a tourist guide?' asked the young man, savouring again the soup, for he had wisely ordered a second bowl.

Somewhere deep in the bowels of the café Mari Wilson sings Cry Me A River.

'I like *your* river,' said the Lean Young Man.

'Ah, the Foyle,' said Gray. 'A mysterious flow. Never the same river twice, as I'm sure you know?'

'Heraclitus,' said the LYM, wringing Gray's hand with surprising force.

At this refreshing bodily contact, Gray felt his spirits rise, allowing himself to believe that his improving mood might indeed be given expression in certain pulsating nightspots, so to speak.

'Epiphany,' he said, 'emotional tourism. Perhaps that's been my calling all along.'

'That sounds truly cosmic,' said the café owner. 'There's no hurry. You can sit all day.'

With this, she gave the Lean Young Man a tofu sausage roll, to take along with him, but he scoffed it there and then, for his journey is a hungry one. The writers kissed as they waved farewell. Permitting themselves to boogey, 'winningly,' as the Young Man said. He paused then on the stairs of the café, in a surprising way, to strum the opening bars of Maple Leaf Rag. The shocked piano, an ancient honky-tonk, was blissfully atmospheric. Seemingly it has been waiting unrequited, for someone with a soul and musical ability, to finger its keys for years. 'But then, aren't we all?' said Gray. He trembled with wonder and not a little fear, as the felted hammers struck the strings, and it awoke and began to twang.

Mrs Green

Despite her problems, Mrs Thelma Green has retained a love of retro. Each Saturday morning, no matter how dismal, she unhitches, in so far as she can, from her scruffy week and, armed with her battered weekend satchel, deserts for a short while her Victorian home, that solitary, decaying dwelling in which she and Daphne had been born twenty minutes apart, in a surprising, private terrace. Some of the dwellings sport quirky little turrets built with old money. Others have purple and amber leaded glass windows. But it was already a faded, jaded house that

Father bequeathed her in 1969. A momentous year in Derry. Daphne inherited the red-roofed bungalow in Port na Blagh, and sold in haste, despite their memories. Thelma, naturally, had preferred to stay put. To soak up whatever sunshine would fall on the just, the unjust, and the just miserable. To endure the drum of Irish rain. The familiar seeping damp. She had been here all her life, which at times appeared interminable. Daphne had vanished to South Australia.

Thelma is on her own, if she doesn't count the woodlice, or each September the annual plague of rodents. It is a steep climb for her on foot, admittedly from the Model School, past the assorted lock-up garages on the right, and Foyleville, now redundant, she supposes, on the left, where Father had died so tragically. She had never meant to put him in a home, but at the time it had been him or her. Dying is all very well in films. Of late it has become quite fashionable to show the nobility of carers, the indomitable human spirit of decrepit old crocks in vans. The real thing is not so damned admirable. Caring brings out the worst in people. Think of the scandals. Now she is old herself.

Hers is a tired, gracious community, with its own grass jungle, where neighbours watch neighbours from windows seldom cleaned. Nobodies who used to be somebodies lurking behind weighted curtains. The Harrigans, the Kerrigans and the Boyles, or what is left of them. Oh, she supposes they are essentially a civilised lot, in the detached manner they all accept, assembling occasionally of a Christmas Eve in some somebody's parlour to sip sweet sherry, or at a wake, if they can't avoid it, to pass themselves. Perhaps, on a summer evening, they exchange perfunctory pleasantries over a runaway hedge, or squint at memories through the gnarled boughs of a poisonous laburnum. One man peeks through a snapping letter box. Obviously doolally. They will all have their toxic thoughts. She certainly has hers.

Around her door she feeds the original ramblers, the ones planted by Father, guarding them, as she had her virginity, to keep them from canker. Blackspot and yellowing leaves remind her of decomposition, and so she sprays them, pumping hard with 'the article,' as Father had dubbed the gun. She feeds them fish and bonemeal from a bucket. Around her feet, she casts tight pellets of chicken dung to make them bloom. Each spring she prunes them viciously, with poor results. They are hell to work with, but Daphne had loved them.

The house retains a spartan elegance, but like herself, its overwhelming ambiance is emptiness. As for the draughts inside, well, they are mighty. Rugs ripple in the winds of March. She employs a menagerie of stuffed dogs behind the doors. Long patchwork dachshunds, bought in jumble sales, with little stupid legs. They appear to make no difference, but nothing will persuade her join the fitted carpet mob. An ancient house needs to breathe, though its lung capacity is reduced. Many of the neighbours have installed wet rooms. How absolutely vile. She retains the original iron bath, though it is years since she soaked naked or saw herself exposed. Nowadays, it holds two breadfruit plants and several struggling coleuses. But the water which gushes into her toilet bowl does so from the original Crapper tank, high above one's head, exactly as it had when Daphne said it would suck them under. The force of it.

Today, she and Daphne – whatever she is doing just now, and however she had spent her day in the antipodes – are both, presumably, in winding-down mode. Though with Daphne you cannot tell. Thelma faces her mirror with some loathing. Old people hate looking glasses. Honesty is to be deplored. She registers some resemblance, she imagines, to those identical girls she knew, the two sisters they had once been, especially about the eyes, but her mouth has sagged lamentably. The cheeks are hollow – like her heart. Daphne was such a firebrand.

Thelma, unlike her twin, had been a lady almoner, as Mother persisted in calling her job, when speaking arcanely to her friends. Mother, long gone, had thought Social Work a worthy, if second best occupation.

And she had foolishly complied, though she could have gone to France, to the Sorbonne. Imagine that.

For she had studied with a bright bunch and with no less a pupil than Indigo Black, currently creating such a splash – she is never out of the papers. What a thrill that had been. How very enervating. For a time, she, like Daphne, had called herself her friend, but the two of them had moved too quick. They were lightning conductors. Still, she had followed Daphne, as Peter had followed Christ, except that she did not betray her. Quite the reverse. If Daphne was queen, Thelma was her faithful retainer. Second fiddle had not been a conscious choice, more of a realisation. For a long time, she had played along without rancour. The text appeared, in retrospect, already to have been written. In Runes or Ogham. But such a challenge to read. For a time, they had, together, unaccountably inclined towards missionary work. It would be a lark to take the gospel to the heathen. Think of the lands they would see. From Zanzibar to Siam. But Father had said 'No,' and when Father said 'no,' that was it. The time for missionaries, in any case, had almost passed. The Empire was in decline. People at home were in greater need of saving. And God help Derry, the way things were going.

Ah, but Daphne. They had been such a pair. They would sail on a boat to Constantinople, and ride horses in Arabia. But only in their dreams. Daphne had lived on a knife edge. Thelma was blunt and dull, as a hand maid ought to be. As befitted her place. Yes, but what *would* they do? No really? Whatever it was, they would remain a duo, pulling together between the shafts. And that was a fact.

But think of the government. Facts are often lies. These lies are the snarled-up memories which Thelma has held for more half a century, their warp and weft intact as she unravelled. As her garments tore.

They could, all things considered, have been teachers together in the Model. But no. Nursing twins in Altnagelvin? Well, almost. In the end they had left Derry on a temporary arrangement and gone to Dublin in the train, through Belfast, to become therapists. This was an expanding field, according to Daphne, who for a while was obsessed with Freud. They would, in time, practise together in Clarendon Street, she said, and this became the plan – their names would soon be emblazoned in unity, on a polished brass plate. 'D and T McCartan. Counselling.' The inscription, like those denoting the establishments of dentists, doctors, and solicitors, would indicate quality, the product, according to Daphne, of time spent strolling through the Phoenix Park, going to church occasionally at Grosvenor, and shopping in Clerys. They would share the journey. She, as ever, would tread in Daphne's footprints. They would explore, as one, the practice of Jung and Rogers, share a flat which Father would select.

But no. The Runes were wrong.

It was during her final placement, with St John of God, where, as it turned out, she was rather happy, that she and Daphne sat down one Sunday to read the papers, in Bewleys. Unusually, the very bentwood chairs, that day, had thoroughly disturbed her. The people around her seemed far away. She'd had a premonition. Daphne, it transpired, had met a – young man in Davy Byrnes. Under the stained-glass dome. An Australian chap, of all things. And she would go with him. Down under. To be buried. They would fly on some sort of Boeing. Barry, for that was the Australian's name, was a rocket man. A boffin, and desperately fascinating. It was destiny, Daphne said, and Thelma would get over it. 'You can always visit,' she said. The pain, which was worse than a gallstone, had gone on and on.

She had not accompanied Father to see her off, remaining instead at home with Mother, and sipping tea, with her head down. That was when she was appointed to her post in the Hospital Authority, because Mother knew someone, the way one did.

All these years later, she is still haunted by the faces of her clients on the wards, along with that of her late husband Walter, who was washed away, perhaps, not far from the little fortress at Culmore. For years she had looked for news. *Man rescued from cave. Body found in Orkney.* A waste of emotion. The tides had been high. The Foyle brutal. She had sought to help others, but when she needed assistance, no one had been there for her. How foolish she had been. *Welfare worker loses husband*, the headlines ran, implying carelessness, as though it were her fault.

Rumination was ruinous. But today is Saturday, and routine is vital. She will not finish up like Father. There are several ways to skin a tabby. So on and so forth. After dumping several empty bottles in the garish, blue plastic bin, she turns the long key in her lock, struggling to apply the extra torque required. The lock is original and full of caprice. For years she has managed with this single key, though once there'd been two.

She sets off with some purpose now, down her somewhat hazardous path. Careful not to trip. A white and yellow profusion of feverfew shoves through the slabs, many of which are cracked. The lupin has gone to seed. Grey furry pods hang, twisted at an angle. In June she'd dealt with a pollution of aphids and a rash of sawfly larvae – the same shade of green, exactly, as the birch leaves which they had devoured with obscene, efficient mandibles. Carefully, she secures the rusting gate, noting how iron, in the end, always seems to swell in layers, and makes for William Street. 'Bomb alley,' as people called it once. This now thriving thoroughfare. She has brought no coat today, for the sky is blue. Perhaps that has been foolish, but coats are so bloody tiresome. The forecast, at least, is in her favour.

Thelma Green, so thoroughly up in her head, can hardly be expected to know all the people she meets on this short descent down Academy Road. How could anyone? But each, she assumes, will have their own sad story. Perhaps they are the sons or daughters of someone once deep in psychosis. Maybe she *had* brought a little comfort along the way and made a difference. Many, though, had not responded. Some had killed themselves to find release. But, no, she will stay upbeat – isn't that the word? She needs to be resolute, yes, that is it, though everything costs so much. Such a slope, and treacherous in frost. She and Daphne were once champions on ice, though few could know that now. Or care. Daphne is a ghost. Thelma selects her steps, passing the pious streaming from Mass at St Eugene's, as she crosses the Northland Road.

McLaughlin's is her favourite shop by far. Such helpful, reassuring staff, and very honest. Shining, stainless-steel cruet sets gleam a welcome in their window, all freshly labelled in confident, no-nonsense, black handwriting, like you used to see, on crisp, white cards large enough to read without glasses. Inside, she will handle the hairy besoms and burnished coal scuttles, the Russell Hobbs steam irons and chirpy metallic alarm clocks, with almost illicit pleasure.

Behind the dependable, wooden counter range a hundred greased boxes full of nails, copper, wire, and brass, she imagines, of all dimensions – nails for her coffin? But, no, stop it. The earnest assistants share their knowledge graciously. She should have liked to work in a place like this, where each screw has a meaning. Every bolt a matching nut that fits. To which people come with pleasure. Or in the Folk Park near Omagh, baking breads, hands all dry oat flakes, on a flour-dusted griddle. She will share these thoughts, in passing, with the staff of McLaughlins, whilst considering a rubber sink stopper, or the purchase of a mouse trap. Humane of course.

'I need a spare like this,' she tells one of the helpful men, dangling the heavy key on the arthritic joint of her little finger. 'Just in case.'

The helpful man nods.

For some time, this whole business has been on her mind. The 'what if' question. Imagine should she be the victim of a haemorrhage, a stroke or something worse. The thought of burly policemen breaking down Father's original oak door is too obscene. She will give the copy to Tim Brolly junior who comes to mow the grass, and with it, handwritten instructions. Time and tide.

'This one's a right old age,' says the helpful man, studying the key, weighing it in the balances, as it were, expert that he is, marvelling at its provenance.

'1912, I believe,' she tells him, indulging in a little pride. 'Before Partition.'

'My God. As old as that.' There follows a deal of rummaging. 'I tell you what,' he says, 'you go upstairs, why don't you, and have a look at the artefacts and I'll see if we have a blank one out the back.' She has clearly set him a challenge. How she longs to go out the back.

Thelma climbs the stairs slowly. Feeling her way. Taking the risers one at a time. Planting her feet with studied care. Unlike Daphne's, hers have always been flat. Fallen arches, she assumes. Probably some logjam in the birth canal. Firmly she grasps the handrail, though her knuckles hurt. Most falls are entirely avoidable. Bones are to be treasured whole, and preferably unpinned.

A slim young woman appears like a welcome breeze. Wearing a golden smile.

'Welcome to the display,' she says. 'How are you, Mrs Green? Are you winning against the slugs?'

How wonderful to have been recognised by someone so – alive and interested. Up here, time has stopped, and Yesterday surrounds her. Once more she caresses clay beer bottles, though she had never warmed to beer. She strokes the high-glaze pottery of the hot water bottles. That lasting yellow sheen. Spotting only superficial varnish cracks. How dependable old things were. And there, serrated, a clutch of wooden butter pats, tied together with string, and with just a little woodworm. A holy picture. Three ribbed washboards, such as Mother's help had used. A galvanised tin tub, which seems too small today for bathing even a premature baby. Two upright pink paraffin heaters standing at attention, side by side, as she used to stand with Daphne, complete with safety strips, *'Don't tilt.'* She sighs. There is a Kodak folding camera, the photograph of a car, one of the black square motors of the past, parked grandly at the kerb, outside this same McLaughlin's shop, but oh, so long ago. A big old Austin, she is sure, like Father's first one.

Despite her resolve, a tear. She can't help it. It is the suddenness. The young woman's empathy. The unexpected and the familiar. She tries, naturally, to overcome her weakness, dabbing at her eyes often, with an embroidered handkerchief.

'Life can be hard,' the young woman says, seeking to bring comfort. Thelma weeps then like an idiot. Her emotions loose and lubricated. She has lived too long in a twilight world of denial and regret, of fading sunsets and bitter dawns. Life is sour and tedious. She wants to ask, 'May I borrow the picture and have a copy made? Trust me, I'll bring it back unharmed.' She could take it to Boots. The chap there would scan it into one of those strange machines. She has only to ask. But she lets it go, fearing her voice will quiver.

Now, deep-seated grief consumes her. She cries for Father, for Mother, for Walter, and, selfishly, for herself. But she does not weep for Daphne.

After this eruption, she can hardly continue the tour. The young woman, sensing her distress, takes her arm, with increasing gentleness. They descend to the ground floor together. She is mortified but does not feel judged. An oldish white-haired man wants Rentokil. 'A right bugger,' he says, of the wood boring lads. Such a simple, normal thing to tell a stranger. But how should one respond? 'This stuff will fairly fix them.'

The oldish man looks familiar. Something about his eyes. Perhaps he had been a colleague? That fresh new Doctor Mulligan who had suggested something once, in the refectory, as she recalls, not long after she started. But maybe not. 'I beg your pardon,' she'd said, like a fool, wanting to slap his face, like in the American movies. But then, of course, she hadn't.

'Will you be all right?' asks the young woman, handing her a glass of water.'

'Thank you, my dear.' Thelma nods, pressing the round, cold chill of the tumbler into her palm. Suddenly, she is aware of the satchel on her back, which is full of – spent dreams.

'I have the key for you Mrs Green,' says her helpful man, emerging from the back. His name begins with S.

'It's a miracle we had one.'

'I don't think so,' she says, perking up in the practical manner she had affected all her life.

'I've never asked for anything in here that you did not stock, and that's in fifty years.'

'Well, there you go.'

He had wrapped the key in thick, brown paper. Securing it traditionally with a neat dab of tape.

'Don't lose it now,' he says, 'it's the last one we'll ever have.'

The key was a precious thing. So recently a blank, now fret-worked identically, should it ever be required. 'Belt and braces,' as Father had liked to say.

Outside McLaughlin's, and opposite the Ex-prisoner and Drop In Centre, with its medals and medallions, her sense of well-being lingers briefly, but threatens to disappear as she continues towards The Strand, and Guildhall Square. But no, she will call at Little Acorns Book Store, in Foyle Street and treat herself to another Alice Taylor, whom she recently rediscovered. What delicate writing. Afterwards, she will gird her loins and scale the 'Heights of Abraham.' Shipquay Street, the ultimate test of legs and heart rate. 'Fortune favours the bold.' Virgil. Having, hopefully, reached The Diamond without incident, she will dither a little. Which café to enter and which antique shop? 'Loneliness kills,' she reads on a hoarding. But despite it all, what a noble city. Employing this deliberate cognition, she attempts to close off history.

All this simmers as she crosses at The Pickled Duck, anxiously watching for traffic from her right, scanning faces in the bus queues as she passes The Gainsborough, which, although established in 1729, looks elegant in its brave new livery. So very black and white.

Last year she had met a local author in Little Acorns. 'For Thelma,' he had written on the flyleaf, 'with kind regards.' It was about salmon or oysters.

The Blue Two

All it takes, sometimes, is one disaster to screw up your life. After that, it's anybody's guess if you'll get it together again. Some do. What makes the difference? Luck, willpower, or something unexpected that comes along years later, that you weren't expecting, that gets you going with new hope. But you're not going to know about that when the wheels fall off your trolley, are you? Crystal balls are exactly that. Balls. Even in magic circles, in cities full of wizards.

Things certainly hadn't been the same over the last fifty years in the citadel for the Derry pair, the Blue Two. Not since the fights were stopped in their tracks. Things had been going all right, back then. But their joint careers got blown to hell suddenly, in syncopation, popping like cheap light bulbs when filaments fracture. Something that started with a ra ra ra had shattered irreversibly, it seemed, and died in tears. Okay though, you could have your cry, but you couldn't keep crying, not in the proud streets of the Brandywell. You had to suck it up. The breaks were over for the Blue Two. There wouldn't be a Big Time after all, and in the meantime, like a lot of ones that didn't emigrate, they had settled for less.

After the debacle, they used their time as best they could, dandering the length of Abercorn Road, and the Oakgrove Bar in Bishop Street Without, opposite the wee nuns. Studying the form. Some days they would even stroll past the hoardings at the jail turret in The Fountain, past all the old pictures, through the Gate, and past the Masonic Hall on the left, between races. Knots of petty criminals huddled inside the railings of the courthouse – there are savages in every town. The savages are surrounded by florid men in wigs who scribble on notepads and are creaming it. The Blues might walk on to The Diamond, to hang about and smoke outside Austins. 'I thought somebody'd bought Austins,' they'd tell each other. 'It's a wild shame. D'you mind the time…' etc. etc., and on and on the way old people do. But they kept their manners, nodding to everybody, the well upholstered women and wee young wans with prams. The Blues had known Johnny Hume, God bless him, and Gregory, they'd talked to McCann and the other Eamon that sang – God rest him. They had loved his breathy voice, especially the number he did about going to Sligo on his own, when he was only a wee boy, and being hugged hard by the oul uncles that met him off the bus in their pony and trap. My God. That was some song. They had had been on friendly terms with Martin too, so say no more, all the way through man. From the first, like, before he was *Martin*, so they knew the score.

Apart from a bit of harmony singing now and again, on a Friday night, the premier event of their week for years had been signing on every Wednesday, in Asylum Road. It was well named, they used to say, ha, ha. But, naw, the staff were nice. When they went together to the Bureau, the girls behind the counter said, 'Look who's here. Come in Numbers 4 and 5, it's the Blue Two.'

The girls were like a welcome committee. This here had gone on a long time.

During the bombs.

After the bombs.

'Yes, girls,' they'd say, with respect.

The staff got a hard time in there, because the punters were stressed, but the Blue Two said to give the girls a break – they were only doing their job – for people that didn't have a job. And that included them. Nobody has a job these days that doesn't involve computers, which is a bloody joke. If there's one thing the Blues are definitely not into, it's technology. So, their lives hum quietly, and they bet on the odd dog.

'Well, why wouldn't they back a hound?' the Long Presenter asks on his radio show. God he was some height, even sitting at his console. He'd been wanting them on for a while, fair play to him. They told him and the listeners that they lived in 'laid back poverty.'

'Isn't that an amazing turn of phrase, folks?' said the Long Presenter after he persuaded them to sing with a song writer called Sweeney.

It's a great song about the Belfast bus, and he's a tasty guitarist.

'These boys are still brilliant, what, and no self-pity,' says the Long Presenter. 'The Blue Two, and Mr Sweeney, consummate citizens and always the gentlemen. They're legends. I don't know about you listeners, but it's a crying shame to have talent like this lying dormant.'

The boys also sang Blue Moon, and it was a mind-blowing rendition.

'Two such loveable fellas, who need to make a comeback,' the Long Presenter says. 'When are we going to damn well wake up to the treasure trove that's right under our nebs in this great mecca of culture? Hey, maybe somebody's listening. Hello, are you there, Miss Black?'

The Blue Two are grand during the spring, they say, when the wee birds are building, but it's rough in January when snow falls, and the pipes freeze. Sacred Heart. Heat or eat. All that stuff. Duvet days all the way then, man. They've been renting the same wee place for years, so they have. The neighbours are mighty to them, 'and rightly so,' says the Long Presenter. He goes out of his way to mention Annie Doherty, formerly of Tillies' cutting room, who still makes them chicken broth once a week. 'So, nobody starves here in this proud city. And proper order. Hot soup, I remember my Granny's, and that's a heart-warming thought for me, but still and withal, it's an indictment of our modern society, is it not? Folks, we need, do we not, as the man says, a whole revolution, when it comes to opportunity. But Annie Doherty. Truly, that's the calibre of the citizens in this corner of our beloved island. Unsung heroes like Annie and her mates, God bless them all. We have to move on, folks, but these fellas deserve a break in the clouds, don't they? That's all I'm saying.'

It's an open secret that the Blue Two are not blood relatives. No sweat. They spent a bit of time together long ago – in somewhere that – gave them street cred. Early on, okay. No need to go into it now. After they got out, they called themselves *brothers*, to give their act a lift. Same as tinting their hair a duplicate dark navy and parting it right to left in identical fashion. Show business was dog eat dog. You needed competitive edge.

After they gave up the other business, for health reasons – they'd become professional grapplers – kind of. Unregistered wrestlers, you know. They were masters of the arm lock, the grapevine and, if things got really manky, the reverse surfboard, which they claim to have invented at Kinnagoe Bay. This is a great tale, but unashamed propaganda, and a lie.

Back then, there wasn't a gymnasium or parochial hall in Derry that hadn't hosted The Blues. In those old penny-jingle, rickety wheel times, they'd had their own dedicated following. Especially in the shirt factories, same as Dickie Rock. They were the climactic bout. The double act the crowd paid to see. The singing wrestlers. The rest of themuns were only warm-ups. In the good old days, you got their bare torsos on the gable walls of Rosemount and Stanley's Walk. Their smudged flyers were in all the bars. The Don and the Monaco. *Blue Two. Melodious blood brothers, Mick and Manus. These muscle men will appear in the Stardust, and the Rialto.* A lot of wee boys got named after them; Manus, Mick, or both, according to the ex-midwives of Anderson House.

But since then, things had gone to hell in a handcart.

This here happened the night they were billed for a tag match against the Prod Gods, from Bann Drive.

'There was a lot of roadblocks on the bridge, on both decks, so you had to hand it to the Prods, right enough, for coming to the Lourdes Hall. One of them was dark, and the other was blond. So, you knew the difference.'

'Fair dos,' says the Long Presenter. 'I hope you boys know where this is going because I sure as heck don't.'

The boys laugh.

'It was a full house that night, a lot of people were standing, as well.'

They had sung a couple of Everlys' numbers to get things going. 'But breathing was hard in the hall because the air was thick. Two stout girls fainted. Smoke, sweat and scent shimmered from the women. The men were lit up too. It was high octane, all right, but it was different times, and nobody'd brought in drink. A whole bunch of girls was swarming at the front. They were all beautiful girls, and they were singing them doffer songs in rounds. They'd paid plenty to get in and by heavens they were going to take no shit.'

'Just mind the language, lads,' says the Long Presenter. 'We're pre-watershed here.'

'They were blowing us kisses and all,' say the Blue Two.

'You couldn't be bad to that.'

'There'd been six bouts already, and two fellas had got hurt. They were carted off by the Knights of Malta,' say the Blue Two. It probably wasn't much, you know, but it could have been brain damage, because with wrestling you never know. People thinks it's all bluff. But you want a see the bruises all over us.'

The Blues had come on, with their skins glistening like seals, smooth as Vaseline, with the secret oil some of the women had rubbed into them.

'There'd been a lot of squealing from the wee back room.'

'Easy, lads,' says the Long Presenter.

The Prod Gods, by contrast, had looked bone white, and hard as drumsticks like, but stale. Aye, too long kept. But they had to be beat. *Had* to be. No contest – in the Lourdes Hall, after the jigs and reels – or as sure as shooting, and no messing, there'd have been a riot. 'Red, white and blue trunks winning in the Brandywell? I don't think so. Are you kidding me?'

'G'on away home while ye can walk,' the women roared. They were flicking peanuts. Petrol lighters flashed like wee eruptions. It was working out a great night. The Gods were obviously yellow b's, but they were letting on to be big lads. Beating their chests, and all, like on the Twelfth and that there.'

'The dark one caught Mick with a forearm smash,' says Manus. 'Not much weight behind it, but it was a warning. Some bloody cheek. I was in the ring now. Headlock. Raised veins. Pressure. You didn't tangle with the Blue Two in them days. The blond Prod was in as well. Back breaker. That was the whole four of us now. The women howled.'

'It was pure madness,' say the Blue Two. 'But we could take it.' They'd been in their primes. They were on the ropes, off the ropes, bouncing and catapulting across the canvas. The ropes twanged. One of the Burke sisters got in with them. She pulled off her top. Black bra. Wired tight.

'Unexpected,' says the Long Presenter.

'The ref put her out,' say the Blues. 'Had to, back in them days. Mick was outside the ring, on the floor,' says Manus. 'He was dazed but still holding his tag rope. He was staggering. Maybe he was only letting on. Were you, Mick? But it looked authentic. The women moaned.' Then Mick was back, full on, clambering on the ropes, dancing like a liltie in the red corner. Jumping like a boy on a trampoline, to get the best spring for his flying drop kick.

'Manus had the blond Prod pinned. Good on him,' Mick says.

The ref, Patent Shoes Kelly from Springtown, was on the deck, with his head cocked low for the angle. I leans in and tags Manus on the hand. It's all legal. The women are chanting, "Easy." They're up wobbling on the folding chairs. Climbing the walls. We're changing over again. Taking each other's place, when the dark prod clobbers me with a seat.'

'Good Lord,' says the Long Presenter.

'I heard it splinter on my head. I was stunned,' Mick says. 'For a second there was silence, like in a power failure.'

'Like in a graveyard,' adds Manus, 'there's blood seeping from the slash in your man here's scalp, oozing in wee rivers down his skull, dripping in slow clots, splashing one by one onto his white wrestling boots. Two hundred frozen faces. The lights dipped in and out. The hands of the clock stopped. It was all over bar the shouting.'

'Pandemonium, eh,' says the Long Presenter.

'The women were wailing, and screaming, "Go Mick, go…" Mick comes round and raises a clenched fist.'

'So do I,' says Manus. 'Oul hands together. "Up The Blues," yelled the factory girls. Right enough, it was pure bloody chaos.'

That was when they'd heard the bang. The entire roof of the Lourdes Hall shifted in a piece. Then, corrugated sheets of asbestos slid from their moorings, one at a time ripping out roofing nails and washers as they careered to the floor, splitting in fibrous shards. 'Asbestos is bad stuff. We know that now. Long cracks appeared in the plaster of the gables, running faster than a ladder in a pair of women's stockings, but opening wider, as the bricks parted company, till you could have put your head between them. Some sort of smell had been released. What the hell is it, we were saying. The hall groaned.'

'I don't know about you listeners, but I'm hyperventilating,' says the Long Presenter. 'Don't keep us hanging lads. Tell us what it was.'

Mick and Manus, and the ref, to be fair to him in his tabby bow, had stayed in the ring. A result was all that counted. The crowd had hung on too, rooting for their team. But their opponents had frigging legged it. Typical bloody Waterside men. Prod Gods my arse. The spectators – no crowd like a Derry crowd – had booed them till they couldn't speak no more, coughing till they were 'spluttering, and retching and holding hankies to their mouths.'

A single shriek. 'They're away for their mammies.'

'No, fellas,' said the Long Presenter, 'I don't believe it. Youse are making this bit up.'

But the Blues are on a roll. 'Nobody else seemed hurt. Which had to be your actual miracle. A crowd gathered outside, beside the grotto. The Hall settled back on its hunkers, holding its breath but the show was over.'

'The thing was, nobody in the Brandywell actually hated the Prods, but they ran away, so that meant they were wimps.'

'Although the results were fixed, it was still wild disappointing. The women wanted their money back. They were all for skinning the promoter, young Father Hasson, from Legfordrum, who was doing his best.'

Then a second bang. An oul wan started the Rosary.

'And that was that. Goodnight. The night ended in a rush for the doors. Everybody out. But it wasn't just the night that died. Our careers were beat. There was a big crevasse in Quarry Street. Water gushing everywhere. A dirty, filthy jet. Muck and glar. Men pouring out of The Bluebell Bar shouting, 'What the buck?''

'Apologies, listeners. Oh my God.'

'The women's clothes were ruined,' say the Blue Two.

'They stood in their heels looking into this hole. Like they were searching for answers. It hadn't been a bomb. It was something about pressure in the gasometer. Thanks be to God. But all the same, you couldn't be sure. The future was uncertain, but one thing was clear. The ass had been blew clean out of the water for the Blue Two.'

Because, after that there, nobody had the stomach for wrestling in halls no more. Time had gone into reverse. The heroes were thrown on the scrap heap, like dead dogs, at the age of twenty-eight, and that was them for years. Through the bad, bombing days that followed, they would tell their story, like curiosities, to as many as would listen, for a pint with the Big Dote, or a half 'un, at the table quizzes in The Park Bar.

Sometimes they went further afield to The Alleyman's down the Strand. Before it was destroyed. But that was later. Once or twice, they'd sung in Bennigans when there was nothing else on. But it was all chicken feed. The heart was knocked out of them. And no wonder. The Long Presenter was right when he said they needed a break. They *had* great voices, but what good had that been, when after a while, the young ones said, 'Who under God are themuns?' Although they meant no harm.

'I get it. I totally get it,' says the Long Presenter.

They'd once been celebrities. Now they are nothing. He has the picture. There is no doubt about it. And it *is* sad. Something *should* have been done years ago. But they needed something to happen now. 'Folks, we need to believe in these guys. Please God, it isn't too late.'

'But no hard feelings,' says Mick.

'Hell, no,' they say. 'We're going nowhere at our age. We wouldn't live anywhere else.'

Judge Scarlett

Many criminals are cynical predators. Deadly as nightshade. Others falling foul of the law have stumbled into felony. Perhaps they never had a chance. Their lives blighted from the beginning. Justice was an inexact science. Some went to prison for foolish repeat offences, only to reoffend upon release. It had been Judge Scarlett's job to see through all that. To get to the core of human behaviour and its consequences. To give a man or a woman a chance when he could. Notwithstanding, he had been dubbed by some 'that bloody judge.' Long ago, he had accepted that some monikers are meant to be, thus embracing his name with a sense of irony, and saying that he had searched for his own Scarlett woman until he found her. She was Penelope, whom he'd met in Clifden one tortuous Saturday full of squalls. She had more than exceeded his expectations, later moving back with him to Derry, where he'd served society for the latter part of the Troubles. Happy to live in the house he loved, and couldn't leave, in ethereal Victoria Park. She would create a garden from the wilderness his father had neglected. But this was no manicured bowling green of fussy, shallow grandeur. Rather it had become a fusion of meadow and wildflowers, of the kind favoured by entomologists, and insects.

After a long day on the bench, the judge endeavours to take a rest from legal matters, given the mental exactitudes of listening, summing up and making determinations. There is nothing more relaxing upon arriving home than to pet Nero, his beloved Lab, and inspect a budding agapanthus. To inhale the residential calm, high above the winding Foyle. More damned character than the Rhine. Of that he remains quite certain, and often says as much to visiting tourists, especially Germans.

To a casual observer, Judge Scarlett might seem like any grey-haired man, parking his vintage Jaguar beside the pergola, entering his pile through open patio doors to take his wife by surprise. To embrace her from behind, inhaling her fragrance. There is also, by way of context, the wholesome smell of cooking. This evening, he will pour himself a generous Bush. Single malt. I am, he thinks, a man almost at one with the world.

Almost, but not quite.

For it is a fractured world of children he deals with nowadays, and the children's parents.

'Nothing is straightforward,' he tells Penelope.

'Did you have lunch at one?'

'Custody,' he says, vaguely. 'Access. A right witches' brew.'

He often forgets to eat. In their dining room, in the snug, hangs a photo of his father, JD, the first Judge Scarlett.

The dining room table is set for four.

'Who's coming?' he wants to know.

'Are you sure your levels are stable?' Penelope worries about his sugar. She's arranging sweet pea. Deep crimson blooms, and purples.

'I've checked,' he says. 'They're fine. I'll shoot more insulin if I have to.' Diabetes would not enslave him.

'I do worry, Henry.'

Yes. Yes. He loves her gentle concern. Her timing too, which is immaculate. The way she reads his mind. How she knows the right evening to ask in a friend or two. The point at which he needs diversion. The night for popcorn and a movie. When he simply wants to read his latest Ann Patchett. *Bel Canto* looks promising. And there is music.

'Go wash your face,' she says, 'and put on a nice fresh shirt.'

Judge Scarlett shuffles towards the stairs. Today he'd made a Freeing Order. That was it. End of, for Theresa, mother of the O'Brien family. She wouldn't get them back now because she had blown it. Permanent separation from her kids. It was for the best. Yet she was not an evil woman. What will these children say when they are his age?

'Good judgement?'

He hopes so. But who can tell?

'The bloody judge removed us. What help was there for our ma when it was needed?' Questions, questions. He picks up the school portraits of Leo, Jon, and Rory, steps of stairs in their jolly Wellington boots. Sturdy grandsons at the other end of the earth. He sighs a little more each time he thinks of them. He should plan a trip. Inertia gangs up on him.

Standing by his favourite outshot window – the house is mid Victorian – he's glad he topped the pines. The tree surgeons did a remarkable job, though they'd wanted paid in cash. Everyone was at that game. If he hadn't scythed the trees, he and Penelope would be living like squirrels. It would have been a machete job.

Below him, the city spreads wondrously, but this evening's mist threatens to shroud it, layer upon dense layer. Just visible stands the historic spire of St Columb's. Not Lord Hervey's earlier, dodgy edifice, but its replacement, reminding him of some poem or other, and the need for radical rethinking. Below the site line, the thrum of traffic. The heart attack wail of sirens. Somewhere out there, in every city, no matter how mesmerising, are the clashing rocks of fate. A fatal crash. A stabbing. Two little ones recently burned to death in a house fire. Perhaps they'd been left unattended? One could only do so much. And that was the way.

Of late, though, he has become exhausted more easily. He is increasingly exercised by the notion of mercy. That quality which should not be strained. But mercy for whom? Families were in such complex disarray.

The judge's tailored shirts hang in a commodious wardrobe of his own. Cohabitation is commendable in a general way, but closets are like cars. They are not for sharing. Penelope's dresses linger daintily in her own cabinet, the blues and yellows, the teal she loves to wear. She keeps her tailored gardening outfits in the plant house, a darkened lean-to, ideal for wintering tubers.

In the bathroom he splashes about, without much thinking, opening his eyes wide, stretching his facial muscles. The bags are worse. He can't ignore them. He'll have to sleep more. But there lies the rub. He'd used to smoke Hamlets. Lear, Macbeth, or someone, has murdered sleep.

Perhaps Penelope has invited his sister Muriel and her daughter Alice. Or Kenneth has flown in from Cardiff. But why four settings? He wants nothing too demanding.

Scarlett studies his belly fat. Penelope is right. The occasional Mars Bar. It's growing all the time. For years he had been careful, but now, it's as if something has slipped, like the wedge from below a door, that's slowly but steadily closing. How long since he's had his cholesterol checked? He's doing himself no favours. Perhaps he should visit Good Futures. Private health care could be necessary, despite his pangs of conscience.

'You have a choice,' he used to tell the guilty in the dock. 'Go to prison and do your time. Mend your ways, and when you come out, society will welcome you back. New start you see. Then you can make a go of it, man.'

And it was mostly men. 'Life is what you make it. It's up to you.' What utter nonsense that all seems now.

He selects a round-collared shirt he bought in Italy. Venice is for the privileged. He had balked at the cost of hiring a gondola. To be poor in Venice? No one talks about 'the poor,' these days, for God's sake. But 'poor' is the word. He had laid aside euphemisms like 'marginalised' years ago. They served a purpose but elevated the grind of poverty to a concept. Sociology was so self-absorbed. Why not use the old word, for all its stigma, when it nails the issue? In truth, it's mostly the poor he's seen in court. It had pleased him to send down fraudsters and violent men, domestic abusers and professional thieves. But the vast majority of the bedraggled people waiting for justice live in a world of which, truly, he has no personal knowledge. 'Dirt poor,' as they say in the States. To know the law is not to know people. Yet how can he meet ordinary, decent people? Once as a boy he'd made a wasp trap. The wasps wore themselves out, swimming in circles, with spidery, hapless legs. Round and around they travelled, but they couldn't get out. At last, expended, they stopped paddling and drowned.

No tie tonight, he vows, no matter who is coming. That way constriction lies.

From his eclectic music collection, he selects Tom Waits. Tom wears his black felt hat and is not smiling. Why would he? Scarlett slots him into his player. His cantankerous Sony permits cassettes. Technology and highfalutin are not his metier but there are certain works which lift him. This week on his way to Omagh, Alexander Armstrong had played Mendelssohn's Symphony in C minor. How come he had never heard it before? Only twenty-seven minutes in length. The melody had wormed into his head.

He should also change his trousers. A looser pair will allow more breathing space. Recently he read an article about holding one's breath. Failing to take in enough oxygen appears to be a problem. He turns up the volume, allowing the music to swallow him. What utter certainty it inspires. He chooses his slacks from TK Maxx. His familiar brown cotton jumper. No formality in his house, thank you very much. Penelope might wear her pearls, but she would let him be. No serial rank, no stupid pack drill.

Except in respect of your sugar, my Lord?

'No gangrenous limbs,' he says out loud, opening a window. How lucky to be here, in this city.

Tyre crunch on gravel. For a moment, he thinks of Niamh Parsons. Of her song about Anne, and the tinkers, yes that was the word in the song, pulling out of some cinder siding. The grass-cropping horses in early morning. Their clopping hooves. He recalls a caravan number by Barbara Dickson. Another good voice. Like himself, she must be a fair age now. He needs to relax. Perhaps he should retire altogether but there is so much to do. So much more to understand.

Whoever is coming to dinner has arrived. Penelope sounds the gong. A little jest of mockery. He peels off his sombre socks. Slips on his lilac crocs. Bare feet. Much better. His toes look fine. No fungal nails. He feels a certain brightness. That promise of light they get over Creggan, that shafts to earth in streaks. The mist may be clearing. August is a wicked month but September, with luck, will be fructive.

Downstairs, two women's voices. One of them belonging to Penelope. The second also does him good. It takes him back to the softness of – other flesh. To the amazing scanty attire of the belle of his year at Queen's, before he set off properly, knowing he'd been blessed. To the exotic, piquant, but unrequited night he'd spent with Indigo Black. They had danced, he would maintain, to 'Je t'aime', heavy breathing and all.

Had it been real live sex? Probably not.

Penelope had known about Indigo, of course, from the start. He'd told her everything. Instead of jealousy, she had loved her instantly, as they all had, and taken her to her heart. This, naturally, had been a tremendous comfort to the younger Scarlett, as it was to him now. Descending the elegant staircase he whistles 'A mighty fortress is our God.' Though he is not a religious man, he attends both cathedrals at Christmas. Hedging his bets, he supposes. One faith would have answered nicely.

His spirits soar now, as Indigo comes into view, standing there in his wide hallway, fixing a loose strand of hair.

'Ah, there you are, Bruin,' she says, 'I'm here on my own. I thought you were in hiding.'

She'd always called him, 'Bruin.'

The judge has largely stopped noticing what women wear. For that matter, he can no longer accurately guess their age. But Indigo is in a peach-coloured dress which gloriously brings out the colour of her skin. What memories. He makes a mental note to share this finding later, with Penelope.

'Indigo, my dear.' The famous bear hug, 'I hear you're organising some sort of shindig.'

'I will not deny it. And you are looking – comfortable, if a little overweight.' She says this, taking a pace backwards, regarding him fondly as one might a forgotten treasure. 'Yes, it will be a major Happening. It's been too long. I was inspecting your tennis court.'

She shakes her voluminous hair.

'It's to be resurfaced,' he says.

There is not an inch of the Lodge that Indigo does not know. Not a cup hook or bevel with which she is not familiar. She is intimate with each peony, every blade of decorative black grass in a way that has probably evaded Penelope, for all her assiduousness.

'But the court, where we played with all our hearts, is full of groundsel,' says Indigo, 'You should get in some eco warriors to clear it up. Bring back its glory days.'

'Uh huh,' says the judge, the way he does at work, 'it's a playground for foxes.'

This said with some resignation. 'It wants a bloody good ploughing.' He knows he's sounding tetchy.

'You wouldn't dare,' says Indigo.

Penelope has cooked pork fillet. Simple and straightforward. No bloody chilies. 'But three is such an untidy number. Could you really think of no one?' she says to Indigo.

'I suppose I could have asked Alan Cairns, Damian H or even Gray. He's free since he left Amanda,' says Indigo. 'But Gray has gone funny, you know. I've seen him with a lean young man. He's supposed to have lost his faith.'

'You mean…' Penelope ladles green beans.

'Oh, I don't know,' says Indigo. 'One honestly doesn't know anything these days, does one, Bruin? And what Gray does is really up to him. But he looked – I don't know – so indecisive, I thought, not like himself. Though he could be unpredictable. All that bother with the radio and so on.'

'Quite so,' says Scarlett. 'Gray *was* always a peculiar chap. What about the Peacock fellow? I thought he was a goer. The old guy with the Lexus.'

'Yum. Tender,' says Indigo, of the pork. 'Too old by far. Most men were never worth the effort, you know, present company excepted, sans doubt. Isn't that so Penelope?' She helps herself to the baby boileds, 'and now that one is past the violent rumpy-pumpy stage, well, the whole endeavour has lost its bite.'

'I'm not sure you mean that,' says Scarlett, rolling up the sleeves of his jumper and patting Penelope's arm, 'though there's more to life than bonking. But why,' he asks, 'did you not consider Ebrington Square for your Happening?' He and Nero adore the Square, the Peace Bridge, the downstream, upstream, views.

Without doubt, Indigo also adores the Peace Bridge.

'It is iconic,' she says. 'I love the squaring of such a broken circle. The military spears into ploughshares. But I need lots of space for tents. Soft turf, Bruin. Lots of.'

'Tents, by God, you *sound* like the British army.'

'The Happening will last three days.'

Penelope smiles. 'You'll have to take your friend Bruin here. He's due a good run out.'

'The idea that every soldier's boot print is being turned into a tourist footfall is marvellous,' he says, still focused upon the conversion of red brick. 'And there is the bakery. The restaurants. The riverfront. The vista. I love the sailor carrying not one bag, but two. There's something hits me hard about that.'

'It's a terrific bronze,' says Indigo. 'And so many buildings which might have seen the wrecking ball. But no, I need the grass.'

'Speaking of grass,' says the judge, 'I met some of the old gang last week at The Brewery. Not that they do nowadays. Craft beers you know, decided flavours, but not dogmatic, subtle in their way. Noel Madden was saying that Derry has been reborn.'

'A rebirth that will go on and on,' says Indigo. 'This pork is great. 'My Happening will be a blaze of renaissance. A uniting consummation of artistic spirits. A collective of harmony.'

'Don't be a stranger,' Penelope tells her, waving at the wine.

'I don't intend to be.'

Indigo pours White Cloud, generously. As ever, it is well chilled. She traces a condensing line on the bottle glass with a determined little finger.

'Linda next door brought it back from Auckland,' says Penelope, 'I don't know why, when we can buy it here, in Winemark.'

'We sat under one of those big umbrellas outside The Brewery,' says Scarlett, 'well into the evening. It could have been Sorrento. Couples in love, walking past and that. Young ones on skateboards. Sun declining below our stunning skyline.'

'A heavenly crimson,' says Indigo.

'Did I tell you, Pen, I met a bat scientist on the train. They get a bad press, it seems.'

Penelope smiles.

'I knew he would come back to life.'

'And we need more poetry,' says Indigo. 'That's what my Happening is really about. Music, song and mingling. The opening of minds. Insight and art. And I'll have a surprise or two. You will be made to wonder, Bruin, but in a good way. Say you'll come. He will, won't he, Penny? Oh, say you'll make him.'

'I've never got him to do anything he did not want to do,' says Penelope, 'but I'll try.'

'Ha,' says the judge, 'now that's my girl.'

Catch-up is good and bad. Good, because hemispheres again unite. Bad, because the process of reconnection simply amplifies the extended gap there's been. Still, the night had begun with banter, and banter, in Derry, as everyone knows, is sacrosanct.

'Anyone for seconds?' Penelope lifts the heavy lid of Monsieur le Creuset. A wedding gift, in terracotta, so long ago. Indigo's mouth is already full, but she points to her plate. This always means 'go on.'

'How has court been?' she asks the judge.

Scarlett thinks before he answers.

'This wine's not bad,' he says.

'Prevarication,' she says. 'I smell deceit.'

She always can. With anyone else he would give the simple but enigmatic Derry answer, 'Grand.' As often as not, it contains the brush off of a lie. But with Indigo – he cannot lie. Never would. Or nothing would be sacred. Communion with others is frequently smoke and mirrors. Often, indeed, sheer subterfuge. But not with her.

'Damned puzzling,' he says.

He and she *had,* after all, shared a bed, though, sadly, nothing had happened. Not through failure on either of their parts, he was sure, but based on preconditions. Hers. 'I'm going to trust you, Bruin,' she'd said.

They'd been well drunk together that night in Belfast's Ridgeway Street.

How different would he feel had he not kept his promise?

Sweet Indigo.

'But here,' she says, sensing some revelation, 'tell me how you see life now, from your seat among the youngsters. If I think you're telling the truth, we'll swap some stories. What do you say, Penelope?'

'I'm like King Solomon,' he says. 'I sell babies to the highest bidder.'

'I wish he would unburden more,' Penelope says. 'He dreams and shouts in his sleep. 'Kicks me black and blue, but, in the morning, remembers nothing. "What happened your legs Pen?" he asks me. I tell him that a kind, generous man did that to me.'

'Oh God,' says Indigo, 'do you really, Bruin?'

'No recollection of it,' he says. 'Not sure that all this heart wrenching in the Children's Court is really me, to be honest. Horses for courses. I'm all right on the flat. No good at the point to points. Old dog. New tricks. All that. Extended families. I hadn't known the half of it.'

'But at least you have the heart, doesn't he, Penny?'

It's Penelope's turn to sigh.

'What a ménage à trois we are,' he says, playing with the dessert cutlery. 'Pray what is the next case? Where is my clerk? Where is the inscrutable Anderson?'

'Crème brûlée, Your Worship,' Penelope says.

'So, is that a promise?' asks Indigo. 'Did I hear his Worship say

"Yes"? Will he come to my Happening, to open his mind and meet our magnificent people, outside the confines of his court, without his restraining judges' rules. Have we a Bible? Did we hear him swear an oath on King James to tell the truth, the whole truth etc., etc.?'

'You heard him say, "Perhaps." If the sinews can rise to it. Crème brûlée,' he says. A seductive little number. A smooth little villain indeed.

Mr White and Miss Marrón

Mr White arrived first at Java. He had often imagined its café window on Ferryquay Street to be a giant television screen, the assortment of regular customers inside as the cast of a Derry soap opera or TV film. Actors who went there every day. Characters he almost knew.

Take the two nodding women with heads together, their matching straw hats nesting on the pleasant table. Maybe they are sisters. The older one looks a little more worn. Age wears you down. Time is a strange affair. He often catches his own reflection, fleetingly, as he passes. This causes him to think of himself as insubstantial. That's it. Less than real. Some seconds are longer than a hundred years. Others blink by unnoticed. The women have that well preserved look that money brings. But their skins have wrinkled a little. Too much sun. Probably smokers. Mr White had smoked in his younger years, foolishly affecting an image of isolation, of the sort evoked by Bogart, and by the marketing company who pedalled Strand cigarettes. But that lonely, hatted man who found solace in a fag had subverted their intention in the end, and they'd pulled the ad. Sometimes he still succumbed and had a drag, but why, back then, had he wished to look so lost?

'Play at a thing long enough, and it will come true, Mr White.'

Thank you, Mother.

Often there is a familiar looking, burly guy, like an American cop, facing the street, with the look of an officer who might someday solve a crime, though not today. Unless he were to gorb another plate of grits. Though Java, he is sure, would not serve grits. Mr White, with the affected eye of a casual passer-by, can tell that Shugh Henderson, the anti-culture campaigner, for that's who it is, has often made himself high on back bacon and maple syrup. If Henderson were to wear a Stetson it would carry the Lone Star of Texas. Henderson, the scourge of waste. Waste is money spent on flower beds, festivities, festivals, and anything bright or beautiful. He is the scourge of 'that schoolteacher woman, turned politician, Miss Black and her "crazy Happening at Prehen." Mr White had heard him on the radio last week. He wonders what drives a man like Henderson. Had he been reared on misery? What twisted mischief is in his head as he grinds his jaws, drinks deep from his mug of tea? He had slagged off Miss Black to the Long Presenter after an item about haemorrhoids. No wonder he eats alone.

'Do you have piles?' the Long Presenter had asked him. 'No, seriously, folks, they can be a big problem.'

But Henderson despised disclosure.

No doubt he is an addicted chocolate drinker who takes four sugars, a two-refill man, who would kill each morning for a freshly baked apple square. A man in the public eye who'd forget to pay. Mr White has heard that the scones sit up smartly in Java, with thick cream already decanted into lovely glass dishes, and home-made raspberry jam, just begging to be licked.

He has window-shopped all his life, because it's free, and he finds it easy to take everything in – from the outside. He has always been an outsider. Usually, he ambles from the direction of Austins, past Specsavers and the Nationwide, though, needless to say, he is not a customer. His is the invisible but well-worn track of the loner who must contend with the counter flow of pedestrians. Who must be careful of the not always crawling traffic, and to watch for approaching trucks. It's amazing how many urgent Transit vans turn into Artillery Street, at speed, with equipment for The Playhouse.

Despite the wafting aroma of Java's coffee, Mr White had never, to date, actually ventured inside. He has never become one of the people in the window. He doesn't so much live life as watch it. Observing his existence as a disinterested stranger. Only once or twice, since his mother died a lifetime ago, has he felt like an actor worthy of his pay, or anybody of any consequence. He wonders, though, about other people. What's in their heads, as they stroll through Derry's parks and chat in the bursting bistros? No doubt, for them, he is that odd fellow they see on his own. The man who appears to be going somewhere but is really going nowhere. The pallid, silent guy in open-work sandals, who paddles past.

'There he goes,' they'd be saying, 'on his own. There must be a story. Maybe he's a pervert.'

'Never with a girl, or a boy.'

Mr White pondered if the women with the hats ever nudged each other, like the girls they used to be, and said, 'Oh look, it's that fella, again' or if the smiley manager whom he'd met one morning at the bus station ever glimpsed his shadow. 'My name's Jack White,' he'd told her. Once, he'd noticed Miss Black in there. Her picture had been in the paper. It was definitely her.

No matter. Today, on this appointed Friday, all that may change. He arrives at twenty past three, to meet his new acquaintance, coiffured, sprayed with Lynx and ahead of time for his tryst. No sign of Henderson. Thank God for that. Mr White has not come, after all, attired as a beachcomber. On this stifling afternoon of Indian summer, as the stones themselves cry out, he proceeds to take up position at the back of Java, well out of the way, in the penumbra, as it were, opposite the amazing steam geysers, to await the arrival of Miss Marrón.

Is this a date or what?

The staff behind the counter are at the end of their shift, but they are still setting out delicacies and engaging the customers. Offering a *céad míle fáilte* to weary travellers from distant lands. The Manager addresses him above the chatter.

'I'll sit down for a minute with you, darling,' she says, pulling out a chair. 'How's the form, Mr White?' she asks him in a tender way, though she's heard his name but once. 'Wild warm,' she says, 'what's the *craic* today?'

When he tells her that Miss Marrón is coming, she gives him a golden smile.

'Miss Marrón. Oh my God,' she says.

But her smile is kind. Her eyes are true. Mr White can tell. 'That's great,' she says. 'You'll be feeling like a millionaire. And what do millionaires eat? Leave that to me.'

It was strange how she had clocked him. He could never manage that in a thousand years with anyone.

'I'll get you a wee Americano, as well,' she says, 'to steady the nerves. On the house, while you wait for your lady.'

His lady.

'I'm sure she'll not be long.'

The Manager nods to one of the girls, who is already filling a mug.

The tourists appear to be members of some club. They are not the heavy, overfed visitors, stuffed full of calories, on sticks variety, though that is a bit unkind. No, these are active young men and women, who might have arrived on pared-back bicycles, in shorts, with healthy leg muscles and rapid hand movements. They cluster like bees around their guide and read aloud from brochures, in English.

'City walls.'

'O'Doherty Fort.'

'Free Derry Corner. A must.'

'The drive down Southway. Amazing views.'

'Two cathedrals. Why two?'

'Why not?'

Their leader, a tall, dark-haired young woman in a yellow top, waves a flashing baton and calls for silence. There *is* silence. Even the Derry wans shut up briefly. She speaks their foreign lingo. Then they are all shouting again. Wanting their photos taken with the local patrons.

'Come everyone,' the Manager says, 'you too Mr White, it's for the *Sentinel*.'

Mr White does not normally 'do' photographs, for several reasons, but on account of her recalling his name, and the unselfish hospitality, he can't say no. So, he stands with the others, sticking out a pale mile among the bronzed, tanned faces. The unabused bodies of these excited strangers.

It is at this point that Laura Marrón choses to make her entrance, glowing like someone who has secured, at great expense, a ticket to her favourite show. She wears a flaming sun dress, gathered at the bodice. Her hair, tied to one side, is secured by a fluorescent butterfly. What age can she be? Who gives a damn? Laura is adorned with a necklace made of sharks' teeth, possibly from North Africa or the Galician coast. As the *turistas* leave, Mr White can hear her asking them this and that in a thick Spanish accent, but in English. No worries. The departing explorers look mystified, but Miss Marrón remains unabashed. Coolly, she glances around Java, allowing her ebony eyes to rest on this one and that one, as she searches for Mr White.

'Ah, there you are,' she says, in her own voice, when she spots him, '*Buenas tardes*.' She rolls her Rs, peeling them off like a stripper. 'To see so many of my fellow countrymen and women makes me glad and sad, all at once, no? I long to be with them cheering in the arena,' she says, 'and waving my national flag. I want to stroll with them down the Ramblas. Run with the strong bulls in Pamplona. I desire to eat with them late in the evenings, tapas, and those little fish they fry so deep. I'm homesick for my native land, Mr White, although I have never been there. Can you accept that, after so many centuries in Derry?'

Mr White does not reply. Instead, he arranges her seat. She smells, he allows himself to think, of mystique and lilies. Just then his coffee arrives. Two large chocolate squares squat sumptuously on tasteful china, well-filled with caramel which oozes extravagantly.

'Do you like millionaire shortbread?' asks Mr White, with an open-hearted smile.

'Oh *si*,' she says. And 'yes of course.'

It is as they share the delights of Java that Mr White, for all his resolution to be measured, unburdens himself to Miss Marrón. He does not tell her all, for that would take too long. But he shares with her his fear of the Ogre. He confides in her his forebodings about the spoutings. The cascades of winter water and the buddleia. Without mentioning the amount of his unpaid rent, he conveys to her many of his worst night fears but also speaks with some hope of the message in the Tio Pepe bottle.

'He would stop at nothing,' says Mr White, 'I am very sure of that.'

'Then move,' says Miss Marrón, with that impulsivity he would grow to love. 'Tell him to eff himself. I'd like to see this bottle.'

Mr White murmurs sadly about deposits, references and guarantors. Life is seedy and short in the slow lane.

'This bad man ogre is a big, prize bastard,' says Miss Marrón at last, with abandon, 'but I have contacts.'

At this point she speaks almost inaudibly, and Mr White, who is due a free hearing test in Carlisle Road, struggles to catch her words.

'I will put out some feelers,' she says, at length, in an assured fashion. 'These brutes deserve a cruel fate. Sometimes it is the only way, believe me. What is this damned ogre's name?'

Mr White looks around Java. It is impossible to tell who may be listening behind their newspaper. Then he leans into Miss Marron, so close he can feel her warmth, and whispers, so near her that his lips touch her ear. His fleshy lips – the second most sensitive part of his body, and they are tingling. Somehow, he has smudged her make-up.

'I'm sorry,' he says, but she laughs. 'This Henderson will be hoisted by his own fooking petard,' she says.

Petard. He would look that up.

After this meeting of minds and bodies, Mr White and Miss Marrón leave Java, and walk to the pet shop near Lidl, on the Buncrana Road, which is a fair stroll, but it gives them more time to become acquainted. Together they look at the soulful puppies, who are well-fed and plump. Miss Marrón buys a dense, heavy bag of glistening birdseed, which Mr White is honoured to carry all the way back to her flat in London Street. This also is quite a walk.

'Do you keep birds?' he asks her, though not, he hopes, intrusively.

'Oh, no,' she says, beaming, 'The seed is for my strange friend Clara, who lives in the Canal Basin in Strabane. Perhaps someday we'll take the bus and go there for a treat.'

'I'd like that,' he says, his face lighting up. 'I'd like that very much.'

After she closes her lime green door, having kissed him on the cheek, Mr White stands for a moment, to reflect on his luck. Wondering if it has really changed. He decides on balance to light a fag. Inhaling deeply, he crosses London Street to stare in the window of The Whatnot antique shop, at the treasures he would like to buy for Miss Marrón.

Spode jug.

Attractive teapot. Staffordshire.

Set of Edward the Seventh Coronation playing cards, 1902, in original embossed box, by Thos. De La Rue & Co, Ltd. He would like to get them all for her.

Sadly, he can but dream.

But Mr White's dreams are improving. He sets off now for the Braehead puffing like a train, with inches added to his step, humming a cheerful air, with more joy in his heart than he has known for a very long time. And with it, he cannot deny, a welcome and lusty stirring in his loins.

John Orange and His Drum

It was a Saturday morning when Miss Black, Rev Gray, Mrs Thelma Green, Mr White and his new friend, Laura Marrón, happened, for various reasons, to witness the following event. Snooping Shugh Henderson also appeared briefly at one point, with a big head on him and bloodshot eyes. Looking for mischief.

By 10 AM the commotion had been going on for a while, having begun as a harmless skirmish before anyone was much about in the Diamond outside Granny Annies. Two frenzied drummers, wearing Glengarry hats with feathers, were roaring loudly in an abandoned sort of way. They were supposed to be on their way from misery to happiness, and they wanted the whole city to know, before they would leave for the next world. They were warming up, whooping, and repeating verses, till there was a decent crowd all swaying dementedly. People joined the melée, not in an avalanche but one at a time, letting on not to be that interested, but craning their necks all the same, and hanging about to see what would happen – instead of going down to the Halifax or into Barnardos, like they had been meaning to do for a fortnight. The singing was infectious.

The lads were Jockey and Strap Nesbitt.

'We're no relation,' they said, 'to the guy in the string vest.'

'Are youse protesters?' people asked them.

'Aye, we're against everything,' they roared. 'We're Antichrists.' Miss Black explained that they meant *anarchists.* Their own hairy variety.

Rev Gray nodded and said something ambiguous to Mrs Green, whom he knew to see. Miss Black embraced Mrs Green and squeezed the bony elbow of Gray.

Mr White and Miss Marrón stood linked.

This was all very well until John Orange McBeth showed up. For years he had stood outside Foyleside on just such a morning, though gradually he'd been moving up the street, as he was entitled to do. These Glaswegians had hunkered right under his tree, to get some shade, on the corner of Shipquay Street, and outside Richmond Chambers.

John Orange was a modern hero from Nelson Drive. He had beaten his way from exclusion to inclusion. Once upon a time an Orangeman could only appear for a parade flanked by a thousand Perspex shields, all held by RUC men, but John Orange was a prophet of the new Ireland. Things, thanks be to God, had only got better. They had changed. There *had* been negotiation. The most unlikely of protagonists had not only got into bed together but in some cases, still only acknowledged quietly, they had actually made love. Happy days.

So, hold on a minute. People had got used to John Orange, who read weaver poetry in Ulster Scots to passers-by, about looms and farriers and the tough times endured by the settlers at the time of the great killings of 1641. He didn't hold a spite about all that now, but it had to be acknowledged. He would open a battered Oxo tin at his feet, for tips.

'The folks' generosity,' he said, 'was *Legenderry.*'

It wasn't original, but nobody minded.

He also told people about the siege. What he said was nothing new. You could read all about it, if you liked, in the Guildhall exhibition. But he gave it his own treatment. 'Have you visited St Columb's Cathedral and touched the hollow cannonball that contained the terms of surrender? A deceitful missile smooched by no less a pair of perfumed lips than those of King James the Second.' King James was a Catholic and fierce eejit that made the planters eat rats. 'I mean to say muckers. There is also a table made out of the tree that the traitor Lundy climbed – to escape the siege.' What a shocking coward he'd been.

'God, is all that true?'

'Oh aye, it is,' said John O.

On your average Saturday, the Derry wans came and went, with their recycled shopping bags, milling about to get their eyes tested and lodge a few pounds, to collect new frames, and open accounts in the Post Office for their weans. They paid little attention to anything except looking sharp and going to the barbers, of which there were many in Carlisle Road, and buying in a few Coors, for the match.

But a crowd gathers a crowd, and when John Orange came along, wheeling his Lambeg drum, as usual, behind him, attached to his old Viking bike, in the big black box on wheels that he'd got made specially in John Street, he got some unholy gunk.

'What the eff's this?' he said reasonably, to the heaving mass of punters.

He was eyeballing the music men.

'Two Glasgow boys,' the punters said, 'they've come from Scotland.'

'I know where bleeding Glasgow is,' said John O, who had travelled extensively on overnight crossings from Cairnryan.

'Years from now, you'll make it to the next world,' sang the foreigners.

'I don't give a monkey's about the next world' said John O, shaking his head and lighting a smoke. 'It's this world that's the problem.' He retreated to the doorway of The Red Cross shop, then to the window of The Lingerie Room on the corner. A lady who knew Miss Black came out, fair play to her, to see if John O was okay.

'He's a bad colour,' Miss Black said, 'but it's pure annoyance.'

Miss Black then phoned the Police Service of Northern Ireland to say that trouble was brewing. Doubtless, there could still be resentment on both sides. Mostly it stayed buried nowadays, but you wouldn't want a riot. The Lingerie Room would have invited John O in, only they were thinking of their customers, none of whom were men, and they weren't sure they could accommodate the instrument, which, as John O said himself, was, 'some size.' So, they fetched him tea in a Free Derry Corner mug, with six sugars in it, and a drop of brandy to steady him. The Red Cross ones loaned him, ironically, a piano stool with a tartan seat that somebody had just brought in. For a moment Miss Marrón forgot her Spanish roots and said, 'G'on take the weight off your legs, John O. God save us all, if an Orangeman can't get peace to beat his drum in his own bloody city where the hell are we all going to end up? Poor creature, I remember his cousin Willy,' she told the crowd, 'he played in the Britannia Band.'

John O sat down like a Christian to see what would happen next.

What happened next was that two women who were leaving The Lingerie Room, and feeling a whole lot better about themselves, saw John O languishing there on his stool. When they heard the gouling of the Scotsmen, they texted their husbands immediately, who texted their sons, who had hangovers that hurt like hell, and told them in no uncertain terms to get themselves across to the Diamond, right NOW, because there was going to be bother.

By the time the PSNI arrived the trouble was well and truly going. Two mobs shoved around the cenotaph. Somebody had lifted the poppy wreaths just in case. A fella was clodding burgers from the Grannie Annies. Two wee girls fainted in the heat and a priest from the Long Tower appealed for calm.

A crew from Ulster Television arrived and set up a van with all their aerials and things in Butcher Street. When they got through to the Diamond, Miss Black assured them the whole thing was a misunderstanding.

But the situation had got ugly. Yes, there was some backbiting. Catcalling, even. It was like the bad, good old days, when shopkeepers had prayed for their windows, and glaziers rubbed their hands.

Two bands, the No Surrenders and the Sarsfield Fifes, arrived in minibuses, on emergency duty. Miss Black spoke to two pipe majors. Rev Gray, as an ex-clergyman, assured Mrs Green, who needed a drink, that it was in higher hands, though he smiled faintly when he said it. The police, Ballymena men, God bless them, played soothing Celtic music from a Tannoy – how times had changed – and told the Scotsmen to pack it in.

'Sling your hooks now, lads,' they said, 'Youse have had your bit of fun.' There was some rough language, but no brutality.

Seasoned community leaders came forward from the Fountain and the Bog, to show their combined mettle. Former mayors and other respected people who had seen it all. And the mob listened.

During all this shemozzle, John O sat on – and on, tapping his feet to some marching tune in his head. He kept serene, despite the furore, knowing, no doubt, that the good sense of the citizens would prevail.

And the end, as they say, when it came, came quickly. The proclaimers stopped proclaiming mid-stream and disappeared. Some wag from Wesley Street said they'd already been spirited to the next world. A space was cleared for John O, his bicycle and the Lambeg drum. Miss Black chatted on for a while, in a serious looking way with John O, who was smoking and nodding and looking mysterious. He seemed to be saying, 'Yes' to a whole bunch of questions from Miss Black, but they were confiding quietly, so you couldn't make them out.

Inside the drum box, the Lambeg, with typical Protestant long suffering, refused to take it bad. It simply waited, John O said, 'like the ones in the siege, for the moment of liberation.' Now that its day had come, its skins trembled in an unexpected and brand-new way.

Slowly, a team of stalwarts, akin to the Apprentice Boys themselves, who long ago had manfully secured the gates, hoisted the drum into daylight, shouting to each other to 'look at the width of her, sir.'

'Swing her round, boys, till we get a decent gleek at her.'

They were jigging like line dancers.

'That's her now,' they guldered, securing her to the person of John O. 'Heavy as hell, boys,' somebody said.

Sense had broken out now in a big way. It was terrific how quickly the whole kerfuffle had subsided, without so much as a broken bottle. But then, Miss Black had presided, and Shugh Henderson hadn't got a look in. He'd have liked a scrap all right. But the city's good sense had prevailed. It was more settled these days than anybody knew.

John O began to beat the Lambeg, rhythmically with two canes, and with feeling, but not too loudly. Not loudly enough to annoy the population or drown out the chimes of the Guildhall clock, which now struck one. This was the signal for the Gaels and Dissenters to cheer together, in solidarity and to say, 'Good on him' and 'proper order.'

Thus encouraged, John O then lashed the drum for Ireland until it was fair bouncing. Pound coins and fifty p's and a lot of euros from Donegal ones flew into his Oxo tin. But later, Shugh Henderson – it would have to be him – enquired if he had a proper street artist's licence.

Miss Black laughed. 'John O is an asset to this town,' she said, 'which is more than I can say for you. An asset, with potential, and an Orange treasure.'

'I thought that went all right,' John O was supposed to have said afterwards, in the Glen Bar. Peter Johnston, the freelance photographer, was there, and he'd taken some great pictures. 'There's a class one of you, John O, with the lingerie ladies. The papers will give you front page. You'll appear in colour.'

'You'll be even more famous now,' said Robbie Hannah. 'Wait till you read the headlines. "Londonderry pulls back from brink thanks to John O."'

'Thank God,' the people said. Rev Gray would tell this story to the Lean Young Man, who would in turn share it electronically with the Nords. Thelma Green would discuss it in a quiet moment with herself. Miss Marrón and Mr White would add the event to their heart-warming adventures, and Indigo Black, who had been privileged to have the confidential words with John O, would look entirely satisfied, for reasons known only to herself.

No doubt, though, Miss Black had seen enough to remind her, if reminding were needed, of the absolute value and indeed the necessity of accepting art and culture at a deeper level of understanding. John O had opened her eyes. Her father would have been worth talking to, God rest him, had he been living. She would value his guidance in preparation for the next Council meeting, when Henderson was sure to leap on the affray, and suggest cancelling The Happening.

'Bring crowds together in this city,' he would say, 'and you're asking for a handling.'

'I can hear him haranguing now,' Miss Black had remarked to Gray, 'But we shall not be moved.'

This struck her later as another of her rather grandiose statements, which, despite an earlier oath, must have smacked of hubris. But then, in a moment of transparency, she had said to his Reverence, 'I may have the body of a woman, but it most certainly is not frail, and it has served me well.' This if anything, was worse.

'Elizabeth the First,' was what Gray said. 'You also have an excellent brain, and brains, so far as we know, are gender neutral. At least they should be.'

Poor Gray. 'Will you come to my Happening?' she asked him. 'I think you should.'

A single tear had escaped the eye of Gray. 'I might just do that,' he'd said moistly. 'It depends. I'll have to see.'

Mrs Green Considers

Riots over drums in the Diamond are all very well, and quite a diversion, but Mrs Green, despite her resolve, has bought an attractive ruby glass jug in the Yellow Yard. What a vintage extravaganza. She needs a little joy, but these sprees of hers are subject to the law of diminishing returns. It's perverse, really. The more she buys, the less she values her most recent purchase. And yet she feels compelled. Following the John O thing, she had eaten brunch in Fitzroys, drunk some wine. And very good it was. Food, and especially alcohol, are still a source of comfort, and she had, all things considered, enjoyed in a transient way the excellent coffee and the petit fours. Towards the end of her solitary meal, though, she had felt the urge to remove both door keys from her handbag, the original and the new key, about which she had done nothing, and place them on her table. The original, of course, was worn. The new one gleamed.

It was all so obvious now. She arranges them face to face, then back to back. No human behaviour is gratuitous. Daphne had been born first, and therefore was her elder, albeit by only a score of minutes. But Daphne was the one who sparkled. And there you had it. Less than a quarter of an hour had made the difference. The duplicate key – with sharper edges. The original, buffeted by the years. But her lock is sticky. Well, there you go. Few analogies work perfectly.

Where is Daphne at this very second?

From the outset, dependence had been a given. Independence, an impossibility. For twenty years, she and Daphne had sailed in tandem, or, to change the figure of speech, like a catamaran, with two hulls, but with one conjoined mind, and heart, she'd liked to think. It had been a partnership. But not a balanced one. They had battled through surf as an uneven twosome. No wonder they'd run aground. Though, was it pathological to harbour resentment for so long? She ought to know. For had that not been her training?

An old woman she met once at Grianan Fort had told her, one windswept day in March, about *her* twin. Thelma and the woman had stood together on the ramparts looking inwards on the rim of that ancient circle, imagining how humans might have related to one another in the forgotten whenever, pondering what could have united and divided *them*.

'I went through labour with her,' the woman said. 'I was here in Derry, in my wee house in Iona Terrace, and my twin was in Tiger Bay. That's in Wales. And do you know, I could feel her every contraction as it happened, as sure as God. You might not believe me.'

But Thelma had believed her, and the memory of that made her worse. She thinks of her solitary journey with horror. As a child and young person, it would have been unthinkable. But the unlikely happens. Years hence you look back and see the unimaginable. How it crept up like a shadowy wolf, only at the time, you hadn't known. You feel deceived and mocked, naïve and bitter. But also, an imbecile.

For a lifetime, she had maintained that distance between herself and Daphne. Lord, how she had allowed the chasm to become fifteen, twenty, thirty thousand Irish miles, and they, as far as she can recall, are longer again. Derry had been built on planting and emigration. Push and pull. The sea spoke of separation. But ghosts floated on the ebb tide, revisiting the great clearance ships that had anchored at Moville.

'I'll write,' Daphne had said, as if that would help. As if a letter four times a year could ever plug a hole. You could not talk in letters. It had been a beheading.

Now in the Shipquay Hotel, and still drinking, Thelma moves the keys this way and that. How destitute she had felt, and yet, how many years until she'd made the trip to McLaughlin's. How destitute she still feels. In therapy one can pre-contemplate, as ancient portals begin to creak. She wonders what is possible. Undeniably the young woman who showed her the exhibition had reminded her of Daphne. Not of her physical appearance. No, it was more the brightness of her smile. Her quick efficiency. All this had been so unsettling. Several times she had wanted to actually call her Daphne and embrace her with love. She shuddered now when she thought of it. How the young woman might have baulked. How *she* would have attempted to explain, but how lame it would have sounded. Sweat beads gathered accordingly upon Thelma's upper lip.

Forty years since Daphne had flown the big aeroplane. Woody Guthrie back to haunt her.

Who can say where loss is stored? What parking lot in the amygdala is occupied by grief? Who can tell why one person's anguish is resolved and another's isn't? Not that it had stayed red raw entirely, like blood dripping. Instead, the wound had become a sort of tumour that had grown and grown. Maybe Daphne had not been physically deported in the legal sense, but she had been stolen from Thelma, and not to Kent or Knightsbridge, but to Woomera in South Australia. Woomera. It sounded like a weapon. She'd recently looked it up again, in the Central Library, with the aid of a first-year school child from Foyle College. 'A throwing stick used by aboriginal peoples,' the child had read, 'used to propel spears with great force over considerable distances.' Exactly. A great distance. 'Thank you, pet.'

Daphne lives in a world of eucalyptus, red clay and mining. Thelma has never been. How could you visit a country with a mine called Peculiar Knob? And saying goodbye would have been too much. Daphne, at the last count, was teaching in some bloody community college, in a voluntary capacity, as a retired person.

Would she care for another drink?

'A small brandy, perhaps?' her waiter enquires.

Does he think she needs rescuing? Normally, she wouldn't. But today is – well, her birthday, so this, she supposes, should be some kind of celebration. Her big day, and Daphne's. But the chasm is too vast. The desertion too brutal. There is WhatsApp, but it has been easier to stay bruised. To expect little and bear the pain.

Even as the cognac does its work, she knows with dread that she's been wrong. Wrong, wrong, all a-bloody-long. That her interventions with dysfunctional clients had lacked integrity. That's what she thinks now, after God only knows how many units. Now there are two keys once more to the oak door. But what will she do with them? That is the thing. How sad am I, she thinks, using 'sad' in the corrupted way she hears on television. She is a fool. Her head spins as she tips the waiter, who seems concerned. Would he ring for a cab? A courteous young man.

Shipquay Street looks steeper than usual, and busier. Loadings and unloadings. A young couple stand at Lunn's window, no doubt selecting an engagement ring. An oil tanker blocks the way. Her taxi man curses. His meter races.

'Can't be helped, dear,' he says, 'your man's taking up the whole street.'

His cab smells of cheap perfume and mints. From her position, alone and imprisoned on the bare rear bench of the cab, she spots Indigo Black. How fresh and attractive she looks as she strides up the hill. What energy she still possesses, this woman of her own age, in those flamboyant red shoes. Indigo's skirt swishes as she increases, if anything, her speed and determination. For a moment Thelma thinks of waving. Thelma in her elasticated trousers. But only for a moment. Indigo has paused, and is speaking now to Rev Gray, who lingers outside the Donegal Shop, smoking, of all things, in the company of a lean young man.

One generally has two options, she tells herself, her internal voice sounding ominous. She'd seen it so often in colleagues. In the clients she'd tried to help. Life should be about choices. The right ones if possible. But frequently the wrong roads are taken because they seem inevitable. The only thing to be done. Often the right choice is avoided because it is too painful. Amazing the insights one has, when one is pissed.

In her befuddlement she produces a photograph of herself and Daphne when they were twelve. In black and white. Their hair in pigtails. She foolishly thrusts the picture at the driver.

'My twin,' she says, 'who lives in Australia.'

'Are youse identical?' he says, without looking. 'How long's she been away?'

'A lifetime.'

'I bet youse are still close,' says the driver. 'That's your man moving now.'

'Oh yes,' she tells him. 'Very close.'

Lead kindly light. For some reason, Cardinal Newman's hymn is in her head. She hums the tune, but the light is far from kindly.

'You in a choir?' asks the taxi man, half-grinning at her in his mirror as he lets out the clutch. As the cab lurches forward. Indigo is still talking to Gray. His face is waxy, and who is that lean young man? What do they all find to talk about? For so long she has existed in a murky fog in which no one speaks, and no one leads. The gloom has most definitely encircled.

Her driver has three girls at St Gobnait's.

'Do you know Miss Black?

'Oh God, aye, everybody in Derry knows Miss Black.'

He points out the window.

'Look, that's her there.'

Naturally, Thelma could so easily sail onto the rocks, complicit in her demise, allowing nature to take its course, as she grows older, more woodwormed, set and stuck. Despite the many letters of thanks from patients and relatives at her exit, and the unread novels she'd bought with gift tokens to read on train journeys she will never take, perhaps it would be best to throw oneself on the mercy of the court, and simply walk, like Walter must have done, into the Foyle.

'Don't be saying that,' says the taxi man.

But had she spoken?

'That's us now,' he says, 'thanks be to God.' The traffic is flowing at last.

Lately, Daphne has gone onto Messenger. She would like to come home, she says. 'Isn't Derry one friendly village?'

Woomera is a different village, a million worlds away.

Thelma needs another drink to become a shade more dotty, or to do something worse.

Is there drink in her house? 'Stop at the wine shop, would you,' she says, taking no chances.

It will be but a short ride home. Insight is a strange commodity. You can have it, but it refuses to help. This is a lesson and a half for a lady almoner to learn, however late. It had been all too much, this birthday of theirs. Just too unstable. Perhaps nothing had been resolved after all by her visit to McLaughlin's, marvellous as the young woman had been.

And yet, like the Virgin Mary, Thelma ponders these things in her heart. She will sit quietly now, allowing the radio jabber to fizz over her. The intercom, if that's what it is called?

'Roger,' says the driver, and all that hooey. How does anyone grasp such garble? In her bag the thin glass jug sits wrapped in white tissue, along with an unnecessary leather bookmark she'd purchased in the Craft Shop. The two keys clank together.

Thelma stands shivering on the kerb where the cabbie leaves her. At the threshold of her empty home. The same weeping, corroding gate. She fumbles for the key. Damn and double damn. Her bottle of wine is rolling about in the taxi. Will the driver drop it off? He will like hell. In the way of tall terraces, her house will be dark. Dismal and, despite the weather, cold. She will draw the curtains. Maybe, if she can stay awake, she'll light a fire. She believes she has some kindling. But is there coal? Oh God. Weariness is not felt in the bones. It weighs heavily in the blood, like liquid lead, blue as slug pellets, poisonous as arsenic A viscous cancer.

Catching the Bus

At first, Mr White and Miss Marrón are simply waiting to get served in the bus station café, in Foyle Street. He carries his ukulele. She holds her bag of birdseed. It is a fine summer morning for them, as they yearn to share a German bun together. You can only get them in Derry. In the interests of simplicity, Mr White has suggested they go Dutch. Miss Marrón felt a childish disappointment at this, but Mr White is a man of principle whom she refuses to push. By contrast, she is a creature of the moment, instant and starlit, a hot decision maker, elemental and intuitive, owing to her genetic heritage, for which she claims no credit. Under the circumstances, therefore, she disguises her emotions. Her growing love for Mr White being a patient work in progress.

The cook in the bus café is known as Delia. Not her real name. She is thought to be from Russia. Probably an Olga. A lot of foreigners take Derry names. A native woman in front of them orders a ham sandwich with mustard, and two large dogs to go, with heaps of red sauce.

'Lashings of it, love. It's going to be tropical today, wait till you see,' this woman tells Delia. 'I for one, am already on factor fifty.'

The woman says this loudly because factor fifty is expensive, and foreigners are deaf. Miss Marrón parks her birdseed in a discrete corner of the café as it weighs heavily on her wrist. A queue forms at their rear.

'Are youse okay?' says Delia, around the woman's head, to two workmen, who are next.

They have hands like shovels. Knee pads, leather tool belts, fists like bricks, red safety hats. The whole nine yards. Naturally, they want the full Irish. You couldn't blame them. Miss Marrón watches Delia peel streaky bacon strips from a polythene vacuum pack and drop them in the pan. Delia also fills coffee pots, wipes surfaces, rinses lettuce, arranges mugs with teaspoons in them, and sets up plates all at the same time. OMG. She serrates tomatoes in zig-zag wedges with a wee slitty knife, swills out glass bowls – and takes the money. She turns the sodas. At times she shouts, in Russian presumably, at the charming but useless Sean Óg.

'A teen,' she mouths at Miss Marrón, 'and most definitely on NVQ.' Mr White nods.

Miss Marrón has no second language, apart from her dozen words of Spanish, but she can tell that Delia is unhappy with the teen. She is directing him to shift his ass, and asking why the hell he is marrying a brown slice to a white slice of Brennans in the same bucking sandwich for the nice lady?

'They never told me he was colour blind,' she says out loud in English, addressing the workmen or some eastern saint.

All the while she is cracking eggs with one hand, without breaking the yolk, and frying them sunny side up for a group of old codgers in baseball caps, who rest on the plastic seats. The codgers belch and watch the clock. How many times has she reported this effing grill for being slow. Her hair, slicked to her brow, shines damp with pride, and she drips like lard.

Before this good weather, it had poured solidly for a week, says the woman in the queue. And she ought to know, because she'd been stuck for seven fecking days in a poky caravan, with three weans and a cockapoo, at Downhill. 'Like what is there in Downhill? Total nightmare,' she says to Delia.

'The caravan and the dog belong to the people next door, oh, don't be talking. I couldn't say nothing.

'But the springs in the bed, I'm telling you, Delia, were pure hammered. It would have broke your back just lying on it on your own, let alone… well, you know what I mean.' Billy was her man. 'You couldn't have whipped a ferret in it.'

'You mean a cat,' Delia speaks from the corner of her mouth.

'What? Aye. A cat.'

Miss Marrón makes eyes at Mr White.

'Then my Billy says, "I'm away to me ma's. I should never have came here in the first place." Too right he shouldn't. Downhill's a hole.'

'Good God,' says Delia, turning the sausages expertly.

'And you know what?' says the woman, flapping at her cardigan, for the heat is fierce, 'he was as good as his word. Off he goes like a tea boy, to his wee mammy in Hatmore. I blame her you know. He's there yet, getting ruined.'

Delia grunts.

'The more fool her, I say,' says the woman, searching for her purse, 'cancelling her outings from the Glenbrook to stand in a pair of bedroom slippers and skivvy for a useless lump like him, stinking the place out with the orange fish he eats for his brains. And why?'

'G'on tell me?' says Delia, grinning now at the workmen.

'That's what I'm doing,' the woman says, 'Derry men never grow up. Don't they not?' The workmen cheer. 'No, that's the God's truth, ask any woman in this town.'

She turns and stares at Miss Marrón. 'Aye well,' she says.

Miss Marrón turns then to Mr White and holds his arm.

'Oh my God,' the woman says, when Laura says, 'Hola.'

Miss Marrón strokes the arm of Mr White with increasing deliberation as Delia wraps the food. Greaseproof, double-layered. She glances at Mr White, alerting him to some hidden danger. But he is far off in his head, thinking, dwelling, she assumes, on the Ogre or his uke. God help him too. She tosses her noble head and speaks directly to the woman.

'I'm glad you enjoyed your break,' she says. 'We also have sand in the bull rings of Spain.'

The woman glares. 'I'll not be missing the Moss Park bus over the head of you anyway,' she says, 'Get out of my road, would you, I'm in a hurry.'

She takes the time, however, to look Miss Marrón up and down in a jealous sort of way. Drinks her all in. The alluring kohl around her eyes, the tanned exotic skin, her primrose Alice band and manicured nails.

'Away you go,' she says, 'and catch yourself on.'

'It's just, I could not help but overhear,' says Miss Marrón, in her richest, most Iberian voice. 'If I may, a word of advice Señora, next time, be more careful, eh? When it comes to men, there is much to know.' She grasps Mr White's free hand. 'It is essential to marry the right hombre.'

At this point she gives Mr White another poignant look.

'I have come to this city from Spain to tell you this.'

The woman, who shoves past her, stops to gawp at Mr White, treading hard on the delicate foot of Miss Marrón.

'He's no bloody oil painting anyway,' she says. Mr White winces. She tramps harder. 'There,' she says, 'that'll fix you, you cheeky bitch and your damned lies. I know rightly who you are. You're from Central Drive and you're not near wise in the head.'

She turns to Delia and the other customers, jabbing a sharpened finger at Laura Marrón. 'This one's never been farther than Bligh's Lane, let me tell you, not once in her manky wee life.' She scowls heavily at Miss Marrón, like an emoji, with the corners of her mouth turned down.

'You've never had so much as your big toe in Spain, darling,' she says, 'so thank you very much.'

At this moment, the hiss of the coffee machine may be heard. Also coughs from the elderly men. Mr White's paleness has intensified as he clings to Miss Marrón. As he plucks at his football shirt.

To be fair to Laura, she bows with grace to the woman and says, 'De nada.' And 'adios.'

The workmen man up and pay. But the German buns are off.

'All gone,' says Delia. She'd given the last of them to the old fellas waiting for their fries.

'Sorry, guys,' she says to Mr White. 'There was a big run.'

So, Laura and Mr White choose gravy rings instead. Tawny, sweet, crisp little lifebelts, but fleshy, and virginal inside. After the commotion, Delia serves them with even greater Russian dignity. The mugs gleam. The tea infuses. They take advantage of the vitamin D outside, for Mr White's benefit. He follows Miss Marrón, still trembling, but clutching in his hands his ukulele. She, in contrast, balances their tray, with reassuring ease.

The forecourt of the bus station is only magical. A floral paradise. Dozens of hanging baskets sway gently in the breeze, lending lushness to the plain brick terminus. The flowers are watered faithfully, she believes, in the early hours of the morning, by Council men, some of whom at least she must have danced with in the darkness of The Carrick. Mature men now, but aroused, no doubt, by memory.

The pinks and blues tumble like petticoats in the bays of the bus station, speaking *Fáilte* to the city but also, sadly, *slán*, for in these places we also say goodbye.

Miss Marrón selects an iron bench, next to a wall which, like an oven, is already hot with comfort.

Mr White has used the gents twice already in the last half hour. But she understands. Men's bladders and all of that.

Their bus is still not in.

Mr White is off again.

'Don't worry,' she tells him. 'I will make it wait.'

The toilet block is visible from the bench. A conical, slated appendage. He is taking his time, but she relaxes meantime and dreams of the Alhambra.

A majestic Goldliner sweeps onto the forecourt, a mechanical monster from Belfast, blasting heat. A blue panting tiger. Its doors swing open. The passengers look parboiled.

Mr White and Miss Marrón are fulfilling their dream. At last, they are travelling to Strabane to visit her dear friend Clara, who breeds the canaries, so bright and enchanting, in the Canal Basin. He will call with a certain Lorcan C. Diver, of Nancy's Lane, who will fix, please God, his banjaxed uke, because he'd dropped it, alas, in Hawkin Street.

Perhaps, admittedly, there is more than this in both their minds, but if so, they do not speak of it aloud. People throng the station now, shifting from foot to foot, like emigrants, anxious to board the coach to Dublin or Enniskillen. Throats clear. Feet shuffle. Trucks race heedless along the expressway in both directions. There is a general murmuring. Youths roar on mobiles.

'I'm not shouting,' a man bawls, 'but stop doing my head in. I will not bloody calm down.'

Old ones tell each other that there's no call for that kind of language in a bus station and listen for the Guildhall clock. 'Things,' they say, 'ran better in the Troubles.'

An inspector strides out of his glass tank office, in his tie and waistcoat, to say that there'd been some kind of incident three miles away, in the village of Newbuildings.

'Just a few stones and things,' he says. 'But it's cleared up now.'

'Aye right,' says a fella and girl slabbering over each other, and well out of it. 'We're going to a party,' they tell Miss Marrón.

'At eleven in the morning?' she says, forgetting to be Spanish.

'It's in the woods at Prehen,' the fella tells her. 'It's on for, what do you call it, three days. Miss Black has teed it up. It's mega. There's this big poetic swimming pool, and stuff. Thousands of tents on the pitches. You can leave and go back.' He shows Laura the inky stamp on his arm. *Admit one*. He gives a smoky laugh. 'We had to go home, like, to feed the piranha.'

That tickles Miss Marron, who understands hyperbole, though it would have puzzled Mr White.

'Seriously,' they say, 'the scuffers are keeping well out of it. Music and *craic*, man, all the way. You wanna bring your fella,' they tell Laura. 'Where is he anyway?'

Laura can see Mr White now. She hopes he is her fella. All right, she might have liked him to be a bit more, what would you say, Mediterranean, but he's White by name and white by nature. Whiteness is in his genes, like Spanish is in hers. So, it's grand.

There he is ambling back now, under the Transit flower bouquets, trying to disguise his angsty thoughts, carrying the precious ukulele on his shoulder, like St Columba's dove of peace, one hand idle in his pocket, fag on his lip – smoking is not so bad – and pretending to whistle when he takes it from his mouth, the way men used to do. Like her da, who had worked on the quay. Borrowed memories of the GIs and the war.

'What's the story?' she says.

'Naw,' he says, 'there is a guy lying in one of the cubicles, with his feet out the door, if you know what I mean, and a pair of wellies on them.'

'On his feet?'

'Aye, on his feet.'

'Colour?' she demands, for the colour of wellies is important.

'Blue, I think…'

'You think?' How could he not know the shade?

'Light anyway,' he says, 'but definitely blue, and very still.'

'His blue boots were still, and you did not poke them? They might have been dead.'

A lot of drinkers pass in public conveniences. This is a tragic fact. Laura has known quite a few.

'Aye, well,' says Mr White slowly. He often says this sort of thing when his heart races. He has been taking deep breaths, she knows, if not hyperventilating.

'Come, sit down beside me,' she says in a motherly way, brushing from the bench some imaginary crumbs.

'I wasn't sure what to do,' he says. 'I called out to him, you know.'

'And what did you call?'

'I called, "Hi, you there in the bog?"'

'Yes,' she says, 'and then?'

'"Are you dead?" I says, to waken him, like.'

'And had he – died?' asks Miss Marrón, who is good with death.

'Naw, he hadn't, as a matter of fact,' says Mr White, taking the weight off his legs. She hands him his tea.

She hopes it's not cold.

Mr White leans his ukulele against the wall.

'It'll be fine there,' he says, 'can I have my gravy ring?'

Miss Marrón wonders if he will cope with the gravy ring as well as the tea, so she holds herself in reserve, in case he may need assistance. Her fingers, she notices, glisten with sugar crystals, so she licks them clean.

This is not lost on Mr White.

'And is that all?' she says with feeling, so glad to have a new amigo with whom to share her life.

'All what?'

'All's about it. I mean what else did you say to him?'

'I couldn't see most of him,' says Mr White, 'but I shouted in anyway, "Are you alright there, mucker?"'

He draws deeply on his fag, continues drinking, ripping the gravy batter apart with his teeth. It comes easily, despite the crispy coating.

What need he has, she thinks. What immense vulnerability. At that moment, a wave of pure tenderness surges through Miss Marrón's enlivened body, as she thinks of Mr White.

'And then?'

'I took a proper gander into the cubicle. It wasn't locked you see.'

'And what did you *see*? Was he breathing?'

'He was doing a puzzle,' says Mr White.'

'A puzzle, in the toilet?'

'Yes, in the *Mirror*.'

'My God, what was he doing with the mirror?'

'It's a newspaper,' says Mr White.

'The *Daily Mirror*?'

'Yeah. With a pencil. Only it was wild dark in there,' says Mr White. 'You know what toilets are like.'

'But what did he *say* to you?' says Miss Marrón. 'Tell me his very words.'

Mr White shrugs. 'The fella turns round to me, and he says, "who the eff are you?"'

'He swore at you?'

'I suppose he did.'

'And was that all?'

'He said he was stuck on four across.'

'Four across what?'

'In the puzzle,' says Mr White. 'He goes to me, wait till you hear, "what's another word for privates. Five letters. No clues."'

'Did you get it?' asked Miss Marrón.

'Naw, I didn't,' says Mr White. 'I'm no good with words. Oh aye, but then he says, "Can a man get no peace in the town he loves so well?" And he starts to laugh.'

'Ah,' says Laura Marrón, whose soul lives mostly in San Sebastian or Córdoba, 'I am familiar with that canto.'

She begins to sing in a low key, which might have surprised Phil Coulter. Skipping a verse or two, her voice brims with ire as she reaches the tanks and guns.

Some of the waiting travellers clap. Though not all.

Mr White chews, sips and smokes.

'After the song,' she says, 'what did you do?'

'I used the urinal on the wall,' he says, 'then I washed my hands.'

'Bravo,' she says with sudden decisiveness, for this is a pleasant thing to discover about a male. Many of whom do not bother. She surveys the other men, thinking bad thoughts about their bodies, and wondering how many of them have also cleansed themselves.

'Did you speak to this welly man again?'

'I said "Good luck to you, squire,"' says Mr White. 'I told him I had to go now for my bus to Strabane.'

'You did right,' she says, as together they make to board the eleven fifteen, though by now it is 12 20. Mr White offers her a manly arm to climb the steps, but in a flash, he says, 'Where is your bag of seeds?'

'Oh, my God,' says Miss Marrón, 'It is in a darkened corner of the café. You are a genius, Mr White.'

'You take my uke.'

'Driver, please hold the bus,' he says commandingly. 'I must fetch the canary bag.'

The driver drums and waits. The bus throbs. Mr White returns clutching tight, in one hand, the bulky bag of seeds. The sun is already a demon. The bus strains on its leash. From some secret hiding place about her person, Miss Marrón produces two cloudy, purple plums.

'Mr White, they are warm, ripe and juicy,' she says, 'like me.'

Part Three

Gathering

The surge is on. From all across the north-western capital, and beyond, people stream to The Happening like they cannot help it. Like it was meant to be. Citizens of all creeds and those with none at all. But people who would see beauty in all its resplendence. Most bedecked splendidly in the colours of their choice. Some, admittedly, have still to realise the stirrings of their spiritual hue, but no one wears beige. There are many black and brown faces among the multitude, which greatly thrills Miss Black. On, on they come, wending their way purposefully on foot to The Happening, from disparate directions. From Racecourse Road and the Collon, from as far away as Culmore and the village of Eglinton. They walk from St Johnston, meandering and flowing like a great, slow current as far as Craigavon Bridge, where, passing the railway museum, and processing past the static red choo-choo, those approaching from the right merge with the multitudes arriving from the left. People from Manorcunningham mingle with their cousins from the Bog. Together they cross the foaming Foyle, using both decks, taking full possession of the space to blend seamlessly with the Waterside ones from Glendermott, Rossdowney and Clooney, from Burndennett, and Greysteel. Town ones and country ones, all drawn to a single destination. And isn't this as it should be?

All of them carry burdens, but they are not refugees. Here the comparison ends. These seekers and travellers are in jovial form, taking selfies and singing as they tramp along. The very stanchions of the bridge join them in harmonic sympathy.

Young men and women sport red, blue and green tops. The weather is warm and so they are sweating buckets. But no one complains. Like pilgrims on the Camino, they are comrades in arms, linked by the lure of possibility, as they gaze on the river, that shrewd old observer who has seen so much. Some notice for the first time that the Foyle is tidal, that the push they had expected to the sea, just then, is a pull of water upstream. The more philosophical explore this allegorically. Someone says their mother once swam across the holy river, in a charity event. She'd had a tetanus jab because, back then it was, 'wild polluted.' But things had changed. Once upon a time, a for-real whale called Dick had gambolled in the river like a wean, high-dipping and diving like a big youngster.

'A shagging whale?'

'No, really.'

There had, quite naturally, been winters of discontent when the frozen earth cracked open, and the river slowed. When it had gone solid and all but stopped. Backed up and caked, like Antarctica. When children swore they'd seen penguins. No kidding. But seriously, this bridge is no novice. Johnny Hume was stopped on it by the RUC. How crazy was that? Lorries evacuated Protestants to the Waterside across it, with their chairs and mattresses piled high in the great migration. Soldiers with rifles had been on it for years. The Craigavon Bridge remembers all that.

Once, imperial troops had bumped along the surface of the Foyle in pugnacious little gunboats, their silhouetted cannon scanning the horizon. Troopers at the helm. Once, the bridge had bristled with weaponry, resounding to the Scouser strains of squaddies on the breeze. A lot of them too had been young fellas from Nottingham or Manchester, Ayrshire and Lanarkshire. You gave your name to the smudged-out faces, without a question, without looking into the reddened eyes, without grasping the opened hand. They checked your mugshot. Lowered their heads. Took a jook into your vehicle. Studied your passengers. You were a civil people, but you hated it. There had to be another way. No matter who you were, or what you thought, you didn't like any of it. You told them where you'd been. And the purpose of your journey. Your place and date of birth. Sometimes, you were held anyway. Thank God those days had passed.

The lower deck of the bridge, especially, had been a cold dripping place, an alien station for a stranger in an alien land, a trouble-scourged, wrought-iron wind tunnel. People on all sides got shot with lead. Often, traffic had clogged for hours, like a thrombosis. You smoked at the wheel, played the radio, fretted and waited. What if the bridge were to be blown up? There had been a campaign for an emergency hospital on the west bank, but it came to nothing.

But thanks be to Almighty God, today is today, and today the people are again on the move, but now they are progressing to Prehen, to take part in The Great Event, as some are calling it, though its real name is The Happening. Many, simply fan across Victoria Road to walk in their hundreds under the trees, but even more choose to trace the imprint of the railway line that had run to Strabane. Singing, they hug the willow shore. Curious sea birds circle. Great black-backed gulls swoop and scoop, diving and winging it, to keep their friends in *craic*. Fish leap frantic from the ripples to get a better view. Such gossip below the surface.

Pilgrims crowd the narrow track bed where carriages once trundled, where iron pistons thumped, and steam had hissed. Two women say they are on a caravan of love. Someone has seen Roddy Doyle.

On the backs of the hikers, knapsacks swing fat-full of 'gorgeous tucker,' according to a returning Australian from Tasmania. A group of musicians blow trumpets. John Orange McBeth is there with some of his percussionist friends, and good luck to him. He walks beside his bike, and behind it, rolls, as usual, his drum. 'There will be other drummers,' he announces enigmatically to those around him. Sometimes the pilgrims walk in step for fun, playing a marching game, increasing and decreasing the length of their strides, to catch one another out, like kids. Melissa McLaughlin has come in from Malin, with her mongrel, Freddy. There are dogs of all sizes and lengths of hair, some on leashes tugging, but most of them romping free, woofing and playing chase.

Oh, the liberation.

It's like the tribes of a nation have at last come together, under the flag of Art, and there, right in the middle of the whole cavalcade, with his eyes like wary beads, is Rev Gray – whose walking appears somewhat laboured. He sports a doubtful, tan tee shirt – and with him, walking, is the Lean Young Man, who may still be in search of wildness.

The multitude carries tents of all descriptions. Old ones, posh ones, simple one-man jobs, many of them green. But many manifest resplendently in rainbow colours. These are not the property of serious Duke of Edinburgh Award campers, but rather the proud possessions of those who have felt the magnetic force-field of The Happening and who cannot stay away. Some oldies reminisce and claim to have been at Woodstock. Poets recite their latest work. The giraffe necks of acoustic guitars protrude timelessly from the corners of restored duffel bags. Bottles clink merrily.

Miss Black, as the instigator of the event, flits like an exotic bird along the road in her recently acquired red Porsche. With the hood well down. She offers encouragement to this one and the other, envying a little, perhaps, the eagerness of the many young people. Sensing too, no doubt, the reviving spirits of the more mature walkers, those who have been on the path for years and who are in need of a pick-me-up. At other times, without inhibition, she walks with the multitude, mingling easily, taking an interest in their artistic aspirations, listening to unexpected tales of their creative endeavours, however small.

And does her heart not leap when she beholds her city so miraculously on the move, a great, seething congregation of good-natured nomads? Yes, she is dewy-eyed, and who wouldn't be? Though, of course, she is not a fool. The Happening will have its unplanned moments, the unfortunate events which can sometimes mar a day. Her nemesis crosses her mind. Where *is* Shugh Henderson today, and what is he plotting? But, no, she will banish the thought of him. There may be heat exhaustion, lost children, unexpected and freak weather, for adrenaline is rampant. But there is plenty of drinking water at the rest-stations. The numbers have surprised even her, the one who dreamed it all up. But she is well supported, and this is no time for doubts. And isn't there so much good in these people, weaving between clumps of friends and rank strangers, to whom they speak like cousins. They all pour together from the great village along the east bank, in such a concerted, cultural direction.

The Red Cross is on hand. The Knights of St Columbanus and the Order of St John are positioned strategically along the route. She had spent long hours with Inspector McAtamney, who was well pleased with the arrangements. With the numbers of stewards and that sort of thing. Space, he had said at the outset, would be tight. But he'd been awfully good.

This is all such a vindication. Like the uncorking of a thousand bottles, the release of ten thousand genies. And what a letting go.

Her job now is akin to that of a midwife. She will deliver Billy Grail, the star attraction, the crowd-pulling sensation from Sacramento. He will appear for the crescendo. The preceding days have been a monumental build-up. What a blistering blast when he takes the stage. The stewards will earn their keep, for Billy is scarcely human.

There had, undoubtedly, been the brickbats. Grotesque posters plastered on hoardings in Spencer Road and Duke Street. A picket in Guildhall Square. Space had been bought in the *Sentinel* and the *Derry News* to vilify Billy and to attack The Happening. Shugh Henderson's work. Some minor religious groups had made common cause with him. They mounted a protest outside the old Brown's Restaurant building at the bridge. Browns, where Miss Black had spent so many happy evenings despite the Troubles, listening with heightened emotion to the stirring voice of a certain curly-haired singer, with whom she'd been half in love.

Worship God NOT Billy Grail

So read the placards hoisted on fresh, white, wooden poles by earnest young men and women, some of whom wore Sunday hats.

'Do come along and enjoy the fun,' she told them.

The protesters sniffed miserably, poor things, and blew their noses. She could not believe for a second that this was their chosen path. She detected sad, old guiding hands. 'Exuberance should not be read as idolatry,' she told them, to no avail. But let them have their way. Such was her unsettled state of anticipation that she had not slept for days.

She would appear at The Happening later, wearing flats, a practical, navy blue pair of slacks and a warm angora jumper, because temperatures could dip. There might even be the dreaded river mist, wafting idly in clouds. So far, though, they had been blessed by Mr Blue-Sky, with his promise of star-twinkle nights and the merest hint of frost.

The crows of Prehen caw mightily in the elms as the crowds sweep past the concrete plinth on which Foyle Fisheries had stood. On, on they swirl up the dry cradle of the disused track, some peeling their eyes, searching for whitewashed memorial words on walls. Remember this one. Remember that one.

Victoria Park, where the Judge and the nobs hang out, is high up on the left, contagious to the enchanted quarry and the Bolies. A number of the pilgrims had once worked in Riverview. Its welfare-slanted roof shines reflectively. What days those days had been. A Child Protection officer remembers the safe, the actual money safe, and the weight of a Saracen, being burgled from the tearoom and dumped on waste ground. He recalls the Nissan huts, the Travellers' camp opposite. The army installation. A tethered donkey in the park. The no-warning bomb in Foyle Road that wrecked the tired old houses and shattered windows. That shook out grannies in their pinnies. Two girls tell how their auntie had watched bullets winging from Gobnascale. 'The Provos were shooting at the soldiers.' This auntie, as a child, had seen them in a blur, from her own bedroom window in Hillview. 'G'on look Teddy,' she'd said, 'them's tracers.'

'But there is no shooting now?' says the Lean Young Man, looking around him at the pilgrims. 'Only in films.'

He jogs along, carrying his equipment and that of Rev Gray.

'Thank God,' says Gray, automatically.

The Blue Two had roused themselves to join the throng. There is a limit to inactivity. Even for old guys. But there is no limit to the appeal of Indigo Black. You had to see it and be in on it. You couldn't not be there. The Happening had got them both going. You couldn't sit at home on your arse, with all this going on. Because you wouldn't know what would happen. It might be what Mick and Manus have been waiting for.

'Do you mind the old Everglades Swimming Pool,' a woman asks her friend, 'before they filled it in? Honest to God, it was as like the real bloody thing. Palm trees and all growing in big clay pots. You could have been in Florida. All you wanted was a few alligators.'

'There *were* alligators. All those old horny males,' says her friend. 'Oul lizards in cane chairs watching us in our swimsuits. D'you remember my blue bikini?'

'Aye, God knows, we were in great nick then,' says the woman, increasing her stride. 'And the long-haired piano player. I wonder what happened him?'

'Sure, that's where you got your Declan,' says her mate.

'Aye, I know,' says the first woman, shaking her head, 'but that, Fidelma, as we all know, is another story.'

Something like wildness stirs, perhaps, in the soul of Rev Gray.

Elevated high above them, Judge Scarlett must hear their voices. Perhaps, like he had half-promised Indigo, he will drop in later.

On, on they plough towards the promised land, marvelling at the honest symmetry of the Star Factory on the opposite bank, with its industrial clock, at the glory of the lush woodland on the distant hills. You can see the City Cemetery from away down here. The tall flagpoles of the Republican plot. Some recall old women telling them about the blessing of throats.

'What throats?' ask two young fellas from Sperrin Gardens. 'We never bless no throats.'

A fella, with a wee girl, remembers a man from Strathfoyle, God rest him, and his war on knotweed.

Wans say the boathouse is a disgrace, the state of it. 'You'd think they could use it for Pilates.'

'They do use it for Pilates,' says a fit-looking young woman. 'I know because I teach it on Wednesday nights, if anybody's interested.' Youngsters like the big swirly writing on the walls, the cool letters. *Oran loves Andrea. True.* 'Graffiti *is* art,' they say.

Rev Gray finds himself nodding, though he's never been into graffiti. But then, as he is learning, things are a question of perspective. He'd dithered in his head about attending The Happening, but Indigo Black, whom he'd known a lifetime, had said, 'You'll come.' After which he'd talked it over with the Lean Young man. And such was their strengthening bond that the Lean Young Man agreed.

But all this chatter, intriguing as it may be, is as nothing when compared to the sheer canvas kaleidoscope of colours on the pitches. The spiralling, kite-blue woodsmoke from fires in safety cages, and the aroma of Doherty's sausages.

So many people. There are all the marshals, to keep order, but you know, it really is an awfully big ask, for the site covers extensive acres of the former city dump, greened over years ago. The Happening is heaving with raconteurs, revellers and rabbits. Someone has seen a heron. 'Is it a myth that herons are monogamous?' Two generations of men and boys have honed their skills on this springy turf.

'Back of the net and there you go.'

Now on Saturdays, girls play soccer. Golfers practise their drives here, greyhounds run in muzzles. At least one Argentinian evangelist once preached under canvas on these very sods. There had been a circus. Van the Man definitely sang Brown Eyed Girl here years ago, on another summer night. The Undertones played it. Ten thousand bodies had turned out to hear them. God alone knows how many are going to lie on the sward tonight, listening to the alternative music of waves lapping, as they ease their collective minds.

The flaps of the large marquee are well tied back. This is the Good Pint Bar beside the stage, and it's mental.

'Are youse two sharing a tent or what?' asks Johnny Torrens from Tullyally, one of the stressed-out guys on the gates.

He is addressing Rev Gray and the Lean Young Man. About their arrangements. His name is on his badge.

'Well now…' says Gray.

'Yes, yes we are,' says the Lean Young Man, politely, but assertively, with well-honed rationality. 'Our tent looks neat, but it is most commodious for wildness.'

'For what?' says Johnny, 'It's ten quid a pitch, mate, for a two man.'

He looks at Rev Gray. 'No, straight up.' People are piling around and shoving from behind. Gray had been sure the event was free.

'That's right, two men,' says his Reverence, desperately, as more citizens advance.

'We have come to enjoy some wildness together you see,' says the Lean Young Man. 'I, for one, was brought up most circumspectly.'

'What the buck is he on about?' says Johnny Torrens to Roisin, who has swung by to give him some help.

'All the twos are at the back, in enclosure K,' she tells Rev Gray. 'Your genders doesn't matter.'

'The back of what?' asks the Lean Young Man, leaning forward with earnestness, in his anxiety to understand. 'Is this where the wildness will be best?'

'Would you get him,' says Johnny.

Gray waits. For a moment, he appears to disengage. But his anxiety rises quickly.

'Technically, it's free,' says Johnny, rattling his tin. 'But all the takings are for the arts.'

He nudges Roisin.

Gray stumps up two Bank of Ireland notes.

'But how will we *know* our pitch?' asks the Lean Young Man, who is fussing about receipts, 'should anyone object, I mean.'

'Talk sense,' says Johnny, lighting up, 'once you're inside paddock K, youse can stick your tent up wherever the hell you like. 'But remember,' and he nudges Roisin, 'if there's any knife crime, or sectarian chanting, I'll personally break your bloody necks. So, be very careful in there.' L.O.V.E. is tattooed on the fingers of both his hands. 'Only saying,' he says. 'In the wee small hours, Johnny Rotten is not exactly going to be your average pussycat. Youse have been warned.'

'Please,' says the Lean Young Man, 'I am not…'

'*Any* violence or carry on, I said,' says Johnny, more sternly, 'because see if there is, I will personally kick youse from here to Kilfennan. I'm wearing my new Doc Martens.'

'What language is he using?' asks the Lean Young Man, thoroughly perplexed, despite a Masters in linguistics.

'Ask *him*,' says Johnny, poking a bitten finger in Gray's face. 'Do I know you from somewhere, friend?'

This is a jarring note. His Reverence looks away.

'Wait for me,' he calls to the Lean Young Man, and toddles off at speed.

Johnny, who most certainly could not have been personally appointed by Miss Black, nicks his fag. He necks a can of Harp. His tin is full of cash.

'I know that oul boy from somewhere,' he says to Roisin. Then he places him.

'Wait till I tell the lads,' he says. 'He tried to teach us RE.'

'Religion. Was he any good?' asks Roisin.

'Naw. He let on to be a laugh,' says Johnny, 'but he was your actual, total moon man. We gave him a hard time. I think he was depressed.'

Miss Marrón and Mr White Take a Circuitous Route

That very morning, after all the carry-on at the bus station, Miss Marrón and Mr White had settled themselves in the single decker, for Strabane. It was well filled with the travelling public, a lot of them on the free blue pass, which meant they were 65 years old, at least. Everyone had to hold tight as the driver wafted them south-west. Miss Marrón had wisely positioned the bag of birdseed at her feet, in case of spillage. The big round wheels of the bus rotated with purpose. Happily, they got a clear run, despite the crowds swarming across both decks of the bridge on their way to The Happening. Below them, the Foyle also surged, wise and wonderful as ever. At the traffic lights, the bus paused opposite Domino's Pizzas for an age, as if it was lost in thought, but then it purred, and they were gone, with the wind at their backs and a ballad in their hearts. Being together and all of that.

Mr White jiggled the ukulele on his knee as they picked their way along Victoria Road, through the technicolour multitude, past Honey Pot Cottage on the left, and the new temporary city. There were indeed campers all over the show at Prehen. He loved the dazzle of the tents but clucked nervously as they passed Newbuildings. For there were a lot of flags. But Laura said, 'Please don't worry.'

'A flag, in itself, Mr White,' she also said, 'is simply a piece of cloth that can do you no harm at all. For example, my own native flag makes me rejoice but it does not instil fear of other flags.'

The rumour of trouble had probably been a lie, she said, with no disrespect to the bus inspector, whom she happened to know was from an excellent family called Quigley.

'I told you it would be fine,' she said as they sped towards Magheramason, where undoubtedly there would be more flags.

Miss Marrón, resplendent in a recently acquired yellow and red sundress, sat closer to Mr White.

'Do you like my dress?' she asked softly. 'There is a secret, you know. It used to be the flag of Spain.'

Mr White, who had looked quite tense until now, began to smile.

Trains trundled, buses bowled, and beyond this Volvo's toughened glass, placid cows grazed tranquilly as the happy couple – for surely by now they *were* a couple – crossed the county border to Tyrone.

'We'll be there in no time,' said Miss Marrón, with spirit, folding her lissom limbs. Mr White appeared, then, to relax, as he sank into the velvet comfort of the Translink seats, his head upon her shoulder. In that very moment, Miss Marrón felt his body, and also his spirit, merge organically with hers, and this caused her much joy.

'God love him, he's beat,' a fellow voyager told her, a large motherly woman with two red setters of her own. Oisín and Flann. Both seasoned travellers.

The world flashed by. They soared over the Dennett, where fishermen stood flicking their rods, in waders. The fishermen waved at Miss Marrón, and she waved back. With her other hand, she salved the troubled head of Mr White, who slept peacefully, for once, without any signs of the Ogre on his face.

'I can see how much you love him,' said the woman with the setters.

On the horizon, wind turbines whirred.

Ballymagorry was drowned in sunshine.

On the outskirts of Strabane, like the hero in some Western film, Mr White stirred on cue.

'You've had siesta,' said Miss Marrón authentically. 'Does Lorcan C know you're coming?'

When faced directly with this question, Mr White said, 'Yes,' for he had certainly sent a message to that effect via a famous darts player he'd met in Poundland, a week or so before.

Having disembarked, Miss Marrón bade him a sorrowful though temporary *adios*, as she prepared herself for the smothering kisses of her odd friend Clara, and the hospitality she would lavish. Full of gratitude to Mr White, she lifted her bag of seeds. She would disregard the cacophony of the birds, who without doubt, would be restrained within wire prisons. Mr White would do his errand. She would do hers. Then they would be together. A fine arrangement and what could be better?

'I'll call at his Mr Whippy van, to begin with,' Mr White had told her sensibly, 'for that is what he lives in. Up Nancy's Lane.'

'I'll see you at five,' she said, 'in Patrick Street. Good fortunes with your repairs and may the Irish sun god shine more vitamins on your face.'

Mr White watched her stride off on her confident, brown legs, then he headed back, a little, the way they'd come, for they'd overshot Nancy's Lane.

The ice cream van in which the ukulele man lived was well up the hill. Though it was easy to spot on account of its bold gaudiness. Mr White also discovered that it was pinkly corroded around the sills. That both wipers were missing, but that its giant cone sat proudly on the roof. The windows were fully glazed, but inside paced two vicious mastiffs.

The van rocked with the barking of the mastiffs, but otherwise, all looked to be in order. No sign, however, of Lorcan C.

'Who will I ask?' said Mr White.

He did not have long to wait. Suddenly, two furtive men in khaki bee suits, obviously sentries, appeared like astronauts from behind a spindly hedge – to look for his credentials.

'You're a stranger,' they growled, from deep inside their bee suits. 'We know by the suspicious cut of you. And your strange town voice.'

He offered the instrument, in its case.

'No, that could be a rifle,' said the more important looking bee man. They both had serious faces, in as much as Mr White could see them.

'He'll be in The Sprocket,' they said, at length, getting over their suspicion, and speaking of Lorcan C.

They stood so close to Mr White that he could smell their honey. Smoke reek rose heavenward, wisping from their puffers. The junior man appeared to have a bee inside his veil – that was supposed to keep it out. Maybe it was a tame bee, and he kept it for a pet.

'You've a bee in with you there,' said Mr White, trying to be helpful.

'What?' yelled the bee man, who must have been hard of hearing. They wore yellow Marigolds on their hands. Surprisingly, the bee man squeezed the bee, and killed it.

'Do you know The Sprocket?' they asked in muffled voices. 'That's where you'll find him.'

Mr White, who was doing his best to follow their intentions, said he had heard it was a great place entirely, and where was it exactly? He imagined himself speaking with a rag stuffed in his mouth, to make him sound like them, so as not to stand out.

'Away on past the phone box that doesn't work a damn,' said the senior man. 'Oh aye, away on yet.' He was pointing at the town. 'Avoid the police station at all costs' – the other bee man laughed inside his suit – 'and cross the Bowling Green, where there's not a blade of grass. After a while, hang a ninety degree at the sweet shop that's missing, and when you pass the church, listen for the bell. When it rings, you'll come to where the doctors be. Are you with me? Continue on another while, then swing due left, take a right and it's the pub with the bicycle nailed to the wall, so you can't steal it, but you'll know it when you see it.'

'A bicycle?'

'God, you know what a push bike is. You couldn't mistake it. It is unmistakably a bicycle. Have you got that now?'

Mr White felt a stab of loneliness without Miss Marrón, but he told them he understood. The bee men stood very still to see him off. 'Go on then, with you' said their leader, when Mr White hesitated.

'It's that way there, you eejit.' They pointed rubbery fingers and flapped their golden hands. 'Away you go to hell.'

Mr White's poor sense of direction was a handicap in these unknown parts, but, like a lot of people, he walked like a man who knew where he was going.

It proved to be a long enough trek to The Sprocket. At one stage he crossed the River Mourne, which, on account of its history, he checked for swelling. Then back again. He asked a lot of Strabane people to help him and was impressed by their humanity. Some even accompanied him for bits of the way, making conversation and offering him cigarettes more than once.

'You're getting close,' they said.

In the end, there it was in front of him. The bicycle was rusted, but it *was* on the wall and a very fine grocer's model it had been in its day. With a lovely basket full of blue, trailing lobelia, to cheer him up.

Notwithstanding, Mr White approached the door of The Sprocket with caution, for pubs have their own codes, and in Strabane, a Derry wan, according to legend, has to be especially respectful.

There were more doors than enough inside, all going in and out, and a lot of thick, treacle darknesses, despite the glare outside. With one hand he clung to the uke. With the other, he manipulated handles.

Some of them more than stiff. It was not the easiest entry he'd ever made.

In the intestines of the building, and far from the thronging streets, he found the inner sanctum of the Sprocket. Six wise men sat on high wooden stools, in cramped but intimate conference around a circular bar. In front of every wise man stood a serious pint of porter. In each learned mouth lurked a fag, though it was against the law. On the top of each man was a head, and on every head a cap. All the heads and caps, and the buttons on the caps swivelled, as one, like synchronised swimmers to stare at Mr White, who, with some decorum, to be fair, approached them in stealthy fashion.

The barman was a woman.

There was not a word. Smoke streamed, blue and steady. In the corner, a tank of neon fighting fish danced, fins flying. He recognised the thrum of an oxygenator, for he knew about fish.

All around the bar there were faded black and white photos of ancient men on bikes. Old upright, bearded bicycles, in the tradition of Strabane, and lads on manly wheels.

'I'm looking for Lorcan C,' said Mr White, now wishing he wasn't.

The heads swung away from him. The barman looked frozen in her apron.

The oldest of the men lifted his pint and drank it down. He pointed at Mr White, who was uncertain.

'What's your hurry, pal?' said the man. 'Will you not sit down?'

There was no seat for Mr White, so he stood.

'Tell us your mission,' said the man, 'My name is Lorcan C.'

'Thanks be to God,' said Mr White.

But Lorcan C, if indeed it was he, did not smile. For this was no smiling matter.

'I've come about my uke,' said Mr White holding it up in its case, which was of limited value, since none of the men could see it inside.

'This is a – bicycle bar, begod,' said Lorcan C.

Mr White knew so little. 'I heard you did ukes as well,' he said.

This caused the men to have conversations in very low tones.

'Has it slipped a cog?' asked Lorcan C, at length, 'and what hell gears are on it? Is it five-speed only?'

Mr White began to shake. It was hard to apply the question to a uke.

'I dropped it in Hawkin Street,' he began candidly.

'Hawkin Street is not in Strabane,' said Lorcan C, spitting with contempt. The other men agreed. They shook their heads.

'It's nowhere near Strabane. Has the chain come off her?' asked one of them.

'The strings won't tighten,' said Mr White, offering to open the case.

'Don't do that,' screamed Lorcan C. 'A lot of them ukes used to be on the fixed wheel. Did you ever hear of that?'

Mr White felt sweat trickle down his arms inside the cotton pullover that Miss Marrón had thoughtfully suggested for today because it was light and easily worn.

'It will be the cotter pins,' said another man with whiskers. 'I had one for years, and damned the note would it play till I changed the pins.' He houghed in his handkerchief. 'Tight divils, cottars. You'll need a soft hammer. It was some job, I'm telling you, to get them out.'

Mr White thought he should offer to set Lorcan C up with another drink, but the barman had read his mind. She wagged her finger in circles, and then, wasn't she pulling pints for the whole lot of them, except for Mr White. God bless us, the Guinness flowed as he scoured his pockets.

'Some of them has cracks in their frames, of course,' said Lorcan C. The other men looked grave. They paid attention and said, 'Oh aye, they have indeed. Especially them English ones. They're out by at least a tone. Oh, the full tone.'

This was some private joke.

'Junk,' they said.

'I knew a man with a champion hound, one time,' said the fella with the whiskers, 'the Pride of Leckpatrick, you called it, and it ran in Lifford faster than any hound before it.'

'But its bicycle broke in two,' said Lorcan C. 'And it, Lord save us, as far as I can remember, came out of England.'

'It did, of course,' the others said, 'don't you know rightly it did, and what would you expect from a perfidious beast of Albion.'

'No matter. I sorted it for him, but afterwards,' said Lorcan C, 'it never sounded the same. And it never ran again. I tried every damned thing with it but when he bowed it quick on the bends the rattles of it were horrendous. It refused to play a reel, whatever was in its head. Not a damned reel would it play. The wheels wouldn't spin in pitch. People comes to me, you know and expects miracles.'

Out of his depth, Mr White hung his head. Miss Marrón was his miracle. This was tough going, but he would see it through.

'Have you heard of our John Dunlap that printed the Declaration for the Yanks?' asked a man that hadn't spoken. 'I'd say he rode a bicycle.'

The other men nodded. 'Bloody sure he did. Your very good health,' they said politely enough, holding up gleaming glasses. 'If it wasn't for pneumatic tyres,' they said, 'we'd all be riding on solid rubber yet, with the balls shook off us.'

'That's no bad one,' they said. 'Boys a boys, no balls would be some state of affairs. A how-do-you-do and a half, no balls, and us running to collect them.'

'Like wee marbles.'

'Speak for yourself,' said Lorcan C.

The men held their bellies and laughed in a sonorous manner.

'How many years have you had her, anyway?' asked Lorcan C, getting back to the business.

Mr White tried to remember when he'd first got the uke, but his arteries had clogged with confusion. He was thinking of Miss Marrón and how long he'd known her.

'He doesn't have a baldy,' the men said, smirking. 'You'd think, by heavens, he'd remember a thing like that. We can all recall our first bicycles.'

'A bicycle needs love, I can tell you that for nothing,' said the barman, wistfully. Her name was Jasmine. 'Do you have a wife yourself Mr...?'

'Oh, White,' he said.

'Mister O'White.'

'O'White,' said the men, 'God in heaven, 'What sort of a name is that?'

Mr White began telling the barman that he and Miss Marrón were in a serious mingling, but Lorcan C stopped him dead, and glared at Jasmine. Then, turning to Mr White, he said, 'we only talk bicycles in here. Cut out that other muck. She should know better. If you want to talk blethers, you can go to The Farmers' Home.'

'But what about the uke?' said Mr White, thinking of how strong Miss Marrón would be in a similar circumstance.

'Throw her agin the wall,' said Lorcan C. 'I'll look at her the next wet day we have. I'll upend her and put her on the bench. Give me a call in a lock of weeks when the swallows sit on the wires and the cows are clamped for the winter, when the crops are stored on racks and the roofs close their pores. Then there'll be plenty of time to tune a bicycle, to oil it and cure its brakes, to attend to its bearings, and all the rest of it. How does that sound? You may run her over there by the fish tank. That's a fierce class of swimmers behind the glass.'

Mr White didn't argue.

Instead, taking his ukulele manfully, and in as mature a way as he could muster, he wheeled it to where he'd been told. Some of the fish were a milky shade of cream, with lions' manes and floaty tails. Even as he relinquished his most cherished possession, worry threatened to hatch like larvae in his gut and his bowel seized. Such an awful spasm. It was then he noticed the many pairs of extracted bicycle forks hanging on ropes, like long front teeth. Black, gold and turquoise prongs swinging from the rafters, and free from encumbrance. He thought of fear and how he wanted rid of it. Of green, blue and cherry worries. He also became aware that the two fans in the ceiling, installed to expel tobacco smoke, had once belonged to choppers, which must have eaten miles.

He wanted to say goodbye or some connecting thing to Lorcan C, about his instrument, but Lorcan C and the men had already forgotten him. They began to discuss a road race held in Sion in 1910, the ins and outs of which were evidently as familiar to them as though it had been yesterday. The bragging, and the bets. The event had been engineered by Herdmans of the Mill. Voices were being raised and it was time to go.

Mr White was sure that Jasmine's hair, which had sat too perfectly, was false, but when he'd paid her for the Guinness, he hadn't liked to stare. At one stage, as he fumbled towards the door, he had looked back, by way of farewell. None of the men looked up. But Jasmine may have waved.

Already blinking in the daylight, he could not be sure where he had been, or which, if any, of the cap-wearing men had really been Lorcan C. He would miss the uke, but in the end, the separation would be worthwhile if it all ran smoothly.

God save us.

After that, he took another reflective wander through Strabane, where he discovered stainless-steel emporiums selling choice chicken fillets, and others dispensing hot breads. Also, resinous stores stocking leather cartridge belts. There were, too, exotic caves stuffed with fishing nets and working men's boots, slick Turkish barber shops and up-market funeral parlours. Relaxed citizens stood good-naturedly at corners in no hurry, chatting in twos and threes, alongside the most affluent of motorcars with four wing mirrors. The traffic wardens wore red jackets, but they were decent looking boyos without film in their cameras, he was sure. It came to him then that he needn't have concerned himself about it raining, for he'd never seen anything like the grey thickness and the height of the concrete flood defences of the Mourne, except for the walls of Derry, which were older and made of stone.

Mr White could not, of course, be entirely sure that he'd see his uke again, but he had survived some kind of test. He was learning to trust his instinct. And his instinct told him that maybe he had been privileged to find his man. It also informed him that he'd been right to follow his nose and to put his trust in Miss Marrón. Things in that department were getting better all the time, and that pleased him more than anything. More than a win at the dogs. Trust is, after all, at the core of every transaction, but it is also a pleasant commodity, and distinct with possibilities.

After a cold chocolate milkshake in a respectable, modern café, where he took the time to consider his life, and cool himself, he bought a cobalt-coloured Frisbee in a trinket store, and threw it for a while in Koram Square with a cub wearing blue dungarees with silver buttons. The dungarees were splattered with what looked like wall cement, because, as the cub himself said, he'd been plastering for some client in Ardstraw. The lime was all over him, but he was a nice cub with an open countenance. On the other hand, when Mr White thought about the Ogre, he felt himself freeze. So, although there was hope, he still had a way to go.

At last understandably, the cub drifted off in the careless way of youth, and it was time for Mr White to go looking for Miss Marrón. This thought was a blessing that warmed his heart. He wondered how she had fared, with her friend Clara in the Canal Basin, and whether she had been as resolute as himself, in holding it all together. He also imagined her skipping towards him, singing in almost-Spanish.

Mrs Green's Chimney

When Mrs Green eventually lights her fire, smoke and fumes come belting unbidden from her wall. Perhaps something has cracked. Thousands are making their way to Prehen for this Happening thing, but she will choke at home, alone.

Yes, she now has two keys to the front door of her decaying house. But what good will they do her if she can't breathe? And she doesn't want to move.

A typical caustic notion.

Before entering her jaded residence, she had stood, somewhat unsteadily, scrutinising the word 'McCartan,' her maiden name. Father had got it blasted in the glass above the door. At this point, stupidly, she had also thought of Walter and his watery reabsorption in the cosmos. The faces too of her many former clients had come back to haunt her. Bizarrely it is the people she sought to help in the early days who surface most strongly, like prisoners of war still doing the crawl in the sewer of her head. She knows she should not drink to smother demons, but drinking has become her way, since there really is nothing to celebrate.

The smoke thickens.

Her heavy wine curtains are infused with years of disappointment, still weighted down with the lead that Mother had inserted in their hems. Exactly as they had been, since well before Father died. Mother, for one, had never liked them but neither had she sought to change them. Inertia inherited. Learned lassitude?

She teeters on the patterned hall tiles, listening to the echo of her court shoes. Wondering at their sneering tone. The floor, these days, often seems to slope away from her and then to rise. She begins to cough. It comes to her now that she has, after all, a half bottle of Powers and an unopened Yellow Tail, though one with a blasted cork in it. Now where is that bloody corkscrew?

She had assembled a few sticks. Crumpled sheets of newspaper. God knows how many paraffin-infused firelighters she had thrown at the grate. Maybe the coal is damp. Once, they'd had an arsonist on the wards. Disinhibited when inebriated. He had burned his grandmother. Drink and fire-setting walk hand in hand. She slumps in her armchair, clutching the bottle. Her room is a haze.

Thelma does not open a window.

On closer inspection, the wine is a screw top after all. My God, she had seen enough lives ruined by alcohol. No cork and she hadn't noticed. You see, she tells herself.

Lifting a heavy Waterford glass tumbler from the press, she splashes it out. Breathes in the smell. Catching it, despite the smoke. Last week she had shattered a crystal bowl of Mother's, and everything, butter, sugar, and coarse-cut marmalade was sprayed with shards.

She had kneeled by the cast iron basket – how long since she'd cleaned it out? And watched Derry men, women and children give way to smoke. Last week's news, in monochrome, smouldering, singeing, flaring, then, turning to ash. That was the way. Collateral clouds now billow around her. This is the worst it has been. She needs a sweep.

Smoke seeps from her wall and into her lungs. For some time now, a month perhaps, she has ignored the fumes. But suddenly she feels light-headed. Avoidance, then a rush of adrenaline. Fear rises in waves. All the gassings drift before her. Old people suffocated in motels. Was that in Castlerock? How long she has sat in this, she isn't sure. The booze is no longer holding her.

She needs a man, but not for sex. God, are you joking? A man who knows about chimneys. Father had swept the chimney for Santa, to let him down. But she had been let down. A man called Sweet had done an awfully good job. But he had died as well. Her magic man was Toots Daly, but he was difficult to get.

Toots, who had subcontracted for Dupont, could crawl through spaces where nobody else would go. He did quality work. Maybe the smoke was clearing. She had panicked, as usual. He'd made a packet in the boom as far away as Galway. Turned 'serious money,' carrying out wood-boring insect surveys, and erecting extensions for politicians, putting up sunrooms, and nearer home, those semis on The Trench. He ran with the big dogs, but he'd kept his paws on the ground. Had never forgotten his roots, the place he came from, that he owed everything to. Bond Street and May Street, though he'd been brought up a Catholic. The folks living there were 'the salt of the earth' and there were 'brave oul craters yet, still clinging for dear life in Barnewall Place,' the steepest street in the Waterside. He told her all this the time her sewers had blocked.

It is hard to see.

Thelma gags and drinks more wine. Perhaps it will lift. She clears her throat. Long ago, when the poor had no windows, they believed that smoke was good for you. That it nourished the tubes if you inhaled it. Something has got dislodged. Maybe it is a brick.

She couldn't care. Disinhibition in drink. Toots, though, is in her mind. She will have to ring him. Doesn't she know his seed and breed? When other kids were playing house, Toots Daly was building bungalows with blocks of wood, scraps of iron, and shiny lengths of copper. The only toys he'd been interested in were hardly toys at all. 'They were rows of pipe I let on to solder.' He had got his da, as he called him, to make a visor out of cardboard, 'to protect my eyes, for welding.' She could be doing with one of those. It is definitely getting worse. Her eyes are stinging. She hasn't the energy to rise.

Toots isn't answering. The fire will burn itself out.

Toots had learned German at the Tech one winter, so that he could read the instructions for installing expensive showers. 'Translations are crap,' he'd said.

Her eyes stream. She sits with the Yellow Tail.

Toots had been lucky. His wife was the former Angela Bradley, Miss Northern Ireland fifteen years ago. They had Italian marble floors in their utility room. She'd seen a picture. And a triple garage. Miss Northern Ireland never cooked. Just ordered in. But that was OK with Toots. They flew to Vegas at least twice a year.

Maybe that's where he is now, instead of taking her call.

Asphyxiation could be better than drowning. And drowning is better than hanging. A game she sometimes plays.

There should be energy in a fire. Toots will know what to do. But where the hell is he? Beep bloody beep.

And then he speaks.

'Hi Thelma, what's the *craic*, pet? I was in the bog.'

He'll be with her in ten. Anonymous, as ever, in his white Transit.

'Why attract the attention of the taxman?' he'd told her years ago.

'What the hell is it, Chicken?' he says. 'There's bloody smoke everywhere. Are you trying to end it all? Have you got a bucket for the fire, and I'll take it out? What's this here?'

He swoops on her bottle.

'Are you on the juice darling? Jiminy be. I cannae breathe.'

She wants to make him tea.

'No, dote,' he says. 'I'll open a window. There's no oxygen in here. Get you into your wee garden and I'll suss it.'

Very few people had ever referred to Thelma as 'darling.'

It was amazing how the smoke cleared.

She could go back in.

'I was away up the back of Glenowen, this morning,' Toots says, trying to lift her mind. He whistles through his teeth. 'Bad news, hi. Oil spill. Whole house needs undergirding. Big bucks. Right into the founds. Floors want pulling up. Major, major. Same old, same old. No bleeding insurance. This here is not a new issue, is it?' he says. 'It's been staining your wall, Duck. Themuns up there are talking a second mortgage. Life sentence,' he says.

'Do you want a drink?' she says. 'I have some whiskey.'

'You're grand,' he says. 'This house smells like a war zone, Thelma. I'd say your chimney's hammered.'

He's itching to get at it.

'Whatever you do, don't fall,' she tells him, her head still pounding.

Toots is outside. He has the extending ladder off the van and he's singing, *Love me tender*… from somewhere very high. She can hear him through the window. He has a good voice. How anyone can climb, she will never understand. This is his external inspection of the breast, the pots, the flashing, brickwork and the slates. Nothing visible.

'The problem's inside,' he says. 'That there's where we'll find the shit.'

How true that was.

Toots must enjoy his food. But she would worry about his heart. He has a belly, and he likes a laugh. It's a pity she only sees him when there's trouble, for as Father might have said, he does her a power of good. Much better than any doctor.

He's squeezing into her loft now, through the tiny trap door. And, no, he isn't afraid of rats.

After a lot of grunting, he disappears, like a miner with a lamp on his forehead, a damp-meter in his hand. His phone on camera. She can hear him scuffling about up there, like a ghost.

She reaches again for Daphne's letter. The one in which she'd talked about coming home. Feeling her way from Australia. Not knowing what Thelma would think or say. How many times has she read it? And what does she make of it? The idea is insane, of course. Whether she's drunk or sober. To come back at this stage, to think that something good could happen, when they're both in the departure lounge. When Thelma is pickled more often than not. When this old house is falling down round her. She will say no. Burnt bridges can't be retaken. She'd seen that written somewhere.

Toots has been gone for some time. As Mother's clock ticks on the mantelpiece, she half forgets about him paddling around above her head, and focusses instead upon a dredged-up memory of Daphne taking honours at the Feis, for verse speaking. It was trivial, she knows. But she, child Thelma, had often been exposed on the stage of The Guildhall, dwarfed by the shining pipes of the organ, and Daphne's talent. They were reciting some Ogden Nash drivel about Isabel, forty girls going over the same awful claptrap one after the other in fit-on accents. '… Isabel, Isabel, didn't worry…' That was a laugh. Her rendition, for once, had been better than Daphne's but the outcome was the same. Beaten by her twin, by a single mark, though a 'credible performance.' Credible in defeat – wasn't that typical of her whole sodding life. A tryer. 'If a little staccato,' according to Maurice Bellingham, the adjudicator, a fat little Fermanagh man, with horn rims and a spotted dickey.

How her stomach had turned that day. And how sour it was now from the wine. She despised herself. But there it was, as the emperor had famously said in *Amadeus*. She had always struggled in the shadows. A rank weed existing in the shade.

How long she ruminated on this inebriated recollection it was hard to say, but it ended when Toots appeared, like a dusty angel of the void, to reveal, at last, his diagnosis. His large, practical head and kindly face were, needless to relate, festooned with cobwebs.

'Good God Thelma, I'm fair bronchitic,' he announces, wiping his mouth. Like herself, he has a sense of drama, and has, foolishly, not worn a mask.

'G'on make me that cup of tea now,' he says, 'if you're feeling up to it.'

She manages the kettle. The teabag. Swirls it round a bit. Fishes it out. Mother would be appalled. She hands the tea to Toots in her NSPCC mug, along with two soft digestives.

'I knew you loved me,' he says.

It is a wonder the wall's standing.

'Your two chimneys merge up there, you know,' he says, reaching for a Biro to draw a diagram, 'but the bricks is loose, here and here.' He draws on arrows. 'Fair enough, there's no damp. In fact, you know what, they're too bloody dry. The mortar's crumbling. Like sawdust. They're just about clinging to each other like lovers that don't want to part, but you know what, someday they're going to break up. Are you with me? A messy divorce is on the cards, love. The lower part of your chimneys has come away altogether. The tops is just suspended you know. There's gaps like rabbit holes you could put your arm in. They're well and truly bucked,' he says. 'There's no other way of putting it. Big ignorant, gaping spaces. They're hanging onto sweet FA, forgive my French, and they're not lined.'

Mother had often been light-headed, though she'd never been drunk.

'Would you not like just a *little* glass of wine?' she asks.

'Honest to God, I would not,' Toots says. 'Not when I'm working.'

The fabric holding her has been decomposing for years. The years have been tolling like St Eugene's bell. Derry has been getting on its feet while she's been losing hers.

'Some clown has daubed the bricks of your chimney up there with white gypsum,' says Toots. 'That says it all. They might as well have iced them for Christmas.'

Funny. She'd been thinking of Christmas.

'Gypsum, sunshine, wouldn't hold nothing.'

That could have been Father. Impractical to the end.

'Some stupid plonker, anyway,' says Toots. 'I'll need to jack them from the bottom. Then I'll drop in the flue liners from the top and build them back up with nice new brick and Bob, as they say, Petal, will be your uncle. Are you getting me?'

She says she is. But will there be time? Daphne. Coming home from Oz, as she calls it? She ought to say 'No.'

'I'll have to act,' she says, sniffing the way Mother had, when she had to take her big pill.

'No worries,' says Toots. 'You and me will be a great squad. I'll scratch the walls before I plaster proper. We'll cut no friggin' corners. You can hang a picture, but you can't suspend a chimney. Did you ever hear that one? It would only be a matter of time, you know. Are you all right Ducksie?'

'Just tired,' she lies, though she's feeling better. 'I hardly sleep at all, smoke or no smoke.'

'Bit of stress?' he says, lifting the bottle. 'Australian? I'll fit you new smoke alarms while I'm at it, and stick on one for carbon monoxide, for the gas you can't smell. The silent killing bastard.'

'It's a big job, then?' she says.

'You've got it in one, partner,' says Toots, 'but together, we'll make it through the night. I'll do it at near enough cost. And I don't want no shite. Okay?'

She pours the tea. Her hand shaking only a bit.

'I have a sister,' she begins, 'a twin actually…'

Toots lights a cigar.

'Didn't know that,' he says. 'Thought you were a one off.'

'No excuses for all this vertigo thing,' she says, 'but that's where my mind has been.'

She reads Daphne's letter to Toots, and in particular, the concluding paragraph;

'… *So, if you do think it's worth it Thelma, after all this time, I'd like to come and try. Do you know what I mean? Time's getting tight… that's all I'm saying. Love Daphne.*'

Toots has sat and listened. 'My God,' he says. Tears glistening in his eyes.

And now she weeps.

'Well, there you have it,' he says.

'You tell me you need to rake it all out and build from the bottom,' she says, 'and with a bit of luck, the chimney will burn brightly with a good draw and there'll be no more fumes.'

'Naw,' said Toots. 'I never mentioned luck. If you do it right, there's no call for luck. But do nothing, and you'll be poisoned or buried when it all caves in. Then it's Goodnight Irene. Nobody can see into the future, Thelma. It's too late when it's all over.'

She gives him a long look. Then she hugs him. How long since she's really touched anyone. He feels so firm. Like a tree she'd embraced at Ness.

He's packing his tools. Folding the ladder.

'Can I use your bog? I've been weein' all day,' he says. 'No pressure. It's up to yourself.'

'Oh, I'll do it,' she says, 'whatever it costs.'

'You weren't listening,' Toots says.

She slips the letter behind the clock. But this time, she leaves part of it exposed, where she can see it, with a triangular corner sticking up, like the listening ear of some paper creature. Can she trust herself?

'Have you heard about this Happening thing at Prehen?' Toots says, when he comes back. 'I see you've a drip in your cistern. That will be the ballcock.'

She had lifted her copy of the *Journal*.

'The world and its mother's going to it,' he says. 'The wife's away, staying at her sister's. I was thinking of dropping in.'

He looks at Thelma. It's also years since anyone asked her to go anywhere. Is this what he could mean? A man young enough to be her son.

'Aye, well,' he says, 'it should be a bit of *craic*.'

She hesitates.

'Did I ever tell you that Daphne and I once skipped our last biology paper to go to Glastonbury?'

'My God. Naw, you absolutely did not.'

'We did. Glorious mud and all that. There was hell to pay, of course, from Father. But for once it was my idea.'

'You're kidding me.'

'True bill.'

'Bully for you, Babe,' Toots says. 'You see, you have it in you.'

He's standing on. Probably calculating quantities in his head.

'Fair play to you, Thelma,' he says, 'you've a lot going on, darling, but you're going to get there, and it never does to leave a chimney. "You see when it needs doing," as my oul fella said, "it needs doing now." Simple as that. You know yourself.'

'That was perceptive of him,' she says, 'I'm feeling a good bit stronger.'

'Now you're talking Angel,' he says. She doesn't mind the familiarity. 'I'll order you up the liners and be back on Monday with the sand and cement, and I'll get you a nice wee pile of pup bricks, wait till you see, from Corrys. A week on, and it'll be tight as a sparrow's arse. You never get nothing done in this world without breaking eggshells. It'll look no better from the outside, but you and I will know it's safe as the bloody rock of Gibraltar inside and that's what counts. And don't be lighting it again till it's good.'

She will put on an electric heater.

Toots stands at the back door with his hand on the handle. Her head *has* cleared.

'If one were to go to this thing of Indigo Black's,' she begins, 'how would one go about it?'

'One would be ready at eight on Sunday night, with one's warm drawers on,' Toots says, 'with one's hat on to keep off the critters, and some boy would pick one up.'

'Would he,' she asks, 'would he really?'

'No bother to him,' Toots says. 'I know the very fella.'

'Have you heard of this Billy Grail?' she asks.

'Oh aye, Thelma, Billy's big,' Toots says, 'take it from me. He's the biggest act there is, and he's going to be there.'

She hasn't told Toots it's her birthday. Only God knows what state her liver's in. How many aeons since she and Daphne had been born upstairs together, like matching piglets, in the front bedroom, which now, she might decorate. Centuries since they'd spoken. Queensland is at least nine hours ahead. Daphne's birthday is already over. How odd is that? She'll be sleeping now in some jerry-built house in Woomera – is it spring or autumn there – just thirty hours away? And here she is in Derry, where she's always been.

She thinks of Toots now, as she finally closes the windows. What is it about human connection? A decent, intuitive, swearing man, sensitive and subtle, who has shown her he understands. What a difference it makes. She breathes in deeply at last. The smell of smoke has faded a little. She had made the call in the end. Been decisive? Well, there were such moments in life. To hell. She would go to this Happening and damn the consequences. At this precise threshold of clarity, the amazing, reassuring Guildhall clock strikes soberly for Ireland, beating the Cathedral by some minute and a half. She takes it as a good omen. Perhaps something has shifted.

Camping With the Lean Young Man

The pitch Rev Gray selected for him and his companion at The Happening, did not entirely please the Lean Young Man. There is not, for example, nearly as much room on the site as he had naively expected. To cope with compromise, then, is evidently an important lesson for this true seeker of wildness. He is learning that life in Derry, though often electrifying, cannot always be perfect. The city, after all, comprises amazing *human* beings, the descendants of unbelievable Planters and Gaels, though not necessarily in that order. It is also important to reflect, he supposes, that life seldom turns out the way you think. Nevertheless, he hopes fervently that this will not apply to The Happening. Indeed, he prays that the wildness of which he dreams will, even yet, triumph in spectacular fashion. That he and Rev Gray will glimpse Billy Grail, even from a distance.

But how can they be truly wild without privacy?

Perhaps his thinking had been altogether too generic. In his mind he had seen an idyllic pasture, with clean wooden glamps. Or at least some kind of corridor between tents. What he realises now, as he stares at the vista, is that the thoroughfares are of necessity narrow ribbons, like tight forest paths, and that although, no doubt, within regulations they are little wider than a rat run. These are the approved arteries for communication amongst the truly free, going about their affairs. Rev Gray, who is sporting a pair of shorts, will be forced to squeeze between two sunbathing girls from Helen Street and a couple of bearded composers from Rock Road.

Also, the Lean Young man ruminates that, despite having once been a boy scout, his Reverence foolishly insisted on erecting the tent with its entrance directed towards the north. This indicated a monumental forgetfulness of life in the great outdoors. A northern aspect might have worked at some woolly stargazers' convention, when the wind was from the south, but sadly the pitches, so he'd been told, were plagued by turgid storms. The Lean Young Man believed that wildness might somehow be related to warmth. That the higher the temperature, the better. He was tempted to remind Rev Gray of this, but thoughtfully desisted.

Well up the list of other concerns haunting the Lean Young Man is their distance from the blue Portaloos, which sway dangerously in the distance. This is not entirely a self-centred niggle, because he wonders how Rev Gray will walk a mile at night to make his water. But there again, he is a novice in Derry, and so, wisely, he holds his peace. It would not do, as an outsider, to complain, and besides, it is a matter of respect for the older man.

Gray, for his part, owing no doubt to extensive training at clerical college, appears to have little interest in practicalities. True, he set up a collapsible bookshelf for his copy of St Augustine, out of habit, but as for any interest in Calor gas cooking – that was hardly even an aspiration. Moreover, the Lean Young Man has noticed that Gray seems to be somewhat internally overwhelmed, since for prolonged periods he has not spoken. Indicative, he thinks, of introspection. It could be indeed, that his new chum is unsettled of mind, and doubtful of purpose.

If he were being honest, the LYM would admit that their physical needs had not been completely anticipated or met. He tried not to feel disappointed with Rev Gray, who had failed to bring the vast sleeping bag to which he had alluded in the upstairs vegan café. The 'big, commodious, common quilt' to keep them warm. He secretly wonders, too, as to whether, in the end, such a prolonged period spent in a confined space together may compromise their burgeoning relationship. Had he considered the whole affair in his usual, cerebral way, he might have declined the offer, and sought wildness in Carndonagh or in the sand dunes of Ballyliffin. But now he is committed.

With this thought, a hungry feeling steals over the spirit of the Lean Young Man. All around them hums the seductive smell of savagery at rest, the relaxed rawness of liberty as the more earnest inhabitants of this flimsy metropolis boil saffron rice and lentils on charcoal braziers, while the more frivolous toast pink and white mallows on sticks.

Their first visitors are two girls who work in Lidl and house-share in the Glen. A Jacinta from Anderson Crescent and a Rose from Cricklewood. They say they work together and keep white rats. The Lean Young Man, who hates rodents, steps back a little, though he practises smiling, and asks how much they eat. The girls giggle.

'You don't want to know,' they say. Perhaps these girls tell lies.

'So, are you Catholic girls?' asks the Lean Young Man, clasping his hands, and inclining his head like a monk.

'Aye, well, she is,' says the one called Rose. 'I'm nothing now.'

'Nothing? You cannot be nothing. You are best friends, and it seems you do not fight?'

'Only over men,' say the girls.

'We would offer you a bite,' Gray says, 'but we do not live by bread alone.'

'Is your man some sort of weirdo?' the girls ask the Lean Young Man, in a confidential manner. Rev Gray looks hurt.

'Have youse any drink?' The girls push their way in, to inspect the tent. 'G'on give us a few of them toilet rolls,' they say, helping themselves to a pile of Andrex belonging to Gray. 'That's brilliant,' they tell each other. 'And they're extra soft.'

'We have some orange Fanta,' says Gray graciously, 'if you ladies can find some glasses?'

'Ladies,' say the girls to the LYM. 'Oh, my God, that's priceless. Where did you find him?'

These words shock and appal the Lean Young Man, who has believed, until now, that respect for others was the number one virtue of the Maiden City. And that Gray was very real indeed.

Now he and his Reverence are squatting on the groundsheet, with these girls. 'Are you very wicked women?' asks the LYM, 'and have you done the wildness?'

'I'm pure wetting myself,' says one of the girls.

'You see, this is why I am at The Happening,' says the Lean Young Man patiently, 'I and my friend here, who, incidentally, is a gentleman, wish to indulge the higher side of our personalities. I was restricted, you see, whilst growing up.'

'God save us,' says Jacinta. 'And what about you, tiger?' She's addressing Rev Gray. 'What floats your wee boat?'

'I have yet to discover even a – discotheque,' says Gray.

'A discotheque,' says Rose. 'You can't be serious?'

'Oh yes, I have become a very dated person,' says Gray. 'I have let the world slide by, and remain concerned with sin.'

'What do you mean, *sin*?' Jacinta checks her lippy.

'We're both wasted,' Rose says, 'but these two are bloody mental.'

'Well, anyway,' says Rose, sticking a bunch of bananas in her Lidl bag, 'it's been great knowing you both, but we're not staying, because our beautiful girlie mauve tent's all sad and everything, without us. I hope we'll see you around.'

As the girls leave, a wave of barely concealed merriment ripples outside the tent. Some tribe of invisible sprites has been listening. The LYM has read of these spirits in a Celtic legends book.

'Obviously sisters in a manner of speaking,' says Gray.

The LYM considers the clues. The girls had not looked alike. One had blonde hair, while the other was dark. He had seen no resemblance.

Next to visit was one of the two composers.

'Hello, I'm Gray,' says Rev Gray.

'We're next to you Gray,' says the musician. 'We're in the what's its name?'

'The groove?' suggests Gray.

'You got it, sir.' The composer wears two man-buns.

'Are you also a local?' asks the LYM.

'Aye, well, I am and I'm not,' says the composer, 'if you get me.'

The young man did not get him.

'What are you into?' asks Gray, in a more modern sort of way.

'You know what,' says the composer, closing his eyes, 'you can make music out of any bloody thing you like.'

'Like what?' asks Rev Gray, 'who, despite his fall from grace, continues to have a yen for Handel and his Hallelujah Chorus.

'Well, you take a bat,' says the musician.

'A cricket bat?' says the Lean Young Man eagerly.

'No, just a regular bat,' says the composer. 'You'll hear them squeaking later.'

English is such a capricious tongue. The Lean Young Man will remember to listen tonight for these squeaking bats, when lying sleepless beside Gray.

'That's where we get our inspiration, do you know what I'm saying?' says the composer. 'From bats and birds. You take a warbler. That's a wee bird. We let him make the notes, do you follow me? We record them in our heads, and reproduce the sound in our studio, beside the Nerve Centre. That's where we crack them out. Easy peasy.'

This is a new use of the verb to crack.

'Can you not record them with some small appliance?' asks the LYM.

'Naw. That's like saying a painting should look like a photo,' says the musician. 'We're into your actual emotional art, mucker. That wouldn't be the same, and you know what' – this is obviously a useful turn of phrase – 'the songs write themselves in our souls, no shit.'

'No shit. I would like to invent such a song,' says the Lean Young Man.

'You'd have no worries,' says the musician, 'I know to look at you, a hundred per cent. What about you, sir?' he asks Gray.

This form of address, which demonstrates deference, is picked up instantly by the Lean Young Man. Does the musician know his Reverence?

'I suppose I play the pipes, in a way,' says Gray.

'Sweet,' says the musician. 'I hope to God you've brought them with you.' His eyes, like the girls', flit around the tent.

'Pipe organ,' says Gray. 'My little joke.'

'Oh mighty,' says the musician. 'Any CDs?'

Gray pauses.

'Not yet,' he says.

'Keep at it, anyway,' the composer tells him. 'And what about you mate?' They turn to the LYM.

'I am an observer at this juncture,' says the Lean Young Man. 'Your city is so musically ebullient. I have not yet chosen an instrument.'

'Maybe you should give the ukulele a go,' says the composer. 'It's a great one to start with. We know a guy up the Braehead, called Mr White, that plays. Loves his music. He's probably here some place. Knocks about with a Spanish-Derry doll. If I see him, I'll get him to give you a shout. You'll like him. He's a sound man.'

'He is also a soundman?' asks the LYM, 'technically speaking?'

'Naw, naw, he's a *sound man*. You know, two words.'

'I see,' he says. Inflection is everything.

As might be expected, these encounters at The Happening both stimulate and perplex the Lean Young Man. He, understandably, feels himself greatly in deficit. Perhaps the lacuna is, despite his talent with languages, like the song in which the river is wide, and the artist singing it cannot get over.

It is also possible that his blood sugar has dropped unhelpfully, and that social exhaustion could so easily swallow him.

There followed a difference of opinion between the LYM and Gray. Perhaps it was about something more profound. For how many disputes appear to be about one thing but are most certainly about another?

In the end, and in the absence of any positive suggestions from Rev Gray about food, and urgently in need of sustenance, the Lean Young Man slipped on the light, skimpy, petrol coloured jacket he had brought with him to the Happening and trudged off hungrily down the rabbit tracks, picking his way carefully over tree roots, sidestepping tents, envying the sounds of rapture within them, the low moans of strangers in poetic ecstasy, the bizarre shadows of those locked in wildness. Patiently he navigated overhanging boughs, as he approached

Victoria Road. A row of juddering food vans stood stark in lurid shades, pumping acrid blue fumes, and serving burgers, as he supposed, with many decks. Loud, unrecognisable music issued from speakers. Perhaps this was the music of Billy Grail. Naturally, he did not ask the young people, who lolled, joked, and kissed. For this would not be cool. Their evening time was highly sexed and sultry. Was this them being wild?

In a winding queue, the Lean Young Man stood apart. Alone in the crowd as he vacantly awaited his turn at **FRIES 4 YOUSE**, slowly rotating the loose change in his pocket, scanning and re-scanning the chalked blackboard. A fine mizzle began to fall. The LYM read as follows:

UR HAPPENING MENU

Plain burger £10.00.
Cheeseburger, (very big) two Kraft £12.50.
Hawaiian £11.50 (heavy pineapple, double thousand island dressing)
All with chips and red sauce on the side
Bargain chips, garlic mayo, cheese £8.50
Chilli chips and cheese £7.50
Small Chips, peas and gravy swimming £6.00
Or
Just Ask

What was *Just Ask?*

'Alright there, sunshine?' asked the van man, washing his hands.

'Yes, thank you kindly,' said the Lean Young Man, stepping forward politely, and pointing at the board. 'But have you nothing cheaper? I possess but a very few coins.'

The van man paused.

'Right,' he said. 'That there depends. I suppose I could do you a *bits* son.'

'What are – these bits?' asked the Lean Young Man.

'Okay, they're the crunchy bits,' said the van man, twirling his scoop thoughtfully. 'You know, the wee hard bits that's left in the fryer. Like crispy toenails, only tastier.'

'Toenails?'

'I'm acting the whack,' said the van man. 'You pile on the old salt and vinegar, and you're elected. They're magic. I trained in England myself, you know, on the Wirral, for a while, with Chip Highway. They called them scraps. But bits is better. I started them here. They're popular late at night. I make sweet FA on them, but sure, life is short.'

'What would this sweet FA deal entail?' asked the Lean Young Man.

'That's what I'm saying.' The van man steadied his tall chef's hat. 'You get the bits with pea wet. That's the water from the peas. It's a winner.'

'And will it give me the wildness?'

'Guaranteed,' said the van man. 'You'll be snarling like a timber wolf. Billy Grail goes for the bits big time. And he's really wild. I'm surprised you don't know that.'

'In that case, yes,' said the LYM. 'I will accept the bits as long as they make me wild. I will opt for them. Can you sell me two portions please, one for myself and one for my friend, Rev Gray, who may be sad?'

'No bother,' said the van man, 'where're you from anyhow?'

'Here and there,' said the LYM, who had done enough talking.

When the van man gave him the bits, the LYM held them to his nose to greater smell the wildness. This was how he would know they were the genuine thing. He carried them carefully back to Rev Gray, who was greatly on his mind because of his unsettlement, for on a number of occasions that day, he had mentioned death. The Lean Young Man wondered if many Happening people at Prehen were also thinking of death. He was sure the founder of the event, this Indigo Black lady, had not been dwelling on death at all when the idea came to her. The bits felt hot and tempting in his hands, as he tried to forget what the van man had said about toenails. Pea wet would be a new experience. Humour, though, was difficult in new lands. He had experienced similar puzzlement in Russia, once, just off Red Square.

Lovers' Return

On their return bus journey from Strabane, Mr White told Miss Marrón of his adventures. 'You did well,' she said, 'to show such understanding. I think you have been most mature.' Miss Marrón, however, sighed heavily as she shared her own experience with Mr White, in the giving way that lovers do. Her friend Clara in the Canal Basin had not been herself at all.

'Mr White, she has become so unpredictable.'

'Tell me about it,' said Mr White.

'Well, there were very many canaries, for starters,' said Miss Marrón. They have been multiplying. She has filled all her rooms with birds. You can imagine the smell of those poor imprisoned creatures. I told her this was cruel, but she flew into a rage and began opening the cages. Clang. Slam. Bang. Birds. More birds. A hundred canaries sweeping from room to room, shitting as they went. You see, they were starved and hungry for sex and seed. This happened for many hours.'

The bus rolled on.

'I think she may be very ill,' said Miss Marrón. 'I should have dialled Emergency. Oh Madre mía, dear Clara. But who, in the name of God, would look after the canaries if she had had to be admitted to – well, you know where, Mr White. I knew I couldn't... I would not be fit to manage a hundred randy birds, you know I wouldn't, but OMG.'

Mr White agreed. He slipped a protective arm around his lover. Perhaps she had a less than total Spanish look about her suddenly, despite her accent. His heart was touched. He adored her beauty and the sincerity with which she spoke. If he could drink her, he knew she would taste like Tio Pepe. This notion had been coming to him of late, with increasing conviction.

'Even in the bathroom they had been making habitat,' said Miss Marrón. 'Everywhere there were the shits. Can you imagine what this was like?'

Mr White could imagine. During his impoverished life to date, he had seen his fair share of shits. Big shits and little shits. The Ogre, for one, was a huge shit. Mr White knew the consistency of shit. Every nuanced element of its texture. He had shovelled shits since as long as he could remember and was therefore entirely sympathetic to the sensibilities of Miss Marrón. And something in her story reminded him of his mother.

'And then her cat called Nilson, he also came out. Cats, believe me and birds do not go well together. This Nilson, it appeared, is an especially nasty feline, who pretended to like the birds at first, you see, and deluded Clara into believing him. He often hides like this,' she said, miaowing and crouching down low beside Mr White, on the moving bus, 'and then, when Clara's back is turned, the savage beast in his deepest self, will spring and slay. I do not believe he even wants to eat the birds, so distilled is his evil badness.'

'That's cats for you, all over,' said Mr White. 'They are like gods. They like to play with birds. It will do for Clara's nerves.'

Miss Marrón's mother, it seemed, had also used this expression, but she was in the City Cemetery, a long time since, and so was quite incapable of speech.

'I'm sorry,' said Mr White.

'They became so manic and did so many swoopings,' said Miss Marrón, 'that we had to proceed outside. Now is that not hellish strange, Mr White? Birds in. Humans out. Where is the freedom there?'

The bus wheels droned. Mr White had never been free, and therefore did not consider himself in a position to say more.

'Hell roast them anyway,' said Miss Marrón, fervently. 'I fetched a neighbour. It wasn't much, but I could do no more. I had feathers everywhere. Down my front, and even in my pants, which I had to remove and shake vigorously in the Canal Basin. Can you believe it? You should have seen me waving my knickers in Strabane.'

Mr White held her closer. 'As for your bicycle men,' she said, 'Pah. We should have gone to McColgans for a wholesome, meaty pie, where were our bloody heads?'

It occurred to Mr White then, with a flash of insight, that Miss Marrón reminded him of a pedigree bicycle with its two wheels travelling in opposite directions.

'What's so funny?' she said. 'Tell me or you die.'

Now was the chance for him to unburden his soul completely, for is that not what connection is about? His face clouded over.

'Is it your uke?' she asked.

'It's the Ogre,' he said.

'I will kill this Ogre, once and for fecking all,' she said ferociously, 'so help me God. But frankly, our day has been so testing and we both need fed.'

'It's been a long road with no turning, until now,' said Mr White.

'A long, morbid wall for you, with no gate in it,' she said, pressing his hand. 'Do you know that the resonance of castanets is directly related to the quality of the wood they use in their construction? Trust me,' she said. 'I know this for a fact.'

Mr White did not need convincing.

As the Ulsterbus passed again through Newbuildings, on the

last percentile of its return odyssey to the melodious city of spires, Miss Marrón arose gracefully from her seat, unencumbered now by the bag of birdseed. Filled with purpose, and still grasping the willing hand of Mr White, she spoke illegally but soothingly to the driver, a dark-haired romantic, also descended, no doubt, from the Armada ones.

'Drop us at The Everglades Hotel, Señor,' she said, with resolve, 'and do not falter, or I take your bus. Mr White and I have important business at The Happening.'

And so it was that she and Mr White disembarked at Prehen, and, linked on each others' arms, like Derry mammies and their daughters on a Saturday morning, they approached together the turnstiles of The Happening, to seek revival.

Most of the campers, and certainly those with nourishment, were already dining. The rain had not been much, and the population of the transitory town sat around their fires, on pouffes provided by the St Vincents. Rich indeed was the bouquet of roasting flesh. Smoke drifted in vertical trails. 'Famishing' was the word in the mouth of Mr White, who had been grieved to see his lady fret.

'Would youse like a chop?' said a blast from beyond.

A round-shouldered man was frying. An old, generous being who had once been somebody. He waved a spatula.

'God in heaven,' said Miss Marrón, introducing Mr White to one of the Blue Two. Was it Mick or Manus? Relax, she told herself. Remember who you are. Your pedigree and all that caper. Just be up front.

'Are you still partners, Mick?,' she asked, taking a risk. She needn't have worried. The unmistakable sound of a guitar came riffing from a nearby tent.

'Manus plays while I cook,' said Mick. 'He's learning flamenco. Are youse hungry? I'm doing lamb.'

Echoes, perhaps, of some Billy Grail classic followed, as Mr White found his fingers clicking to the beat. As Manus gave it the twelve-bar treatment.

'I'll get youse two beers,' said Mick.

Sheer magic. Mr White looked at Miss Marrón, who clapped staccato, and took short little steps. Could this be their defining moment at Miss Black's Happening?

Perhaps.

Kick Back

Yet, all had not gone smoothly. Miss Black was right. She had known there would be doubters. Even in Doire Colmcille. Gainsayers. Blamers. Reluctant begrudgers like Shugh Henderson. You couldn't necessarily tell by looking at them, but there *were* Derry wans who had descended from aberrant, straggly lines of the genetically discontented, whose ancestors had always been thinking that it wouldn't be long now.

'What won't be long?'

'You don't need me to tell you. You know yourself.'

This sounded cryptic, but everybody knew them. They came from Bards Hill and Woodburn. From Heron Way and Shantallow. There weren't *many* of them, relatively, but you got them in offices, schools, meat plants and retail. All hellbent on disaster. They were in the hospitals, in the bun shops and tattoo parlours, in hairdressers and shops that repaired leather-soled shoes. You found them languishing in off-licences behind the racks of crisps and in the churches. The sort who'd support a man like Shugh Henderson.

And you could hear them.

'I didn't like the look of Father Harry at nine o'clock Mass last week, Fergus. I thought he was very short on it.'

'I know, Mary. And he's getting shorter.'

'What way, shorter?'

'In his breath.'

'Oh aye, his breathing's shocking too. He has no puff.'

'Did you hear him wheezing at the altar?'

'I never liked him, you know, God forgive me.'

'It will have been his mother.'

'How do you mean his mother?'

'She never had no puff.'

'All them McDaids was the same. Wild smokers.'

'Say nothing, only our Grainne was telling me.'

'Your Grainne knows everything.'

'They brought it on themselves. That's what I'm saying.'

It was the same on the other side of the what do you call it.

'I see the forecast's bad for the Twelfth.'

'It's the same every year Edith.'

'You'd think the other crowd was running the weather as well.'

'They soon will be. Remember I said that.'

'Where is the Twelfth of July next year?'

'It must be Limavady. It's bound to pour.'

'I hope there's enough buses this time.'

'Is your Wilma coming home from England?'

'The whole shower of them's staying for a month.'

'You're mad. Your head will be fried.'

'The fun's away out of the bonfires. All them pallets has ruined them. They're too tidy now.'

'Too regular.'

'That's right. Too professional.'

'You're not wrong. Too fussy looking, like you'd got them in B&Q.'

'Here, that's a good one. Too controlled.'

'Don't be talking.'

'Shugh Henderson wants to stop them. All the bonfires. On both sides.'

'That's him all right.'

The gloom merchants *were* in the minority, but you still got them, though Miss Black had their number. All the same, though, Shugh Henderson had his fans, and he'd tried to block her Happening.

'An ego trip,' he'd said. 'One woman's self-centred journey into fantasy land.' Henderson had lobbied the Chair of the Sub Committee. Leaned on Archie Robinson's crowd, threatened Sinead Brown, of all people, in a lift. Why would any man be so frightened of a woman and of Art? Where was the soul of Shugh Henderson, if he had one? Even after he'd lost the argument, he was still sniping away.

'I hear you're bringing in some dodgy character from America.' He was speaking of Billy Grail.

Dodgy?

'I thought we supported home industry. Are there no tinsel pop stars here? Could you not have got somebody a whole lot handier. And what about Daniel?'

There was nothing wrong with Daniel O'Donnell, but Henderson's lies stank like slurry. They were pollution multiplied.

'She's importing a cowboy.'

She certainly would *not* be moved.

'What do you know about the entertainment business, anyway?' This in front of the Mayor. 'Somebody's filling their boots.'

A lesser mortal might have cracked, but Miss Black's pedigree was long and colourful. She would not be intimidated. Her paternal grandfather Hubert Black had been a high-class artist and decorator, with a thriving business in Sackville Street. A master craftsman, akin to Michelangelo, some said, he had lain on his back on hard scaffolding, plying his brushes and tempura, painting the ceilings of churches, chapels and secretive Masonic halls.

A previous Miss Black, the formidable Briony, had been a suffragette. A family legend who had travelled by steam train, with a flotilla of women in cloche hats, to Lisburn, to smash windows in its cathedral. It had pained Briony to cause destruction, but she had done it in the cause of equality. One had to have backbone. How could the contemporary *Indigo* Black be a lesser woman one hundred years later?

Indeed, it had often been remarked, in a city renowned for 'can do,' that Indigo, as an infant, must have been inoculated with optimism, as well as immunised against polio. It was for displaying this positivity that Henderson and his honchos despised her most. Her insouciance and projected self-assurance.

After the election they'd suggested her vote was rigged. That votes had been for sale. But it was all lies, damned lies and a fear of the aesthetic. There were rumours of orgies and other calumnies.

'Her apartment is full of nudes,' Henderson had told the High Sheriff.

Indigo knew this for a fact. She made a point of dining with the High Sheriff, who was reassured. She went through the figures meticulously with the finance people, with the Mayor, and also with the Deputy Mayor, both of whom asked many searching questions. It was a pleasure to be thorough, she told the press, but it had not been easy at a time of restraint to secure overwhelming support for an event such as The Happening. She had prevailed not by charm alone, but with persuasion, conviction and the sound economics of emotional investment. And, yes, she was loved by most men, but it was the power of argument which had carried the day. The vision and the intrinsic good which would accrue. And despite the provocation, she had avoided taking cheap shots.

There were other examples of slander. It was put about that she supported euthanasia. That she had docked her poodle's tail. (Miss Black did not possess a dog.) She was on for prostitution. She had taught history from a biased point of view. Honoured violence. This fabrication was particularly hurtful. There were dark thoughts in the recesses of her mind which could be dangerous to children. Those trips she had led to the Burren had been a corrupting influence. Why had she been in Boston?

And now, having climbed 'the greasy pole,' as Henderson parroted, she was 'promoting herself shamelessly at the ratepayers' expense.'

'This is what the so-called Happening is really all about. Make no mistake.'

These chilling winds had swept relentlessly around Miss Black, ruffling her skirt, giving her goose bumps. Politics was a dirty game. Toland had been right when he said, 'Beware.'

She'd banked his words.

Fight fire with fire, she told herself.

Trouble With The Poetarium

When overseeing the purchase of The Poetarium Miss Black, accordingly, had been doubly vigilant, knowing that procurement was the graveyard of reputations. Yet it had been a must for artistic legacy, and she'd had to pull it off.

Super Sauna in doubt for Happening, ran the headline. Henderson's work. The Poetarium was so much more than a sauna, though naturally there would be steam.

It was shipped via Harwich to Ringaskiddy and thence by special container to the northern end of the island, accompanied first by an Garda Síochána outriders, and from Aughnacloy onwards by the PSNI. A slow stately ship from another galaxy. After The Happening, it would be mainstreamed, as they say, continuing to provide diversional and integrative cultural services to the freshly swelling ranks of those converted to poetry.

The city engineers had laid extensive pipe work. A fleet of JCBs had shunted earth, in great staccato grabs. The ultra-modern solar panels on The Poetarium's perfectly pitched roof initially gave trouble, but a senior woman came from Dublin to realign them. The new owner of a firm that made buses, a very fine man, indeed, and well known to Miss Black, arrived to give advice. Harland & Wolff, in a gesture of goodwill, sent two consultants. Crowds had gathered at obscene, early hours to take selfies against the red, profiled jibs of cranes. They could not tear themselves away, as The Poetarium dropped into its bed of sand.

In the end, the plumbing had all matched perfectly. Water drawn from the Foyle was filtered and pumped by wind power into a chamber, then heated geothermally, until at boiling point it softened naturally. Finally, after the removal of sodium and magnesium ions it flowed into the Turquoise Pool where it cooled to the approved temperature. To witness all this was healing, classical and mesmerising. There were smaller, more intimate caverns for more immediate encounters. The Poetarium, according to Miss Black, was where change would happen most intensely. She had seen it in a dream.

But even after installation, Henderson alluded to some negative report, alleging Legionnaires', in some doubtful publication. It is always easy, is it not, to drop in words like 'lurking' and 'hidden' and 'suspicion of.' He would genuinely love to feel secure, he said, but he didn't know how. Better get shot of it altogether if they could.

But it couldn't go back. It was bedded in, and installed, and like the pyramids of Egypt, was there for the duration.

Miss Black was forced to give an interview on screen. Unusual crow's feet had appeared around her eyes. She had felt compelled to post a YouTube video in which she looked lopsided. Henderson was Scrooge, with that lying face of his.

His opposition to The Poetarium arose from pure fear. Fear of exposure. Fear for fear's sake.

Well, by God, she had thrown herself into the fray. Had swiftly learned about filters, and storage, water circulation, and chlorine. Henderson's antics caused the Council to wobble. But it prompted Miss Black to seek reassurance far and beyond the commissioning standards demanded by the bureaucrats.

She flew to Oslo, to the plant which made the product. It was so easy for that bastard to sow doubts. To refute them would be harder. And, what, oh God forbid, if there was something in it? Sweet Lord, it was unthinkable. She had long ago realised that a person one loathed could nevertheless, make a valid point. 'Try to be objective,' she had told her girls. Sleep was now history. For what did she know of hydraulics? Her world was art.

The owner of the company was one Sven Olrig. A calm, white haired old man who was fond of Robert Frost. That had set the tone. Indigo sailed with him, on his boat, for fully three days and nights. When they returned to Oslo, Olrig announced a speedy, independent, and international inquiry via the Norwegian Government, who, as he said in perfect English, would cancel his life, should faults be found.

The team could hardly wait. Delias Fernando, Buck Finley from Texas, Rossi Romano, the Italian filter king all engaged. And when they were done, The Poetarium was lauded to high heaven. How wise that Olrig had been. What confident rationality. Following this result, the Swiss placed orders, the French, and also the Germans, who were not known for rashness. More exports, more tax revenue, more reputation.

The story made *The Economist*.

Indigo had phoned Judge Scarlett. 'That's it,' he said. 'Exoneration. God smiles on the righteous. Its future is secured.' His words.

But it was now that mattered.

Miss Black had already immersed her body luxuriantly in the waters of The Poetarium and listened to *Station Island* being read from start to finish, by Heaney himself. What a wonderful, rich, musical voice. And how restorative. But God knows it was all needed. For, although she felt like a new woman, she had also begun to nurse another secret concern. Namely, that something was wrong with Billy Grail. So far, she had received three garbled voice mails, so indistinct and, oh, sweet Mother, possibly not from him, for scams rage wild and unbridled.

Despite her growing turmoil though, she welcomed personally countless aspiring artists, joining in their joy, standing with them for pictures whilst affecting unconcern.

'We are not a Sunday School,' she had announced. 'Swimsuits are optional. Freedom is everything.'

The Council had surprised her by agreeing this policy by a large majority, to the professed disgust of Henderson. A man known for prurience. Naturally, The Poetarium was for adults only, but even so, and understandably, many of the Derry wans were reluctant to remove their kit. It was a matter of choice. Though, honestly, how shame of the human body was in anyone's interest, she failed to grasp. How much more empowering to jettison constraint and live in the moment. She, herself, had no conscience about nakedness, but one couldn't insist, for this would be re-enslavement.

She was hugely moved as ordinary culture seekers also responded to recorded readings of Longley and Hewitt. That their minds were eased and stimulated by the authentic voice of Maura Johnston. But why was one not surprised that they were transported most by the softly spoken bard himself.

And wasn't it more than a happy coincidence that his old Alma Mater, now Lumen Christi College, could be seen, standing sentinel, not far away, on the opposite Western shore?

Great and multiple were the connections being made in The Poetarium, in that penultimate day of The Happening, as time ticked by, and the seekers got to know themselves and each other better. Many were the surprising conversations between citizens who otherwise might never have spoken, as their spirituality increased, and their awareness grew.

Miss Marrón, for example, was soon deep in discussion with Judge Scarlett, who recited 'Digging' with feeling. 'Bravo,' she said. 'You are highly convincing as a poet and performer. This could have been your calling,' she said. 'I think you will sleep tonight.'

A Long Day Dawning

But there was more to occupy the mind of Miss Black. An indifferent dawn staggered in from the east, on the last morning of The Happening. Miss Marrón and Mr White had clicked with the Blue Two, as none of them were vegetarians. They had dined richly the night before on the fried chops provided generously, by Mick and Manus. And drunk red wine and sung long songs together, in the priceless, occasional manner of transient pilgrims, who would remember it all with high affection in years to come. Happy days. And sweet dreams, for Mr White and Miss Marrón had also bedded down together under a borrowed blanket and slept like babies. The tent was, admittedly, overcrowded as day stole in. But it was quiet. A seasonal but heavy dew lay on its sloping canvas. As the friends slept on, breathing easily in and out, the fantastical, prescient heart of the city joined with theirs, to pulse in sympathy.

In their dreams, the delectable and totally tanned Miss Marrón swam ethereally in Alicante, while Mr White already played his freshly restored ukulele. The Blue Two snored in harmony, as they often did, sliding mesmerically in and out of each other's fantasies, in the interchangeable way of familiar partners, unconsciously cherishing the opportunity to show hospitality to new friends. The impossible was becoming probable in the land of nod. They were the backing group for Billy Grail. Vamping the doo wahs. Doubtless, they had also been aroused by the glamour of Miss Marrón – for who could fail to be – and astounded by the attack on her by her friend's canaries, which she had openly disclosed, at some unearthly hour. Mick and Manus declared it a truly unheard-of act of aggression. And certainly not a common occurrence in the Brandywell or in Upper Bennett Street. 'Those psychotic birds were on something. Let me tell you. They were out of their tiny skulls.'

A smile played on the lips of Mr White.

But Miss Black did not sleep on. At an earlier hour she had called upon Judge Scarlett.

'Indigo,' he said. 'I adore your Poetarium. I was there last night, and I want to go back. Penelope is still comatose. We'll take the Jag. You drive.' Miss Black might have preferred to walk, but she gripped the judge's wheel.

'Park up at The Everglades,' he said. 'They know my motor.'

'When we cross Victoria Road, Bruin,' she said, 'you will hold my hand. I want to walk the site.'

It was while they were making their rounds, nodding genially to this one and that, inhaling the scent of wood smoke, as the light increased, that they met Gray, who sat like a beaten prophet outside his tent with the Lean Young Man, who also did not look so sharp.

'Is that you, Gray?' asked Scarlett.

'It is, and he is hurt,' said the Lean Young Man, without introduction. 'He is not used to wildness and has pulled some tender psychological piece of himself, most horrendously.'

Gray shrugged. He appeared to be disabled.

'Can you rise?' asked Judge Scarlett, out of habit, though he was keen to take a seat.

'He cannot do much,' said the Lean Young Man. 'It appears his mind may, after all, be padlocked.'

'Good God,' said Scarlett.

'We have had some talks,' said the Lean Young Man. 'A girl in the next paddock tells me with great sincerity that his Reverence is a beaten docket. I do not get this reference. Perhaps you can explain?'

Gray looked pained.

'What did you do to yourself, man?' asked Scarlett.

'Something atavistic,' Gray said vaguely.

'Have you been to the Remedial Tent?' asked Miss Black, perhaps, on reflection, a little too severely. 'We have a Dr Eric up from the rebel county. He is a hybrid psychologist, I believe, with many strings to his repertoire. I have no personal experience of him. And you may find him eccentric, but I hope he is insightful. Drop in on him after eleven. No appointment needed. His services are free at delivery point to those in trouble. For once our many indigenous therapists were unavailable,' she said to Scarlett. 'But he comes highly recommended by Bord Fáilte. He's multi-purpose,' she said, as a parenthesis. I hope he earns his keep. Paddock D. Will you remember that? D. Here I'll write it down. Tell him I sent you, Gray. Let me know how you get on. You must not neglect your... whatever it is.'

'Oh well,' said Gray, who seemed quite absent.

The Lean Young Man shook his head.

'I worry about him. I do not swallow his blurby *craic*. *I* believe he has many inner fears.'

'Don't we all,' said the judge, 'but that's a very convincing line of patter, young man. You're fairly coming on at the lingo.'

'You know him, then?' Miss Black enquired.

'The Lean Young Man? Well, yes, I've – met him before.'

After the departure of the judge and Miss Black, Rev Gray sat muttering in a disturbed kind of way. Then, sometime later, without bidding farewell, he slipped off to see the man from Cork.

Sleep had not visited Gray, for dark and dreadful demons had paraded before him in the night. Accusers upbraiding him. Random and terrible had been the ghastly thoughts which assailed his mind. Perhaps his guilt would totally un-rock him. At times, during those forever hours, he had wondered as to his sanity. Indigo Black was a fine, if exhausting person, but he was not used to assertive women. Was this a sign of chauvinism, of an inability to cope, a lack of ego strength? At desolate times like this, the 'in sickness and in health' promise he had made came back to smite him. He'd been thinking of Amanda, and the time he'd had pneumonia. When he thought he was a digger-driver mining Mount Moriah, with Abraham and Isaac his son who was about to be sacrificed. The horror had gone on and on. His wife had fed him pork ribs and marrowbones. And nursed him back to health. This could not be denied. But it had not been enough. He shuddered as he navigated the rabbit holes. His body felt quite chilled as he made for Dr Eric.

Paddock D, he imagined, was contiguous to Foyle Search and Rescue, to which he had often contributed money and sincere words of thanks, when in his pulpit. He now became aware of wings. He was not alone. In the ghostly glimmer of his confusion his closest companion was not a human or celestial being but a cranefly. A humble daddy-long-legs. Unsteadily he cupped it in his hands, wondering what was in its mind, and how long it was for this world.

Dr Eric's pointed tent was bright amber, and highly visible, even to the most bleary-eyed depressive. But it danced like a jester in the mind of Rev Gray, and this was most disconcerting.

'Where am I?' Gray asked himself, existentially. You can't knock on the door of a tent, so he cleared his throat several times, outside, and waited. 'Wait till I call you.' He read Eric's notice. 'Try to be patient.' Gray hung about, tapping one clenched fist against the other. And both against his temples. Struggling to pick up the hum in his head, he found only emptiness. No sign of the Cork man.

During this hiatus, he imagined giant creatures stamping on him. Tramping on his bones. Monsters as big as elephants, but more aggressive. 'Where am I?' he repeated again and again. 'And where am I going?' What good would this Dr Eric do him? Never in all his decades had he felt so alone. At one point he became convinced that Billy Grail was inside the tent and that he would pray with him. Perhaps the therapist was Billy Grail, and he would summon an ambulance to whisk him to Grangewood. Life journeys were so fractured and overwhelming.

All across the pitches, in that vast encampment, ordinary men and women, with regular lives, were stirring drowsily, emerging slowly into a tolerable uncertainty. As they brushed their teeth, they would look skyward and say, without a shred of evidence, that it would be 'a lovely day.' He saw no lovely day. The entire site would soon be one great rattling of pots and pans. The smell of sizzling bacon should have been a delight to Rev Gray, but he tasted dread and pain.

It was possible that the Lean Young Ma regretted having met him. Perhaps he'd been pretending to enjoy his company. Gray's congregation had often played games with him. Or so he had come to believe. If it wasn't some deception about Communion, it was about money or Daffodil Teas. Daffodils. Teas? Maybe he was a man to be deceived. To have always been running away from himself. And yet he had tried. The problem now, he divined between delusions, was perhaps that, unused to freedom, he was construing it as wickedness. But what was wickedness? In practical terms he was a novice. And, after all, he had done no training in wildness. Just gone for it blindly, like a fool, and made a donkey of himself. The Lean Young Man would be so disappointed. Gray was not without insight. His physical symptoms, he knew, were an outward manifestation of inner fragility. Not everyone can be constantly attuned to their inner world. He was holding on by his fingertips.

Later, he told how a bell had clanged in Eric's wigwam. And of how the treble voice of a holy man appeared to be calling out in a high register, the way you might expect a goat to speak, if goats could talk.

Gray approached the flap of the tent, he would maintain, cautiously, still expecting some more definite signal, such as a Damascus light, to summon him. Just then, a head of black curls, hopefully attached to an invisible pair of shoulders, poked through the flap and he thought it said, 'Boo.'

It wasn't the greatest start for a man in trouble. But Gray, recognising this as, perhaps, the greeting of a guru, also said 'Boo,' though in a dejected way. His head was scrambled.

'You in bother, brother?' This was what Gray thought he heard. 'Bother brother, brother bother. I like the sound of that.'

In the absence of the rest of him, the multi-stranded psychologist had the peculiar appearance of someone hanging upside down by his feet from a trapeze. Gray trembled. Flight would have been his natural response but some essential part him resisted.

'Miss Black has sent me,' he heard himself say. 'It's my knee, as it were.' He clutched his patella.

'Are we a little defended, and if I might have your name?'

'Gray,' said Gray humbly.

'Gray, Gray, I say. Don't know any Grays. But Gray is good, don't get me wrong. Though I hear ye are overrun with grays up here. They will never sign a treaty, I can tell you that. I believe a fierce pile of them are being – what should we say – dispensed with on our Emerald Island, if you catch my drift, by the pine marten flying columns. Say no more. Smart boys, and mighty ruthless.'

'Well,' began Gray… He'd always been into history.

'I know I'm in the black North and that you're not a squirrel,' said Eric. 'Not remotely. Sure, what, after all's in a name? That's an old one now for you. It's the lack of a tail that does it. That's the dead giveaway. Not a squirrelly thing about you. But, no, I shouldn't jest. For there's trouble on your face and haven't we all made a pile of blunders in this life? God knows, are you coming in or are you going to wait there for the second coming?'

Gray had once believed in the second coming. He limped towards the tent. This Dr Eric was clearly a dexterous man, physically as well as mentally. For in a matter of seconds he had flipped himself over, was standing athletically outside the tent, and looking almost human. The tent gaped open-mouthed. When Gray looked in, what he appeared to see was a fully fitted consulting room, with a high adjustable couch, albeit with electric, coated cables, like cruel distributor leads, and a hundred bottles of healing liquid, every one of them a poisonous shade of green.

'Hop up,' said the doctor, who might have worn a loin cloth, and cranked his generator.

Hopping up, literally or metaphorically, was not an easy manoeuvre for Gray. With restricted muscle movements he mounted the therapeutic platform. Eric pulled some hidden lever and raised him higher.

'Now I can get a look at your mind, so to speak,' he appeared to say. 'Tell me this, would you be on for Cork? The Lee is a great river, is it not? A powerful waterway. I'm all for rivers. Although the Foyle is all right too. Is your head comfortable?'

He felt Gray's head.

'Ah, God no,' he said. 'I can feel the conflict.'

Gray had still not spoken about his condition. For how would he describe it? He was hoping for a spiritual and alternative dimension, for since he had joined The Happening, the strangest thoughts had been jarring his mind, especially in drink.

'You see,' Gray may have volunteered, 'I was married a lifetime, but something has always been wrong and, more and more, I have been feeling miscast. Like I'm in the wrong play. Feeling that I need to start again with a different... what is the word... orientation? As if my lines have been crossed, if that makes sense. I came to this Happening to explore possibilities, but then I took cold feet and swithered. The young man I am with must think I am a fool. What day is this?'

'You mind is bursting,' Eric seemed to tell him. 'Are we a member of a rambling club?' This, with his eyes tight shut. 'The week that's gone, you went to the Giant's Causeway maybe, looking for answers, in a way? Perhaps you cavorted virtually on the basalt pillars like a two-year-old, but it didn't help you, and now your mind is crippled. Would I be right or wrong?'

And more. And more.

During his peroration, Eric probed and prodded and goaded the mind of Gray this way and that until he groaned aloud.

'You're feeling it,' said Eric. 'By God, I know you are. But no pain, no… I needn't complete a saying like that for a gentleman like yourself. You'll have to work hard at your transformation.'

Gray's mother had told him about mind over matter. He thought of her now as he surrendered.

'I was at the very same thing a while ago.'

What did Eric mean?

'I had a bit of a personal crisis. I know how it goes. You'd be surprised at a man like myself being triggered. So how long have you known about all this here? Tell me the truth, have you ever been to Cork, hypothetically speaking? It's easier said than done. Did you know that what's in your heart comes out in your groin?'

But what had come out in his groin?

'Life's not easy,' said Eric to himself.

Did he adjust the loincloth? 'Looseness of mind is the quare man. You'll not see many garments like this so far north, but Cork is full of them. I need you to visualise a heavenly state, like a good fella.'

Then Eric spoke earnestly to Gray in a quieter, different, more intimate kind of voice.

'Why are you really here, Mr Gray, at this Happening?' he said. 'Can you tell me that? Are you wild for the music? Or are you looking for genuine answers? I'll pop on Enya if you like. Are you fond of Billy

Grail? He's not my dish of kefir, to tell you the truth. Do you eat kefir? If you don't, will you promise me you'll start today? The whole of Derry should be on kefir, without delay. I know that much. I can get you the grains for thirty euros and I'll post them to you, discreetly. Or are you having me on?'

'I thought I was a roast beef and two veg man,' Gray heard himself say, 'but then I thought I wasn't and now I'm not sure. I left my wife because I couldn't put her through the…'

'So, there is a *Mrs* Gray? Why didn't you say? I'm sure she's a lovely lady.'

'Yes, she is,' said Gray. 'But that's not the point… she is indeed.'

'Do you know Miss Black well?' Eric must have asked. 'She thinks I'm a great guy because I have the Multi-Stranded Cert. It's all a question of direction. My professional opinion is that you're stuck. I'm going to yank your psyche, are you ready for that now?'

Gray moaned.

'Do you want to live a lie? Are you ready to take a chance, Mr Gray? You know, it's peculiar, but I don't think you are. Not a bit of you. It's not all about insight. It's also about courage. The pain you're feeling is dissonance. Do you know the concept?'

Gray squirmed.

'That's the bad acid leaving the system. Like the way the British left Cork, after they burned it. Do you believe in crossing borders?'

This was the nub of it. Gray still wasn't sure. Eric, he assumed, was an allegory, like Daniel in the lions' den. He would have to decide. But without a guiding star, what help was there for him? He yelped, as Eric applied more pressure on his soul.

'God, that resistance is tight,' Eric said. 'Healthy mind, healthy body. Are you feeling poorly?'

Then, springing to his feet: 'The poison's in the heels. Metaphorically speaking, I'll have to bruise them both. There's a hell of a lot of toxin inside you. I suppose you've explored all that?'

This resonated with Rev Gray, but it was brutal. In desperation, he prayed for the first time since he'd lost his faith. Each word of supplication wrung agony from his being. But the heavens remained as brass. His prayers were going to limbo, somewhere between hell and nowhere.

'We all pray, in extremis,' said Eric. 'I was a sloth for a while, could you credit that? Mostly in the trees, but it gave me time to think. And I never stopped praying. I was in a shocking state but look at me now. I found a way through. What do you see when you look at me? Go on, tell me. From small beginnings. What did it teach me? Faith.'

'I lost my beliefs,' said Gray. 'My mind's at war.'

'Now we're getting places,' said Eric. 'I'm seeing movement.'

Maybe Gray should have given up any idea of wildness, before he ever got started. Abandoned the pleasures of the flesh. But it wasn't just the flesh? That made him sound perverse. There was something beautiful about the Lean Young Man. Gray clenched his mind. But where was *he*?

'What the hell are you doing that for?'

Was this really Eric speaking? Eric, who somehow, seemed to know.

'I can't help a man who clenches his mind,' he was sure he heard him whisper. 'That's serious resistance. A lot of us men do that, but it's a dreadful habit and one that, like an arse, should be well kicked. Of course, it's up to you. And maybe you should do nothing at all. Simply yield to fate. Go west with the wind. Do you get my drift?'

Gray had read of inverse paradigms, but this was too much.

After it was over, he saw himself lying, whether in reality or in some other dimension, with a single sheet over him that smelled of thyme and balsam. His psyche had been stretched beyond what he thought possible. Gray had imagined angels who should have mothered him – how strange that was – of harps that could have strummed. Of a blackbird that might have sung once on an ivy bunch, before it lost its feathers. Wherever he was, he had known insurmountable darkness descend upon him, like black death on the broad playing fields of Prehen, in the surreal tent of some awesome therapist. Or was he the madman? His location had become a thin, unresolved place of loss, such had been the perceptive caprice of his torturer. Paranoia may also have been at work.

And then, perhaps, he slept.

When he awoke, he was still, in every sense, alone, though rainbow light filtered through the fabric of his brain. In his soul he sensed the sound of music. Possibly from some Joseph and his Coat. It sounded real, at least.

He wondered where Eric had gone. Had he been substantial? And what was *real*? Worst of all, was he real himself? And if he was, was he really awake, or was he still asleep? In the ice bath of his inner nightmare, in a land of threatening shadows, he coldly sweated, believing that he didn't matter. That he was doomed. That one dream was much the same as the next. That any dream would do.

Where he subsequently went, mentally, literally and tangentially, it would be difficult to say. He had come some distance, but had it been too far? Not far enough? Perhaps God, like Eric, had abandoned *him* and not the reverse. It was a heavy cross to bear.

The result of this turmoil would shortly come to the attention of Miss Black, who was to discover, with alarm, that Gray had disappeared.

The Happening advanced climactically on the playing fields of Prehen. The revellers reflected that they had expanded both their bodies and their souls. Most felt uplifted by simply being there. Others gained strength owing to new connections made. A number of serious campers had plunged headlong into the ancient woodlands, close to the golf course, kingdom of the red squirrels, to commune with them and to dwell on eternal questions.

But those who truly knew Miss Black – the friends who loved her to death – could see beyond her mask. They observed that her exuberance was clouded by distress at the disappearance of Gray. This concluding period of The Happening, designed to be extraterrestrial and sublime, was therefore both less and more than she had imagined. Indeed, it was turning out to be, without equivocation, a time of the utmost agony for her. And rumour was rife.

She sought out Dr Eric personally. Doubtless, Gray had been conflicted, Eric said. He had given 'considerable time to him.' Gray had been hallucinating. Perhaps he had 'taken some substance.'

'I hardly think so?' said Miss Black. 'He's an ex-clergyman.'

'We covered a lot of ground,' said Eric, spreading his arms. 'I felt he was fragile.'

'And you let him go? In that brittle condition?'

Eric had advised him to speak to his medical practitioner after The Happening and 'left it at that.'

'Left it at what? Could you not tell that he was vulnerable?'

'He's an adult,' said Eric. 'I couldn't lock him up. He said he'd go back to his tent. He's camping with some young friend, I believe. I hope he gets sorted out.'

This was merciless and impersonal. She blamed herself. She had missed a trick. An awful dread seized her. Gray was lost. Really lost. Through her negligence. It was obvious when she thought about it. What he had needed was nurture. She had not been paying attention. Was too caught up. Less than person-centred. What, she asked herself, if anything, had she known of this so-called Dr Eric, when she engaged him?

'Where was your intuition? Did you not see?' she said. 'Could you not tell he was a soul in trouble?'

Eric's casual answers did not please her for a second. Had he no back-up? No protocols in place? My God, she had taken all this for granted.

'He is badly mixed up,' said Eric. 'A lot of men are like him. But I cannot say more. My service is confidential.'

'Your service is shite.'

But this would do nothing to find Gray or secure his welfare. A savage blizzard now raged in the breast of Indigo Black, as doughty hope battled giants of despair. Gray would have to be found.

Over the Rainbow?

A schizoid twilight filtered oddly that evening through the trees and around the historic Prehen House, where the musicians, who had not yet yielded to the pellucid waters of The Poetarium, sawed swiftly with well-rosined bows. Many too were the young and not so young who found it enriching to be close to nature among the fairy bowers and dells. There they gathered the delightful fungi growing under the canopy, in supportive little clumps, clustering together on lichen-covered stumps. This was a land which sunlight seldom reached, and so the psychic was not unknown. These campers, no doubt, had yet to hear of Gray.

Soulful were the dirges which issued from the throats of the singers. Macaronic ballads, with multitudinous verses, issued through pale, white lips, as Irish and English, in turn, strove for coherence.

To the uninformed, this might have sounded like despair. Ireland's woes being lived all over again. But this was to misjudge these artists at work. Rather, they were delving into the slow, deep leaf mould of the past, prior to quickening the tempo of the future with a reel or polka, presaging the momentum which would sweep the gathering and society at large, when brightness would entirely appear. Since only the truly iconic had assembled in these covens, all this was mutually understood. As Donal Óg gave way to the Mason's Apron, someone remarked that the sound of the violin was the nearest to the human voice that ever God had invented. There was no dissension there.

The musicians had entered a place of fortitude. After an interlude, a large ukulele player – no doubt known to Mr White – with an even larger pair of hands played ecstatically, his own evocative version of Somewhere Over the Rainbow. Approving nods in the shadows. A song to meet their needs.

But where was Grail?

And where was Gray?

Battered guitar cases lounged in the undergrowth among the ferns and bracken. Somehow, at the end of the session, they would be reunited with their occupants. Fiddlers, prepared to play till dawn, holding with a light touch the instruments to their ears. They all had perfect pitch and not a bit of time for tuners. Foxes peeped from copses, as saintly men and bare-legged women, wrapped in rugs, arranged themselves on mossy banks, in clearings and in amphitheatres. These were the true bearers of Derry's spirit, the holders of the dream.

This was where Rev Gray had fondly longed to be finally knitted together, according to the Lean Young Man, with whom he had shared this secret. This same Young Man who was now scouring the pitches in desperation and speaking non-stop to Foyle Search and Rescue.

'I have not seen him, at all, for many torrid hours,' he told them tearfully. 'I think we had, how do you say it, words? Or lack of words. A silent bust-up. A dripping fog fell and tipped us in the shits. Is that what you call it also in Derry? I believe he may be alone and greatly challenged.'

'Did he mention the river?' asked the volunteer.

The LYM could not be sure.

'He might have spoken of the river of life. He was, you see, so very exercised, but in a bad way, for alas, he was dislocated in his emotions. I would say it was not easy for him.'

'Are you his nearest relative?' asked the volunteer, as he radioed Control. 'A nephew, his son, a brother?'

'He is my confessor,' said the LYM.

'A priest?'

'No not a priest. A clergy, but not anymore, a clergy. A dear, dear man. He at first was sure, you see, about wildness and then he was not so sure, but I thought – and now I am no longer certain of anything. I suspect he may be sinking.'

'Had he been drinking?' asked the volunteer, who was speaking to Control. 'Yes, yes, he *could* be in the river.'

'My God, after some wildness he *was* indeed drinking,' said the Lean Young Man.

And so, as the multitude prepared to be stunned by the arrival of Billy Grail, a mega search was mounted for the departed Rev Gray. Campers began to fan out and beat the grass. Miss Black shared his details, in impassioned tones of anguish over the Tannoy. 'If you see him or have any knowledge of where he is, engage with him and comfort him, hold on to him, don't let him go, and in the name of God contact me directly at 07791779908. You could be the one to save a precious life.' In this way, the angst of one troubled traveller was belatedly broadcast, and the rescue boat, lights ablaze, set off with energy. The orange-suited crew had scrambled faithfully to search for Rev Gray.

'If he's in the water, we'll find him,' said the crew, helmeted and securely life-jacketed. A bereaving moment for Miss Black, but such was the confident look of compassion and determination on the serious faces of the volunteers that her spirits and those of the Lean Young Man were buoyed a little.

'I have been wheel-sleeping,' said the Lean Young Man. 'He is a good man who does not deserve to perish.'

Sorrow welled in his voice but the steady drone of the inflatable's engine and the steely fortitude of Miss Black suggested trust, rather than despair.

News of a missing person could never be welcomed. Good God, no, not by anyone. But Shugh Henderson, bending the elbow like it was going out of fashion, and with a face on him, was supposed to have said, 'I warned them about that bitch.'

Those at sea level said that whoever he was, poor creature, they hoped he'd be found alive. 'Please God.'

The March of Time

Meanwhile, as evening continued to fall, but in complete accordance with the detailed plans laid by Miss Black, a squad of bold musicians, percussionists, to be precise, and led by none other than John Orange McBeth himself, proceeded along the skyline, on the eastern bank, high above The Happening. They were a fine marching army of talented insurgents from Newbuildings, on their way to a ten-acre field, kindly granted by one Piers Mitchel, near Gobnascale. Such had been Miss Black's vision of merging two disparate hemispheres. What a cultural triumph. From Strabane Old Road, the drummers could observe the camp below. The expectant rows of glowing tents. The illuminations and spiralling smoke. They could also make out the lights of the rescue boat, but may have been unaware of the unfolding drama as they pressed on steadily, beating Lambegs for Ireland, each bearing cheerfully their heavy, rounded burden.

Any danger of being mown down by vehicles had been cleverly avoided by the laying of new red and white traffic cones, and the wearing of flashing armbands by the many stewards. As they approached their destination they rested respectfully, while a lone drummer tapped a single beat. That drummer was John O. Owls, it was later reported, hooted in time. Perhaps the assembling of this muscled army, embracing all genders and persuasions, would yet be the greatest legacy of The Happening, for despite the meticulous attention of Miss Black, Billy Grail had yet to arrive. The field was strewn with bunting of every hue and every marcher received a shot of Quiet Man whiskey, and a specially embossed copy of a certain seminal poetry anthology by the Man Himself. The marchers were just ordinary folk, from Primity Crescent, with day jobs, but they were showing, under the influence of John O, a reassuring and thorough commitment to art, in all its truth and beauty.

Meanwhile, in the warm, all-enveloping waters of The Poetarium, Judge Scarlett, unaware of the increasing turmoil being suffered by Indigo on behalf of Gray, was locked in learning mode with Mr White, who for years, he gathered, had been in care.

It had clearly been a most unfortunate period in the life of Mr White, whose mother had loved him desperately in her own way. But following her demise, he had barely survived a life of gut-wrenching terror from a number of adults, and other children. His mother had been taken when he was eight.

'I was without protection then,' Mr White told the judge, who found this hard to hear.

'How can I safeguard children without harming them?' he asked Mr White. 'How did you manage at all?'

'I turned to nature,' said Mr White.

'He has a lot of birds' eggs and a display table,' said Miss Marrón, who, like an attentive mermaid, was swimming close by. 'And a message, in Spanish no doubt, incarcerated in a Tio Pepe bottle, which we have yet to open. But he is frightened of the Ogre who haunts his dreams and refuses to fix his spoutings. He also grabs his rent.'

Judge Scarlett was disturbed to hear of this also. Despite, and perhaps because of their different starts in life, he felt, as The Happening neared its conclusion, an attraction and common bond with these good people, wanting to know them more thoroughly, though in the end, he had not been brave enough to remove his trunks. Mr White, on the other hand, with the encouragement of Miss Marrón, had abandoned this inhibition.

'Is this your wife?' the judge asked him, although he'd seen no ring.

'We met at The Coffee Tree,' said Miss Marrón. 'Do you know it? Their produce is most exquisite. And they are all so smiley. My people are from España.'

'You must be enjoying this wonderful warm water then,' said the judge, 'it's like the bloody Med.'

'*Si,*' said Miss Marrón. She had also shed her things, and clung now, limpet-like, to the needy, translucent body of Mr White.

'We have decided to be wed,' she said modestly. 'After we open the Tio Pepe bottle, which we will do tonight, for luck. It will be the best thing. I asked *him* and he said, "Yes," less than an hour ago. You are the first to know. Now, what do you think of that?'

'Honoured. Very fine,' said the judge, wishing he could stay in the womb of The Poetarium for ever.

'He will moonlight from Braehead, and to hell with the Ogre,' said Miss Marrón. 'At the conclusion of The Happening, Mr White will come to me in London Street, where we must renovate tired wood with paint, and build a nest together, for his taste in art and artefacts is excellent and he does not want canaries. Also, he will strum his ukulele most romantically for me, after the Strabane man who thinks it is a bicycle returns it. We hope to God it stays in tune, though whether its wheel will be fixed completely is another thing.'

'I hope everything works out,' said the judge, sifting these disparate elements. 'I must say, I'm damned pleased for you both. I've been married to Penelope for a lifetime. She's not the only one who ever excited me, of course, but after we got hitched, I never looked back. I wish you the best of luck.'

'Do you think this singer Grail will ever come?' asked Miss Marrón. 'It is getting so late.'

'I have no doubt he will,' said the judge, seeking, as he was forced to do at court, to look omniscient, but wondering about a towel. 'I know the organiser of the event rather well, as a matter of fact.'

'Oh, do you now?' said Miss Marrón. 'You and she have shared some moments of intimacy, no? Do you hear that, Mr White?'

'Why do you say that?' asked the judge.

'Because, Señor, I am a woman,' she said, 'and I can tell these things.' Mr White nodded.

'She's clairvoyant,' he said. 'As well as being a mermaid. A Spanish one.'

The night, alas, was upon them and Judge Scarlett, for all this diversion, was thinking about Indigo. She had seemed so sure of Billy Grail. Even now, he hoped and prayed, as it were, that she would be all right.

The Arrival of Thelma Green

The last patrons to be admitted to The Happening as it teetered suspensefully towards the finale were Toots Daly and Mrs Green. Thelma had avoided the temptation to consume more drink. To her surprise, she had showered and washed her hair, even spraying a little eau de cologne behind her knees. God knew how old it was. Toots was not her date, but he *was* a man, and he would be calling for her. She had resisted the obvious conclusion that he pitied her. This was *her* choice. He was an honest human, and humanity was what she missed. Daphne had been the one for splashing perfume on her body. She, Thelma, plain Thelma, had seldom used it. Walter had liked her the way she was. Or so he'd said. That might have been his problem. It might also have been hers. Too easily pleased.

'Youse just arriving?' asked the Blues, whom she had never met before, having seldom been in the Brandywell or in Upper Bennett Street.

'Has Billy Grail played yet?' asked Toots. 'I want Thelma here to get a load of him.'

'Naw, he hasn't,' said Mick. 'We don't even know if he's here.'

'Maybe we'll have to stand in for him,' said Manus, 'that would be some bloody comeback, wouldn't it, hi?'

Toots winked at Thelma.

'Singing only,' said Mick, 'no wrestling.'

'I'd say something's happened to him,' said Manus. 'You can never tell with these big shots. They're always tossing their rattleys…'

'Out of their prams,' said Toots.

He was taking a long look at Mick and Manus, the way you would if you saw your oul car in Horace Street with somebody else driving it.

'Wait a minute,' he said, 'weren't youse pair once the Blue Two?'

'We always will be,' said Manus and Mick,' checking simultaneously the matching retro watches they'd bought in the Yard, as if for confirmation. 'We are definitely not spooks.'

'Naw, God, I know that,' said Toots. 'But the Blue Two. Unreal man. 'These guys are legends,' he said to Thelma. 'Lourdes Hall and all that there. My ma told me about them. 'Youse should be in Madame Tussauds,' he said.

The boys grinned.

'But, no messing, you know what I mean. You don't have to be dead to be in the waxworks.' They smiled more warmly, still showing a few teeth.

'My Auntie Winnie lived in Bluebell Gardens,' said Toots, 'straight up, no coddin.'

'Winnie Dooher?' said the Blue Two. 'The nice wee one that turned?'

'Turned where?' asked Thelma.

'You couldn't write it,' said Toots. 'Aunt Winnie had to become a prod when she married my half-uncle, on my da's side, the cop from Corrody, that rid the motorbikes.'

'Aye, so he did,' said Mick and Manus. 'BSA Bantams. At the start of the bother. God, that was a while ago.'

They wagged their heads. Then they shook hands with Toots.

'You must be, what, then, Stevie's son? Stevie the sign writer? He's like him, too. Isn't he Manus? He's a dead ringer for his da. That's right, your ma came out of Harding Street.'

'What do you know, Thelma?' said Toots, 'these ones remember my ma and my Auntie Winnie.'

'And the time you were born.'

'Her and him had to leave,' said Toots. They went to live in Bally someplace, near Coleraine. And they never came back. Not even to burn Lundy, or for him to watch the Twelfth of August. That's the Gospel truth. They might as well have been in Australia.'

'Fuck's sake,' agreed the Blue Two.

Thelma did not speak. But a slow tear trickled down her face. Then Toots as well.

'Awk now,' he said, 'we've started her off, don't be blubbering Ducksie. What the hell are we like Mrs G, you and me, eh? A couple of friggin' cry-babies. Don't mind us, fellas,' he said. 'Our heads is pure distracted with cracked chimneys, but, come here, we're on a night out, Thelma and me. We have a wee thing going. Don't we, pet?'

The Guinness Tent

As the weather broke at Prehen, there was still no sign of Billy Grail or Gray. Some campers had wisely taken advantage of a quiet time to lie in their tents, to read and count their blessings. Other more extrovert Derry wans made their way under the trees, to the big marquee, to drink Guinness and pull together, like they always had during bleak days of adversity. Some people were saying prayers for anybody that needed them. Aggressive raindrops bounced madly on the wide canvas roof, as vigorous debating began.

Miss Black circulated freely, but her colour had drained. No one, it seemed, had seen Gray for a very long time. Long enough for something monstrous to have taken him. The strain was telling. Steam rose from the drinkers in the Guinness Tent as the humidity got higher. The white-coated waiters were flat out.

'I'll be with you now, love.'

Vocal cords loosened. A bunch of non-forest-loving musicians was at one table, a crowd from City Paint at another. Lorna McC from Rushcroft, with her luxurious head of hair, as usual, looked ten years younger than she was. She was with her wee dog Max.

'I wouldn't have missed The Happening,' she said, 'and neither would Max. Would you, darling?'

Max licked her lipstick, but Lorna didn't mind, because she loved his little ways. 'I think we'll both have a nice cool drink of Harp, Max,' she said. 'Would you have a wee saucer?' she asked a friendly barman.

All the tables were filled. People tried not to think the worst about Rev Gray.

Melissa McLaughlin, who worked in the tyre place down the Strand, said her ma had been far through one time, but she was all right now. Her ma had went to Nexus, and themuns had pulled her through.

Nods all round. Everybody's heart went out to Rev Gray and, 'may

God be good to him.'

'Did you ever hear the like of your man Henderson, all the same?' somebody said.

Who was Henderson?

'You know, the plonker that's always on about waste. That hates Miss Black, that organised this here.'

'You get people like that. Two pints love, when you can.'

'Aye, that's what I said… and a big bag of smoky bacon, mucker. Sound as a pound. Naw, he's a bloody bad animal.'

'Our Amie works in the Council,' said Gerry Canning. 'She takes notes at meetings, and stuff.' Gerry's tongue was deep in the creamy head of his stout. 'Henderson tried to stop The Happening – from happening, you know.'

'Nice one, Gerry,' said Stumps Ferguson.

'No, but he wound up the Health and Safety people something shocking,' said Gerry, 'and Environmental Health, and the Roads ones. You name it. He had a two-hour meeting with The Water Service, two hours, bloody hell. He met with your man McGuire, the Fire Chief, and he was on to Translink. Henderson and his hoods. That's what they call them. He made a speech at the General Purposes Committee and tried to pull the arse out of Indigo Black.'

'That was his biggest *foo pah* ever,' said Melissa. 'We all think he's wild looking. Every woman in Derry wants to stab him with a screwdriver. He was on the Long Presenter's Show, did none of youse hear it?'

Nobody had.

I don't know what youse be doing,' said Melissa.

'We're all bloody working,' said Stumps, 'that's what we be doing.'

'I was on a half,' said Melissa. 'Feck away off Stumps Ferguson'

'Do we want to hear this story or not?'

Gerry was working on his pint.

'Ok,' said Melissa, 'so, we're on the show, Henderson speaks first.

And he says – this here's Henderson speaking – that he's, 'as good a what do you call it as anybody in the town but this here project is money right down the toilet, so it is, like Hallowe'en and Gay Pride.'

'What?'

Four dozen voices.

'Another crazy scheme from an even crazier woman.'

'Sacred Heart. That's misogyny.'

'I told youse,' Gerry said.

'I know.'

'The phone lines were jammed with women ringing in, and men as well, are youse listening?' said Melissa, giving them her stare.

'Proper order,' said the men.

'But Henderson batters on.'

'Nothing like stopping when you're ahead,' said Stumps.

'Aye, but wait till you hear the best of it,' said Melissa. '"I have nothing against wholesome entertainment," he says. Wholesome. Henderson. "I'm not out to spoil anybody's fun" – I hear you – "but quite frankly I'd never heard tell of Billy Grail, until we had all the carry-on about this Happening, or whatever the hell 'it's going to be. It'll be nothing but drink and drugs."'

'Feckin' hypocrite.'

This was the same man who, when he was rotten, had insulted Miss Black in the dining room of the Bishop's Gate Hotel. That story had got about.

'Bastard.'

'Excuse me,' said Melissa, 'if it's not too much bother Gerry, I want another Pinot Grigio. A large one this time. Here's the Long Presenter on the airwaves, "Well, that's one side of the great debate, folks. A strong case being made by Councillor Henderson, a proud Derry man who speaks, I'm sure for a significant number of our citizens. What do you say to that, Indigo?"'

'I'm sure he does,' said Stumps. 'Who's Indigo?'

'Would you just listen to yourself, Stumps, I told you, she's Miss Black. She was on with the Long Presenter.'

'Go on, Melissa. Shut up, Stumps, and let her finish.'

'And the Long Presenter says, are youse ready? Here he is, "I guess you're a woman of experience, Indigo, but let's face it, you're the new kid on the block." The Long Presenter's great, but that was wild cheeky. "I know it's your baby, and all," he says, "but how well have you really thought this through?" That's his exact words, as sure as God. But Indigo bloody ate him. She taught me at St Gobnait's, you know, me and Gertie Arbuckle and she was only BRILLIANT. She told us we would go far and so we have.'

Cheers.

Billy Grail had still not arrived. But somehow, Miss Black held herself together. Had Henderson threatened him? Or her? Paid him out of some slush fund, not to come? And more important, where *was* Gray?

'I loved her too,' said Melissa's friend. Then Gerry, who was on his fourth pint, said that his Nanna Nelis – on his ma's side – had been as good a singer as Cissie Parlour in her day, and that was saying something. His nanna had been born in Artisan Street.

'Artisan Street was the nicest street in Derry,' said Patsy Burns, who'd just come in, looking half-drowned.

'I don't see how youse can all just sit and say stuff like that,' said Gerry, also known as the Plumber's Brother. 'Beauty is in the eye of the what-do-you-call-it.'

'Like a soldered pipe,' said Melissa.

Everyone laughed.

'I've seen a cracker print of Artisan Street,' said Patsy, 'I'm telling you, it was totally gorgeous. All these wee cottagey houses and taller ones with fancy bricks round the windows and youngsters in the street skipping, because there was hardly any cars in them days, and it was safe for the weans. Honest to God, it was like fairyland.'

'I bet you a fiver the picture was painted by Bridget Murray,' said Melissa's friend. 'She's my favourite artist of all time.'

'Better than van Gogh?' asked the Plumber's Brother.

'What would *you* know about van Gogh?' said Melissa. 'Sure he only painted sunflowers.'

'Away you go.'

'Nanna Nelis sang for General Balbo,' said Gerry. 'He was an Italian that flew in to Derry for his dinner. All his batmen had these big waxed moustaches. They were a right sketch. You want to seen them.'

'*You* never seen them anyway,' said Stumps.

'I know,' said Gerry, 'because they were Fascists. But I seen them in a book.'

'Italians make the best ice cream in the world,' said Booboo Harrigan. 'Me and Monty Collins used to never be out of Fiorentini's.'

Monty was Booboo's dog, but he'd choked on a chicken bone.

More nods.

'Italians are geniuses, in my book,' said the Plumber's Brother. 'Look at what the Romans did.'

'Aye, but the Romans never came to Derry, did they,' said Booboo, 'because they didn't want to show themselves up.'

'I'll tell you who the best Derry singer of *all* time was,' said Marcella Tinny – now where had she come from – 'it wasn't Dana, or what do you call him, Josef Locke, it was Mickey McWilliams.'

A buzz went round the tent. 'Aye well, Mickey was a quare singer all right. A great bloody singer.' People's grannies remembered him in The Hall. 'Not a dry eye in the house.'

'But how the hell can you know a thing like that when all the people have passed?' said Stanley Ferris, who was a kind of philosopher. 'The best singer and all that there.'

'Catch yourself on, Stanley.'

'Naw, but that's right, it's a good point,' said Stumps.

The rain was easing.

'They say he's an Irishman,' said Gerry.

'Who?'

'Billy Grail.'

'*The* Billy Grail?'

'The one we're all waiting on.'

'Oh aye. His great great-granda came from Galliagh,' said Gerry.

'There was no Galliagh, then,' said a bald fella from Belfast that nobody'd noticed, and and everybody said, 'Who's he?'

'You're up the left there mucker, no harm to you,' Gerry told the bald fella.

'I'm telling you. There's no Grails in Derry' said your man, who had some bloody nerve. 'And there never was.'

'God save us.' Gerry was going out for air.

'There's a man missing,' said the bald fella, and somebody said, 'Whisht, would ye? Would youse all dry up a minute?'

After all the clinking of glasses, and laughing, and roaring, the silence was deafening. But only for a second. Because then you could hear it. The pounding of rotors. The big, thirsty thrust of engines.

'It's the Brits,' some eejit yelled.

The walls of the Guinness tent were sucked out as the wind rushed in. Everyone poured outside to look heavenward. And as they did, the clouds, which had so recently dumped on them, parted company, and a gap opened, reminding them of the goodness of God. Then through the gap flew this giant bird, shining and splendid in the arc lights, and whirring its tail. Down it came to rest on the turf, rocking only for a moment. With the grace of a celestial capsule, it settled perfectly, only yards from the drinkers.

Two men from Goshaden unfurled a new herringbone carpet, made specially in Ardara. The crowds gasped as spots picked out a translucent woman in a red sheath dress, colour-coordinated exactly with the livery of the aircraft, walking with her head high, on the sharpest of heels, with the poise of a ballet queen towards the chopper. That woman was Indigo Black.

Who, though, could have truly comprehended her complex spirit, titillated and tortured as it was, as she strode towards the personalised conveyance of the super-galactic Billy Grail, who, thanks be to God, had come, at last, against all the imprecations, no doubt, of a certain lowlife called Henderson, arriving apocalyptically, as she had said he would, on Derry's holy ground?

But Gray had still not shown.

The people clapped. Some danced. They linked arms and did the conga. Dogs howled in ecstasy. It was four hours from the finale of The Happening.

Landings

As the Ardmore men stood to attention, the staircase of the swirling ship descended. For a moment, on the threshold, Billy Grail waved, like a man delighted to be home.

By now the night was dark.

From a barge on the Foyle, fireworks spangled the sky. Gunpowder stars exploded, in words of English and Irish and Ulster Scots. What a glorious touch, to usher in the future, and Billy Grail. From the direction of the Bolies – that high, ancient grazing ground above the quarry that was filled with quivering aspens – came the unmistakable, cross-community brattle of a mighty Lambeg, as John McBeth himself beat out a welcome to the Maiden City.

What faith this Orangeman had shown, thought Miss Black, wishing she could dry-freeze time. Oh, that she could preserve this moment forever, in aspic. But where in the battered gates of hell was Gray? Other drummers drummed on snares, two hundred strong at least.

And now that almost everything was in place, and *almost* everyone was where they ought to be, Miss Black, despite her deep concern, held out her superlative arms to enfold the hypnotic Grail. Ten thousand pairs of eyes watched that most memorable moment of union. When the drums ceased, a most intense silence fell over the assembled revellers, none of whom had lost faith in Miss Black or at the end of the day, in Billy Grail. Speechless, Miss Black continued to hold him as the emotion of the entire city welled through her.

Years later, people, by then in their seventies, would undoubtedly swear they had observed the thinnest of blue electric currents sizzle and connect them. Scientists would decry their testimony, but since when did science have all the answers, and how can one calibrate the energy between two humans?

Miss Black, in some completely imperceptible manner, must have been speaking to the cohort on the hill, though no-one had spotted a phone.

With sudden ferocity a fire ball blazed, huge and explosive, flaring like a combusting meteor. Never before, since the Troubles came to Ireland, had such a sound been heard. A sound at once localised and spreading out wide above the heads of the campers. The earth in the field where the fire burned was said to have vapourised, so intense was the heat. The wild creatures, badgers and the like had, in some prescient way, anticipated the events and moved to higher reaches. The light was intense. It had ushered in a bright, brand-new, hyperbolic day in the dead of Stygian night.

In other, lesser cities, the population might have run. But here they stood like shirt factory girls together, as Miss Black had known they would. Wasn't it typical of their character, to be strong and to see things through. The sense of pride which filled her breast could hardly be described. This was far from the hubris she had prayed to avoid, but rather an ache of affection for her family, her greater tribe, her people, whatever their religious label, and it was without parallel. The thrill of that pyro-spectacular, combined with the pulse of drum skins, could surely have been achieved only with the aid of divine intervention, whatever and however that had come about.

Derry was that sort of place.

'Dear God,' prayed Indigo. 'If you love the world, let Gray turn up.'

The drums continued to beat as giant flames leapt skyward and lovers held lovers, as Billy Grail stood on terra firma at the bottom of the steps. He did not, like the Pope, kiss the soil of Erin, but he did stand in his pink suit, with the wildest possible flares, in the arms of Miss Black, long enough for the city to embrace them. Pictures of their enmeshed bodies were immediately beamed to New York, Joburg and Tokyo – to the vast diaspora. Billy was even more handsome than his pictures had suggested. Unlike the later Elvis he had not become obese. Here was a star who had kept to a strict regime, for himself and for his fans.

A number of young girls were understandably overcome and fainted, in the same way as their grannies had done half a century before, when they'd queued at the Ritz in Belfast to see The Beatles.

But all this was nothing compared with the uncontrollable hysteria they experienced when Billy began to sing. Miss Black, now standing alone, had taken the bother to beckon one of the Ardmore men. She was clearly asking him questions and pointing at the river.

By the look of her, he had heard something good. He nodded. 'Are you sure?' she seemed to ask. Yes, he was sure. She nodded too. Some lip reader, standing close by, swore that she said, 'Dear Jesus,' and 'thank you God.'

It was generally felt by the many students of human nature – and Derry has more than its share – that something of astronomical import had come about. Something which would allow her to proceed, as anguish gave way to triumph.

The evening soared accordingly.

'A legend is being born. I mean it,' she had said. 'I want every adult and child in every house in Derry and beyond to hear Billy Grail, live, as plainly as we'll hear him in Prehen.'

She wasn't disappointed. His amazing voice carried via radio to Muff, Magheramason and Donemana, but he was also streamed to the world.

The Blue Two were called to the stage on the orders of Miss Black, to whom they'd been introduced. Billy would have sung with them no problem, but they were old pros who wouldn't perform at a thing like The Happening without rehearsal. Standing between them, though, Grail hoisted their arms, much as Bono had once jacked up the arms of certain politicians. The crowd sang You Raise Me Up.

'I'm told these guys are the real deal,' said Grail. 'And tough as well.'

'WE will return, no worries,' said Mick and Manus into the mic. They sounded good. Strong and clear. Everybody heard them. They couldn't get out of it now. They were back in their prime. Their comeback was in the bag. It would be vintage Blues and totally insane.

Mr White kissed Miss Marrón fully on the lips and told her that he loved her.

Miss Marrón, despite her deprived upbringing and lack of education, spoke several new words of Spanish. '*Que maravillosa*,' she said, returning the *besos* of Mr White, moistly, again and again.

'Now I can write my book,' she said, like one who had been freed.

Judge Scarlett embraced Miss Marrón, now that she had her clothes on, and oh, by God, how he kissed Miss Black, vowing to bring Penelope to The Poetarium and to spend more time in the company of Mr White, with whom he again shook hands, and from whom he would learn so much.

Thelma Green, bright-eyed as a doe, and looking younger, resolved to mail her twin sister Daphne in Woomera first thing in the morning about her chimney, and to give her an invite home, without a vestige of rancour and with a heart full of gratitude to Miss Black and the gallant Toots Daly.

In all, not a living soul in this corner of Ireland or beyond could have missed hearing Billy Grail's broadcast on that night of investment, reward, faith and mystery, even if they'd tried, and certainly not the Lean Young Man, whose woes had threatened so seriously to engulf him. Not in the end, thanks be to the Good God, who was looking down from heaven on the whole thing. Rev Gray, although a swimmer, having learned as a child in William Street Baths, was exhausted when Foyle Search and Rescue hauled him to safety. Even as the current made to sweep him past Sainsbury's and under Foyle Bridge and drag him, helpless towards the open sea. Thanks be for those volunteers.

One can only imagine the reconnection he and the Lean Young Man must have made in A and E, and the care with which the nurses, aided by the LYM, wrapped his Reverence lovingly in tinfoil to fend off doubt, shock, and the challenges they would face together, after this ghastly baptism. According to the papers, Miss Black appeared by his bed, like a visiting angel, before the night was through. 'Poor soul, he has rested at last,' she said, 'with all his emotion spent.' But something 'cathartic,' she was convinced, had 'solidified in the body and the soul of Rev Gray.'

'I am what I am,' he'd said.

She was convinced that he would make a full recovery in time, pursue his true artistic way, and no longer walk alone. The demons which had tormented him would at last desist. She was sure of it. He would learn to walk more softly, and to abandon guilt.

What a terrific bonus for him, for Miss Black and the city as a whole. Even Mrs Gray, who manifestly had committed no offence, could, with a fair wind, please God, begin to understand him more, and be again, against the odds, his very special friend. She might even aspire to become a close confidante of the Lean Young Man.

Neither, at the last round-up, did the dismal, duplicitous Henderson himself escape completely the spell of Billy Grail and what was happening. Oh, he tried, as you would expect, to block his ears, to disregard the message of hope, like a man refusing to be saved, but without success. Some goodness, thanks be to God, is just too hard to stop.

Endings and New Beginnings

It was five in the morning when Miss Black, her well-preserved body still pumping adrenaline and clothed only in the most translucent chiffon, made the Guatemalan coffee she had promised Billy Grail. She served it straight from a seldom, if ever, used cafetière, on the balcony of her crucially located riverside apartment. There had been no need, on that shortest of nights, for heat to be generated geothermally, for they had not slept at all. Indeed, without so much as referring to the weather forecast, Miss Black had kept the windows open. Yet, despite more showers, the temperature had risen. On her balcony now, they stood together, in consummate communion.

'My greatest and deepest regret is in hiring that serpent Eric,' she said to Billy Grail. 'If ever I've learned a lesson. And I've heard of irregularity at the turnstiles. Men cashing in.'

'Human nature,' said Billy. 'Give yourself a break, Indigo. Come here to me.'

He held her fast, as the seabirds mewled on the waterfront, as they circled, spinning and crying to friends, in their own avian language. Across the Foyle, that greatest of rivers, lay the refurbished stone railway station – how truly amazing it was, and what a delightful, authentic restoration, with its history and inside foliage, its sepia evocations, *play me* piano and double tracks. What a great job McCann and his group had done to keep the line open, to ensure connection. She and Billy watched the day's first train depart. There had to be leavings as well as arrivals. Oblivious, the gulls skimmed, rising without effort on the thermals, diving and dipping in their subjective aerial display.

How very apposite.

A strawberry blush of day. The morning after. Beyond, the wooded horizon of the Waterside, and to the west of Altnagelvin's tall healing cube, residual wisps of smoke still ascending from where the fires had been. Refining fires, she reflected, which would burn brightly in her heart always, in the hearts of Derry's people.

She later swore to Scarlett, and to Toland, the doctor, that John O and the drummers had played on and on in the distance, knowing full well that sound reverberates for ever.

In the deepest blue of blue heavens, a jet aircraft glinted silver, at thirty thousand feet, headed for the States.

'You see,' Billy began, his suit thrown on her bed, 'it was such a damned close squeeze. I tried to get you, but our cell phones failed. Nothing went right. There was a problem with the chopper. God knows. Only for some fancy footwork by the mechanics… I can't think what would have happened if they hadn't… I mean, for a while we thought it really was no go… I can't imagine. It looked like curtains.'

And she had thought it was Henderson. 'Shush, Billy,' she crooned.

It had been *such* a comfort to learn of Gray's rescue on the cusp, on the very cusp. And to witness his joyful tears and those of the Lean Young Man, that same young man with whom she had seen him some weeks before The Happening.

So much had taken place.

'But what were you thinking?' said Grail. 'Did you imagine I'd stand you up?' With enchantment, she shook her head.

'Rest easy,' she said.

Below, the waters sparkled.

And the sun, she thought, the sun.

He tried again.

'Tush, tush,' she said, placing a finger between his pulsating lips.

'Look, Billy,' she said, with tenderness, as she directed his gaze, 'what does that yellow lollipop say to us?'

Billy regarded the expectant orb. Its undying gleam. He would leave at midnight from Dublin.

'The future has arrived,' he said without hesitation. 'It speaks of hope. That's what it's telling *me*.'

For the second time in a matter of hours, time stopped for Indigo Black, as she stood with her thoughts and Billy Grail.

Just then a fleet of Council scarabs with shiny, aluminium carapaces, all stuffed no doubt with yard brushes and shovels, and busy as beetles scuttled in convoy along the quay in the direction of Craigavon Bridge. Heading for the clean-up at Prehen.

A light breeze now wafted Miss Black. She struck a slender match, lit two cigarettes, and held them, oh-so-briefly, in her mouth, tasting, momentarily, the dry thinness of the paper. One was for her – the other was for Billy.

'Linger with me on my balcony a while longer, Billy Grail,' she said, with abandon. At that awesome moment, the Guildhall clock struck seven, but time had ceased to matter.

'Savour this moment with me,' she whispered. 'For all too often I am alone.'

Acknowledgements

Thank you, Arts Council of Northern Ireland and Derry City and Strabane District Council for your amazing financial support. Words really don't begin to cut it. Thank you, Carousel Aware Prize for Independently Published Authors, for shortlisting *Smokes and Birds* in the anthology section in 2023, and for awarding *Smokes and Birds* Best Cover award. It was a timely shot in the arm.

Thank you, Laura Jaworski, for generously giving me permission to use your great words as a signature quotation. Huge thanks to Derry artist, and my lovely neighbour, Bridget Murray, for once again producing such evocative and arresting artwork. Thank you, participants in the True Colour Workshops, sponsored by Derry City and Strabane District Council; deep appreciation to participants Mark McGrath, Faustina Starrett, Martin Boyle, Katherine Kay, Nina Quigley, Anne Tracey, Eamonn Baker, Susanne Nolan, Eilidh Patterson, Geraldine Toman, Nonie O'Sullivan, Margaret Cradden, Paddy McEvoy, Hazel McEvoy, Margaret Hough, Una Morrison. Thanks to Sinead Coxhill, Ruth Holloway, Kirsty Mowat, Janet Peace, Robin Holmes, Esther Reid, Noreen Kane, Emma Kane, who took part in a Coleraine-based workshop. Thanks to every member of This Writing Thing, and North Coast Writers groups who also offered astute and imaginative feedback in our regular sessions.

Thanks Sylvia Lester, who read an early version of the manuscript and gave valuable commentary. The many responses I received were positive, perceptive and challenging. I took many of the points on board. It's been a highly interactive journey and a lot of fun. Thank you, Derry Central Library, Foyle u3a and Coleraine Library for your generous provision of accommodation. Thank you Sue Divin, Mary Farrell and Maureen Dunseath for your good offices in arranging the workshops. Thanks to Hilda Quinn, my patient and faithful first reader.

A huge thank you to Garbhán Downey at Colmcille Press for having faith in me, and to Jenni Doherty in Little Acorns for her encouragement. Thank you to all the stores who stock *Smokes and Birds*, and once again, to John Boyle for the photograph. Thanks, in spadefuls, to my computer guru Paddy McGill and the amazing Felicity McCall, who, without doubt, inspired me to press on and who gave affirmation. Without her expertise and energy I might have flagged. A big thanks to Siobhán Prendergast and all at Dingle Publishing Services.

Thanks as ever, to my lovely, long-suffering wife Jen, who has lived for so many years, not only with me, but with the characters who come out of my head. Lastly, thank you Derry for embracing me, a blow-in from Belfast, for allowing me to become part of you. Your indomitable spirit has been my inspiration. I hope I've done you justice.

James Simpson

James Simpson grew up in East Belfast and studied at Grosvenor High School, Banbridge Academy, Queen's University Belfast, and the then New University of Ulster. After a career in the Health Service, and helping to set up Oakgrove Integrated College, he began writing. He was a runner-up in the Francis McManus Short Story Competition in 2013 and longlisted in the RTÉ Guide/Penguin Ireland Short Story Competition.

His work has been included in literary anthologies: *On the Grass When I Arrive*, and *Blackbird Vol 2*, published by The Seamus Heaney Centre, QUB. A participant in the Irish Writers' Centre X Borders in Transition programme 2018/9, he was also a winning finalist of the Irish Novel Fair in 2019. He has been read on RTÉ and been featured on Radio Ulster's *Your Place and Mine*. In 2019 he graduated from The Seamus Heaney Centre with an MA in Creative Writing.

James has performed at the Listowel Literature Festival Open Mic, Armagh Food and Cider Weekend, the Gasyard Open Mic in Derry, and at Ten x 9 in Limavady. In October 2021 he published his debut short story collection, *Smokes and Birds*. This anthology, generously supported by Derry City and Strabane District Council, was shortlisted for the Carousel Aware (Fiction) Prize for independently published authors in 2023, when it also won Best Cover award. In April '22 James had appeared at the Dingle Féile Na Bealtaine in County Kerry, where he was in conversation with *New York Times* and *Irish Times* writer and journalist Douglas Dalby. He has delivered workshops and readings to groups in libraries, including Linen Hall, Belfast, to This Writing Thing, Derry, North Coast Writers, and in Foyle u3a.

True Colours, has been extensively workshopped in draft form. It is in receipt of both DCSDC Individual Artist funding and financial support from the Northern Ireland Arts Council's SIAP programme. His as yet unpublished Belfast coming-of-age novel, *What Peter Knew*, made the pre-longlist first cut of the Bridport Prize in 2023. Pre-Covid he ran a creative writing club for students in Derry's Lumen Christi College. He performed his flash fiction piece *Thenums* at the John Hewitt Summer School of 2023. James, who has been married to former beekeeper Jen for fifty-one years, spreads himself between Derry and Dunseverick, on the Causeway Coast. He has three grown-up children and three grandchildren.